THE BANKER

Banker #1

PENELOPE SKY

Hartwick Publishing

The Banker

Copyright © 2019 by Penelope Sky

All rights reserved.

Contents

Siena

My grandmother left me a small house outside Florence. It was old, a living antique. The pipes were original, and I could hear the water running through the entire house when I flushed the toilet. There were cracks in the stone outside, and the glass in the windows was so aged that they were constantly blurry, regardless of how many times I cleaned them. It was a short distance from the city, so close that I never felt like I was really out in the middle of the Tuscan countryside, but it gave me the quiet and peace I craved. Every morning in spring and summer I could hear the birds chirping outside my window. It'd been a haven to me for a long time—since I'd turned my back on my family.

But right now, this house couldn't protect me.

I sprinted up the wooden staircase, the creaks screaming beneath my feet as I moved as quickly as my body could carry me. There was no point in being quiet—not when they knew I was here.

"Run, bitch." Damien led the chase, his two cronies behind him. "It's more fun this way." His sinister tone reached every end of the petite home, as if he were speaking over a sound system that amplified every single syllable.

"Shit." I made it upstairs and slid across the hardwood floor toward my mattress. Tucked in between the two pieces of the bedding was the revolver I kept for emergencies. I'd disowned my family years ago, so I'd thought I would never need it.

Guess I was wrong.

I turned off the safety and prepared to shoot Damien right between the eyes. I wasn't the kind of person who hesitated when they squeezed the trigger. It was either him or me.

It certainly wasn't going to be me.

Damien took his time moving up the stairs, his heavy footfalls beating like the sound of steady drums. "Sweetheart, I would check that gun if I were you." His deep voice carried down the hallway, his smile so audible I could actually see it behind my eyes.

My hands started to shake.

I opened the barrel and looked inside.

Empty.

"You've got to be kidding me…" They must have hit my house while I was at work, stripping away all my bullets so I would be unarmed when they came for me. It was smart on their part—because I was a good shot. "Fucking asshole."

His laugh drifted down the hall, the sound getting louder because he was so close. He seemed to move slower the closer he approached, as if he wanted to savor this for as long as he could. He cornered me like a rat—and he wanted me to squirm.

I was no rat—and I didn't squirm.

I opened my closet and pushed back all my shoe boxes until I found my sword—a samurai sword given to me as a gift from Kyoto. I removed the sheath and prepared the blade, ready to stab my attacker right through the neck as I'd been taught. I wasn't a master of the sword, but I certainly knew how to stab someone.

I pressed my back against the wall and waited for Damien to walk through the open doorway.

Damien cocked his gun before he moved inside, his gun held at shoulder height. "Sweetheart, you know I love it when you run—"

I slammed my blade down fast, aiming to sever his arm right at the elbow.

Damien must have been expecting me to hide there because he dodged out of the way. "Ooh...you look pissed."

I slashed my sword at him again.

He jumped out of the way and kept his gun aimed at my right shoulder. "And sexy." The corner of his mouth rose in a smile that looked more like a sneer. He was enjoying this way too much. His jet-black hair flopped down in front of his face and hid some of his left eye from view. He was the top dog in the organization—because he loved his job so much.

I stabbed my sword at his gut, wanting him to bleed out all over my floor.

He backed up toward my bed. "Sweetheart, I will shoot you."

"And I will stab you." I put all my strength into the move, preparing to drive my sword right through his gut and into the wall behind him.

He pulled the trigger.

I didn't feel the bullet enter my shoulder, just the jerk of my body at the momentum. My shoulder jutted back and my body shifted because the force was much stronger than my own velocity. Smoke burned from the tip of his gun. The smell was suffocating—along with that of my own blood. I dropped my sword but stayed on my feet. It was the first time I'd ever been shot, and the shock that washed over my body protected me from the pain.

I stayed on my two feet—refusing to fall.

I held his gaze, my eyes narrowing with a promise of death.

Damien dropped his smile, and against his will, he showed a slight look of respect. "Damn, you're stubborn."

"Damn, you're a bad shot." He'd hit me in the shoulder, missing the main arteries and organs.

"No. I hit my mark perfectly." He kept the gun trained on me, this time aiming it between my eyes. "Drop the sword. Or die." The barrel didn't shake as it stared me down. "What's it gonna be, sweetheart?"

I wanted nothing to do with this life. While I loved my father, I'd told him I wanted nothing to do with his business. By putting some distance between us, I'd thought I could have my own life, a reputation untarnished by the criminal underworld.

It looked like it had followed me anyway. "What do you want from me?"

"Drop the sword."

"What do you want from me?" I hissed. Blood was ruining my clothes and dripped down my arm. Dizziness settled in my brain. My strength was slowly starting to drift away, but I kept myself upright, like I had something to prove.

"What does it matter?" He tilted his head, his eyes narrowing in irritation.

"Because I need to know if it's worth dying for." I wasn't the kind of person who could be a willing prisoner. Instead of surrendering, I'd much rather die. Maybe it was my family bloodline or my Italian roots, but I was the most stubborn woman on the planet. I'd rather die for what I believed in than submit to anyone.

He shook his head slightly. "You've always been a crazy bitch."

"I take that as a compliment."

The corner of his mouth rose again. "We have your father. If you want to save him, drop the sword."

I continued to hold my pose, my heart beating harder in my chest. My father was being held captive, and if I died then and there, I wouldn't be able to help him. Damien had me cornered, and he knew it.

"Continue this suicide mission and die," he said simply. "Or come with us—and we'll work out a deal."

"Work out a deal?" I hissed. "You'll just take me and kill me too."

"Normally, yes. But I have another use for you. Drop the sword."

My hand wanted to keep gripping the handle, but there was doubt planted in my mind. Even if there was nothing I could do to save my father, letting myself die now wasn't an option. We fell apart a long time ago, but my loyalty had never waned.

I dropped the sword.

He grinned wide. "Good girl."

2

Siena

THE MEN STOPPED THE BLEEDING THEN STITCHED UP both my entry and exit wounds, like this was an everyday occurrence. They didn't give me anything for the pain, and I was too stubborn to ask. A thick piece of gauze was wrapped around my shoulder, hidden underneath my t-shirt so I didn't stick out like a sore thumb.

I was thrown in the back of the Escalade before they escorted me into the center of Florence. It was five in the evening, but the sun was still bright because it was summertime. We ventured down the narrow streets until we approached an old building. With a tap of a button, a door to the underground garage opened, and we descended.

It didn't bode well that they allowed me to see where we were going.

I could have broken the window with my elbow and jumped out of the car at any time. But if they really did have my father, running wasn't an option. Regardless of our differences, we were family. He would lower his weapon for me in a heartbeat…at least, I hoped he would.

We plummeted into the darkness of the underground garage. Other expensive cars were parked in the spaces, all SUVS and all black. After we parked, we got out of the car. The two sidekicks tried to handcuff me.

I kicked one in the shin. "Are you kidding me? I surrendered and I've been shot."

He clenched his jaw before he snatched my wrists again.

Like a horse, I slammed my leg back and bucked him.

Damien raised his hand. "Let her be. Nothing she can do anyway."

The guy finally let me go.

I kicked him again anyway, hitting him in the ankle.

He didn't hesitate before he backhanded me, hitting me hard across the cheek and making my body turn with the impact.

I moved with the momentum and almost tumbled to the ground, but I regained my balance before that humiliating event could occur. I righted myself again and glared at him, ignoring the tingling sensation in my cheek.

He pointed in front of him. "Walk, bitch."

"You know, I'm getting a little tired of this nickname." I stepped in front of him and followed Damien.

Damien opened the door and led the way. "I hope not. It fits you so well."

I was tempted to kick him in the back of the knee, but Damien would do something worse than slap me. I was already suffering from a gunshot wound, and I didn't want a stab wound to go with it.

He led me into the building and past a bar where the lackeys were enjoying their booze after a long day of criminal activity. Most of them looked me up and down like I was a plaything they would enjoy sometime that evening.

Not gonna happen.

I was led into a private room. With black walls and black-framed mirrors, it looked like a private room in a club. There was a bar in there too, but instead of having a bartender, there was just an older man in a black suit. He sat on one of the curved leather couches that faced a black coffee table. There were three glasses of scotch on the surface.

I was certain one of them was for me.

The goons shut the door behind us, leaving the three of us alone.

"She's damaged goods," Damien announced as he sauntered into the room. "But she didn't give me much of a choice. Pulled a samurai sword on me. She was pretty good at wielding it too." He approached his boss then turned to me. He snapped his fingers like a man calling to his dog.

I refused to cooperate. I probably would have sat of my own free will because booze was exactly what I needed to mask the pain. But comments like that weren't well received. My eyes narrowed, full of murder.

The man in the suit studied me with an unreadable expression. He had a gray beard that matched the hair on his head. His skin was tanned and tight, but he looked to be in his fifties. His age hadn't slowed down his muscularity, and he filled out the suit well. He still possessed enough strength to be a formidable opponent. "We treat our guests better than that." He rose to his feet then indicated the leather couch across from him. "I'm sure she's thirsty after the day she's had. Damien, get her a few painkillers to take with her scotch. No need for her to suffer."

If this guy were trying to kiss my ass, it wouldn't work. If he had a demon like Damien on his payroll, he definitely wasn't trustworthy. But the booze and pills were calling my name, so I took a seat. If they wanted to kill me, they would have done it already, so I knew their offering hadn't been poisoned.

I took the pills and washed them down with the scotch. I drank the entire glass, needing every drop to steady my nerves. Like my father, I didn't show fear in the face of danger, but a good glass of booze always made it a little easier. A drop dripped from the corner of my mouth, so I wiped it away with my forearm. "Let's skip the power plays and the bullshit. I need my father, and you need me. Elaborate." I rested my elbows on my knees as I stared at the gentleman sitting across from me. He seemed harmless, like a grandfather who only punished you when you really deserved it. But I wouldn't let the false kindness in his eyes overshadow who he really was.

He held his glass in the hand resting on his knee as he smiled at me. "Like father, like daughter."

"Not sure if that's a compliment or not." I'd inherited my father's hardness but not his lack of morality. I also had his eyes, but that was as far as our shared attributes went. Everything else I had I received from my mother, who'd been dead for many years.

"I'll let you decide." He took a drink before he set the glass on the table.

Damien sat beside him, his predatory eyes glued to my face. Lust and hostility shone in his gaze. He wanted to shoot me again just to get off on it. He was a demon without a leash. There was no telling what he might do.

They obviously needed me for something. Otherwise, I wouldn't be alive. If they wanted to torture my father and punish him, it would make sense to execute his only daughter. But I was still sitting there, the painkillers kicking in. "On with it." Perhaps I was bolder than usual because I knew I had some sort of power in this game.

"You know Damien well, obviously," he began. "But we haven't had the pleasure of meeting. I'm Micah."

"And you know who I am," I said, not bothering with an introduction. "Where is my father?"

"In the building." Micah wore a gold ring on his finger with a green emerald in the center. His hands showed his age, the veins mixing with the wrinkles. He must be a few years younger than my father. "The specifics don't matter."

"They matter if you want my cooperation." My father taught me to always be strong, regardless of the opponent I faced. Earning your enemy's respect was the only saving grace you would ever receive. And if your fate was unavoidable, it was best to go out with honor. I was too proud to kneel for anyone—because that was how I was raised.

Damien gave a slow grin. "You're lucky you're alive right now."

I glanced to him. "As are you."

He widened his grin farther, hating me but wanting me at the same time. His green eyes were set in a handsome face, his masculine cheekbones complementing his full lips. He was a beautiful man, but he was tainted by such evil, his handsomeness got lost in translation.

Micah ignored his right-hand man. "If your father remains in my captivity, I will torture him and kill him."

I maintained the exact same expression, just as I would in a poker game. My brother was part of the family business, but he hadn't been mentioned once. He must have disappeared before they could get to him—and now they had no idea where he'd gone into hiding. He would never tell me, so it was pointless to ask. "I assumed. What do you want from me?" I didn't have special skills or any interaction with the family business, so I didn't have much to offer. Even my information was useless because I'd turned my back on the trade. That should be obvious to them—if they did their research.

"We'll make a trade with you," Micah offered. "One man for another."

I narrowed my eyes automatically, the fear involuntarily controlling my reactions. The only person they could possibly want was my brother—and that was a trade I refused to make. They could threaten to kill me again, and it still wouldn't make a difference. "You have a building full of capable men at your disposal. Why are you asking me?"

"This man is untouchable." Micah pulled out a folder from the inside of his jacket and set it on the table between us.

I didn't open it. "If he's untouchable, I'm a terrible person to ask. I may be a good shot, but I'm no assassin." I couldn't pull off any kind of stunt. I lived a quiet life outside of Florence. I went to work every day at the gallery, spent time with my friends, had a few dates here and there, and then went home.

"We don't want you to kill him." Micah pushed the folder closer to me. "We need this man alive. Bring him to us, and your father goes free."

I couldn't allow myself to think about my father's condition. He was probably locked up in a room with no windows and barely a cot. Maybe he deserved it because of his business, but it broke my heart to imagine him that way. If there were anything I could do for him, I would. "As I've already said, I have no skills. I'm an art buyer."

Damien watched me with those malicious eyes. "Give yourself more credit, sweetheart."

I kept my gaze on Micah so I wouldn't rip out Damien's throat. "Who is this man?"

Micah grabbed his glass again, but instead of drinking from it, he held it in his palm. "Cato Marino."

That name meant nothing to me.

Micah must have recognized the blankness in my eyes because he elaborated. "He owns the biggest bank in the world. He hides money for the Chinese, has ties with the vaults in Switzerland, and half the debt of the United States can be attributed to him. There may be banks under different names, but they're all owned by the same man."

"Jesus…and you think I can touch this guy?" I laughed despite the seriousness of the situation because it was ridiculous. "He's like the richest dude in the universe. You think I can just walk up to him and ask him to come with me?"

"No." Damien watched me without blinking. "But you could get into his bed."

Now it became crystal clear. They wanted me to spread my legs and seduce this man. They wanted me to bed him like a whore. Once I gained his trust, I could trick him into being caught by the wrong hands. "I'm not in that line of business." I grabbed the bottle of scotch and refilled my glass.

"Then you better find another plan," Micah said. "It doesn't matter how you pull this off. As long as we get Cato Marino, your father walks free. It's that simple. Do nothing—and I will kill him." The gentlemanly attitude was long gone, and now his true colors rose to the surface. He squeezed his glass with his fingers. "Your father encroached on our territory and was stupid enough to cross the line one too many times. I was kind enough to give him a warning—but no more."

My father ran a cigar business, exporting them all across Europe. They were high quality, sometimes costing eighty euros just for a single one. But that wasn't how he made his money. His cigars were stuffed with drugs—the finest drugs in this hemisphere. He smuggled them where they needed to go under the clever disguise. The problem was, Micah was in the same line of work—and Italy just wasn't big enough for the both of them. I warned my father that his good luck would run out, that he would take a bigger bite than he could chew. When he didn't listen to me, I turned my back on my family—because I wanted a simple life.

"You're a clever woman, and I respect you." Micah had just threatened me, but now he'd flipped his attitude like it hadn't happened. "You didn't approve of what he was doing. You warned him this would happen. You left your family and started over. Unfortunately, the rest of your family didn't inherit the same intelligence."

"But I'm still here with you…so I can't be that smart." I should have left Italy. I should have moved to France or London. Or better yet, I should have crossed the pond and started a new life in America.

Micah gave me a slight smile. "You can blame your father for that."

Yes, I could blame him for all of this. I wanted nothing to do with his criminal life, but I somehow had been dragged back into it. "What do you want with Cato Marino?" I didn't know anything about this guy, but I knew he wasn't innocent. If he were, Micah wouldn't be risking his organization to take down such a powerful man. There must be a good reason.

"Our business." Micah took a drink. "Not yours."

Why did I expect anything else? "And if I say no?" I had every right to walk away right now. I'd warned my father so many times. Even when my mother was murdered, he didn't stop. That was the last straw for me. He was blinded by greed and power. Fortune was more important than his family, more important than the woman who gave him his children. He got himself into this mess, and I should let him suffer for it.

Damien cocked his head slightly, as if that answer was the one he was hoping for. "Then you can join me in my bed." The threat was palpable, filling the air around us and permeating our skin. His lust matched his hostility, and there was no evidence of a bluff. "And when I'm done with you, I'll throw your dead body into your father's prison—naked and dripping with come from every hole."

Like bugs were crawling across my skin, I felt my body being twisted under invisible hands. My breathing picked up slightly, and my fingers flinched automatically, wishing I could grab a glass and smash it over Damien's head. But I already had a gunshot wound, and I wasn't craving another.

Even if Damien hadn't threatened me with that terrifying image, I knew my conscience wouldn't allow me to abandon my father. If he were anyone else, I would have kept fighting until the last drop of blood left my veins, but my loyalty wouldn't allow me to flinch. If I managed to pull this off, I would save my own life as well as my father's.

And the little girl inside me still wished we would have the fairy-tale ending I always wanted—a simple life together. Family dinners on Sunday. Putting up the Christmas tree while the frost pressed against the windows. Drinking wine at our favorite vineyard just when the harvest finished. I'd felt alone my entire life—even when my family was just a few miles away. "If I bring Cato to you, you release both my father and me?"

Micah nodded. "As long as your father shuts down his business."

My father loved that business more than me, but perhaps being locked up for god knows how long would change his mind. "Fine. But I'm not sleeping with him." I would do anything to save my family, but opening my legs wasn't an avenue I would take. There must be some other way to make it happen.

"It doesn't matter to me how you do it," Micah said. "Just get the job done. But if you fail, there is no deal. Until Cato Marino is in my captivity, your father will remain here. And if you can't deliver what you promised, I'll be forced to kill your father. So, if I were you...I wouldn't take your time."

Damien smiled at me. "But after I capture you again...I'll definitely take my time."

3

Siena

THIS WAS WHAT I'D GATHERED ABOUT CATO MARINO.

He was stupid rich. Multibillionaire.

He was self-made. I couldn't wrap my mind around the achievements of this single man in his single lifetime.

He was young. He just turned thirty in March.

How did someone so young accomplish so much?

And the most surprising revelation of all…he was hot.

Inexplicably gorgeous. So beautiful it was unreal. Over six foot of steel—and probably all steel in his pants too. Every picture I saw of him showed off his caveman shoulders, his muscled arms, and tight waist. Whether he was in jeans or a suit, the hardness of his body couldn't be denied. Sexy from head to toe, he was model material, not just banker material.

I hadn't planned on seducing him to accomplish my goal, but now I realized that plan wouldn't have worked anyway. A hot billionaire like him was already getting too much ass to handle. He could have any woman he wanted, so there was no way I could impress him. He might glance at me, think I was pretty. But an instant later, he would already be thinking about something else.

I did as much research as I could, and it was safe to conclude this man was impenetrable. Every photograph I could find of him showed his security team in the background. The only public appearances he made were for work. His personal life wasn't disclosed. There wasn't even a picture of him going to the grocery store to pick up some orange juice.

No wonder why Micah put this on my shoulders.

There were a few places Cato frequented in Florence, so I decided to get a view of him in person. Perhaps if I studied my prey, I'd gain a better understanding of how I was going to pull this off. Marching up to him with a gun wouldn't accomplish anything. One of his men would take me out in a second. I probably couldn't even walk up to him at all, not without being intercepted by one of his bodyguards.

I didn't have a lot of time to waste, but I had to take this slowly if I were going to accomplish anything.

I went to one of his favorite clubs in Florence. I didn't have a clue if or when he would show his face, so I made an appearance three nights in a row, wearing a different dress and heels each time. The bartender thought I was a lonely alcoholic who had quickly become a regular.

On the third night, I sat alone at a table when I finally got some luck. My hands were wrapped around my glass of scotch as my eyes watched the commotion at the doorway. Bouncers moved out of the way so Cato could lead the pack. With three other good-looking men in suits, they entered the bar, all heads turning their way like they were beautiful women in heels. Women weren't the only ones looking, but men too, probably envious of a man who was so rich and handsome he could have any woman he wanted—at any time.

A special seating area was cleared out just for them, and before their muscular asses pressed against the leather seats, a sexy waitress in a dress that hardly covered anything appeared out of nowhere to wait on them.

I focused on Cato and ignored his three friends. Even in the darkness of the club, he looked exactly the same as he did in his photographs. Rugged, handsome, and confident. He wore a gray V-neck that highlighted his muscular arms and chest. His shoulders were broader in person than they were in the pictures. With blue eyes and brown hair, he was a very pretty man. His tanned skin implied he loved the outdoors, even though I'd never seen a single photograph of him hiking or yachting.

I continued to enjoy my scotch as I stared from my chair, trying to glean as much information as I could. The three men with him seemed to be friends, not security detail. The men in charge of keeping him safe stayed near the entrance, their eyes scanning the bar and everyone near it. Hopefully, they didn't find me suspicious, just a woman who was debating making a move.

Just as the waitress returned with their drinks, a group of confident women joined them. All pretty and dressed for the occasion, they flashed their smiles and their long legs, knowing exactly who Cato was.

I assumed a handsome guy like him was a playboy, but I wasn't prepared for how extreme of a playboy he was.

He grabbed the woman closest to him by the wrist and gently tugged her toward him. His hands guided her hips over his thighs until she straddled his lap. Then he gripped her lower back and pulled her in for a kiss, her dress riding up and showing her black thong to everyone.

The other guys didn't seem the least bit surprised.

The bar staff didn't rush over and tell her to stick to the dress code.

With my jaw hanging open, I watched Cato make out with a complete stranger. Like he could do whatever he wanted, he took control without asking permission. His hand dug into her hair, and he kissed her with his full lips, treating her like he adored her rather than had no idea who she was. His fingers tucked her hair behind her ear then he gripped her ass.

Even though he was a total pig, it was still pretty hot. He certainly knew how to use that rugged mouth of his.

He ended the kiss then gently guided her into the seat beside him. His arm rested over the back of the couch, and he turned to talk to her, perhaps to actually ask for her name, but another woman straddled his hips and stole his attention.

Then he made out with her next.

"Jesus…" I took a long drink of my scotch.

She kissed him harder than the previous woman, her hands scratching his chest as she ground against his erection in his slacks. She showed him her best moves, doing her damnedest to erase the woman who had just pulled the same stunt.

The kiss lasted a while before he directed her into the space on the other side of him. Both of his arms now rested on the leather of the back of the couch as he claimed both women for the night, one under each arm.

"Wow…what a pig."

The other guys found their women, and then they spent the night drinking and talking.

I'd had my fair share of playboys, but nothing of that caliber. That man didn't even need to hunt for pussy because it hunted for him. All he had to do was wait thirty seconds, and a beautiful woman would appear to replace the previous one. When the night was over, he would probably take both women back to his place with the intention of bedding them both. They probably hoped they might catch his attention if they were adventurous enough, but like all the others, they would be gone by morning.

And he would forget their faces forever.

Just when I finished my scotch, another woman appeared. She straddled his lap, and another make-out session commenced.

I'd been sitting there all night without attracting an admirer, while Cato was getting more pussy than he could handle. "Fuck…I need another drink."

―――――

I HAD a few friends in high places, so I used that to my advantage to get an audience with the right man.

A hitman.

He specialized in killing high-profile targets and making it look like accidents. He'd retired a few years ago, but he'd had an illustrious career that garnered him a great deal of respect. Bosco Roth was a good friend of my brother's, so I called him and asked for an introduction to this famous killer.

Now I sat on the bench at the bus stop in the middle of the night. It was two in the morning, and everyone was at home. The only company I had was a bum sleeping across the street in the alleyway. The sun had been gone for hours, but the humidity still hovered over me in the darkness. I was in jeans and a t-shirt, but even that was too warm to wear.

Heavy footsteps sounded to my left, and that's when I turned to see the huge man covered in sleeves of tattoos. He was terrifying in appearance, especially when he clenched his jaw like that. He didn't look the least bit pleased to see me, like this favor he was doing for Bosco was nothing but a pain in the ass.

I rose to my feet and stood under the lamplight. Like always, I didn't show fear, even though this man was much more terrifying than Damien had ever been. "Bones?"

He stopped in front of me, keeping several feet in between us. We were visible under the lamplight, but he didn't seem to care if we were seen. He was in a black t-shirt and black jeans, matching the ink that covered his arms and disappeared under the collar of his shirt. "I'm only here because Bosco is a friend of mine. I'm not in the game anymore, and there's nothing you can offer me to change my mind. If we're done here, I have somewhere to be." He spat everything out as quickly as he could, like just one more second of this meeting was too much for him.

When I was part of my family, I was used to luxury. We were a wealthy family, so I always had everything that

I needed. Perhaps if I had stayed, that would still be the case, and I would have a lot more money to offer him. Unfortunately, all I had was the deed to my house, some jewelry my father bought me, and my car. "There's a million euros for you if you can help me." To me, that was a fortune.

But based on the coldness of his face, that was just a few pennies. "I said there's nothing you can offer me. I meant it." He slid his hands into his front pockets, and that's when I noticed the black ring tattooed on his ring finger.

"I don't want to kill this guy. I just need to get him from Point A to Point B." Now that I'd observed Cato with my own eyes, I realized how difficult this mission would be. He was impossible to access because he was never alone, and if he was alone, he probably had a woman's tongue down his throat. This was completely out of my league. "It's a simple mission."

"Then why do you need me?"

"This isn't really my forte…"

He continued to look bored.

"Look, I'm mixed up in some serious shit, and I need help."

Bones still look irritated, like every moment he wasted was precious. "I have a guy who can help you. But a million euro isn't going to cut it."

"Then how much?" Maybe I could scrounge up some more money somehow.

"Depends on the target. Who is it?"

I glanced around us to make sure we were alone. "Cato Marino."

Recognition immediately flashed in his gaze. "No one is gonna take the hit for less than a hundred million."

My eyes snapped open. "You can't be serious."

"He's a high-profile target. I'm not even sure it can be done. A hundred million is a conservative guess."

"I don't have that kind of money…"

"Then you don't have Cato." He took a step back like he was going to leave the scene. "I've got a wife and kid at home. I shouldn't have come in the first place."

"Wait, please."

He stopped and burned his ice-cold gaze into mine. "I just told you I can't help you. You're on your own, woman."

"Could you at least give me some advice?" I tried not to beg, but my voice slowly rose. If no one would help me, my odds of completing this mission were even more unlikely. Killing Cato would be a much easier task than delivering him to Micah. At least then I could hide on top of a roof and aim my weapon. "How would you capture Cato and hand him over?"

"Cato Marino is a powerful man. He's got security on him at all times."

"Hence, why I'm asking for advice." Maybe I shouldn't be a smartass right now, but I was losing my focus.

He narrowed his eyes. "You don't stand a chance. If you have no men and no money, capturing someone like him isn't possible. You only have one option, and even then, it probably won't work."

"What?" I asked, crossing my arms over my chest.

He stared at me for a few seconds, his eyes steady and

wide. He didn't blink often, adding to his aura of constant hostility. "Fuck him. Fuck him hard."

———

THERE WAS a coffee shop across the street from one of Cato's banks, and he'd been seen grabbing a cup of afternoon coffee there once in a while. He had been dressed in his suit and tie, and it seemed like he'd spent all morning talking about money until his brain was fried.

I sat at one of the tables outside with a latte and a book, hoping he would stop by sometime that week. A few days passed and he didn't make an appearance, and I was almost done with my book and would soon have to replace it. Thankfully, the gallery had been slow for the past two weeks, so my boss didn't need me as often as usual.

I could keep stalking my target.

Finally, Cato Marino showed up. It was two in the afternoon when he crossed the street and stepped inside the bakery.

I could watch him through the windows. He was in a gray suit and black tie. His trousers hugged his rock-hard ass, and he held himself with perfect posture. He stood in line and waited to order as he casually glanced at his expensive watch. Then he rubbed his fingers across the shadowy beard that started to pop up along his chiseled jaw.

I wondered if he'd gone home with all three of those women from the bar.

Wouldn't be surprised.

He moved up to the front of the line and gave his

order. He dropped a hundred euro into the tip jar when no one was looking then stepped away to wait for his coffee to be prepared.

So the guy was generous.

I didn't know what these stalking sessions would accomplish. It didn't seem like I was gleaning any helpful knowledge in the process. So far, all I'd uncovered was that he was getting laid constantly and he looked damn good in a suit. He was also a generous tipper. But none of those things would help me get him into Micah's hands.

And regardless of how hot he was, I was not screwing him.

I'd have to find another way.

The barista handed him his coffee, and he took a sip before he walked out and crossed the street. He didn't look at me once because he didn't notice me in the center of filled tables. That worked out in my favor, because if he did notice me, I wouldn't be able to follow him anymore.

I watched him as he opened the door and stepped inside the bank, over six feet of muscle and pure masculinity. The suit fit him so well, clearly designed just for him, and he moved like a god rather than a human. The door shut behind him, and he was gone from my sight.

How was I going to do this?

―――

I PULLED up to Barsetti Vineyards and left my car in the gravel parking lot. The sun was high in the sky, and out in the middle of Tuscany, there were iconic views of the land that made it so famous. The smell of olive trees was in the air, along with the succulent scent of grapes in the vineyard.

I walked onto the property then made my way into the main building. A friend of my father's ran the vineyard, and from what I could recall, he wasn't just a winemaker. His hands were just as dirty as my father's.

I checked in with his assistant before I stepped inside.

The last time I saw Crow Barsetti, I was just a child. His features weren't easy to remember because I was just too young, but I did remember his eyes. They were unique with their green and hazel color. Now decades had passed, and he was a different man from the one I'd met all those years ago—but his eyes were still the same.

He rose from behind his desk and joined me near the door, examining me like he was trying to place me in his mind. "Siena Russo…are you Stefan's daughter?"

He had a good memory. "I'm glad you remember me."

"Vaguely," he said simply. "How can I help you, Siena? Your father well?"

"Uh…not really." I crossed my arms over my chest and hoped this man would risk everything to help me. It didn't make sense why he would, but I had to try. Maybe he would take pity on me.

"What is it?" Tall and strong, he was a man who had aged well. Spending his days working at a winery had obviously kept him in shape. There were pictures scattered across his desk, probably pictures of his family.

"My father has been captured by Micah and his men. My brother is missing, and I'm not sure what's going on with the business."

He sighed quietly. "I'm sorry to hear that, Siena." He seemed sincere.

"Micah made a deal with me. If I bring him a man he wants, he'll let my father go. If I don't…he'll kill me and my father." I left out the rape part. That was a subject no one ever wanted to discuss.

"Who's the man?"

"Cato Marino."

Crow sighed as he rubbed the back of his neck. "So he gives you a mission you have no chance of completing…"

"It seems that way."

"I'm sorry, Siena. I warned your father he should walk away from the business. A criminal life will only last so long…before that luck runs out. I stopped my weapons business when I married my wife. We both wanted a simple life."

"Good for you. I wish my father had done the same." Perhaps my mother would still be alive right now if he had.

He gave me a look full of pity. "I know you're going to ask for my help. But before you do, I have to tell you about my family. My brother and I have been running this winery for thirty years. Now I'm grooming my son-in-law to take it over. I have two grandsons. Reid is two and Crow Jr. is one."

I smiled. "He was named after you."

"Yes." His happiness didn't mirror mine. "I've fought many wars over my lifetime. I can't do it anymore. I'm very sorry, Siena. Truly. But I can't put my family in jeopardy, not when we finally have the peace we worked so hard for."

How could I argue with a man who just wanted to protect his family? He'd made the right decision when my father didn't. He'd walked away from his business and criminal ties to protect his family. He wasn't greedy and selfish like my father. He'd made the right call. "I understand." Crow Barsetti deserved the peace he'd fought for —and I would never take that away from him. "You're right."

He tilted his head slightly, his eyes full of pity. "Want my advice?"

"Please." I lifted my eyes to meet his.

"Run."

My heart started to palpitate.

"Your father wouldn't want you to risk your life for his. He wouldn't want you to attempt this mission and get killed. And if you fail, Micah will just hunt you down. Take whatever money you have left and run."

It was good advice, the same advice I would give to anyone else.

"Stefan had his chance to choose a peaceful life. He didn't take it. You shouldn't be punished for that, Siena."

He was absolutely right. I shouldn't be punished for my father's stupidity. "I agree with you. But my loyalty won't allow me to give up. His blood is my blood. I know if our places were switched, he wouldn't give up."

"That's different. He's your father. That's his burden —not yours. And as a father and a grandfather, I can promise you he would want you to run. He would want you to leave him to die. If my daughter were in that position…I would want her to run as hard as she could. My memory would live on with her anyway."

It was a sweet thing to say, especially since it was so sincere. "I still can't do it." I couldn't let my father rot in that prison until they tortured him to death. "I would never be happy anyway. I would constantly wonder if he'd been killed yet. And if he had been killed, the guilt would haunt me forever. He doesn't deserve my loyalty...but he has it anyway."

———

AFTER I FINISHED work at the gallery, I walked a few blocks until I reached the café Cato liked to frequent. This time, I didn't stop by in the hope of seeing him. After the long day I'd had, I wanted an iced coffee and a muffin to rip apart with my fingertips.

Most people hated the brutal summers here in Florence, but I didn't mind them at all. I'd grown up in this treacherous heat, and I couldn't imagine my life without that experience. So I took my coffee and muffin and sat outside. I had a client who'd recruited me to decorate his summer home in Tuscany, and now I was studying images of his living room and dining room to determine the size and color of the frames as well as the artwork that would complement each one. That was my job—finding artwork for rich people. Sometimes people just wanted cheap stuff to cover the walls, but occasionally, my clients had more refined taste and preferred masterpieces by local artists. Those always took longer to locate, but since I charged by the hour, that worked out in my favor.

The chair across from me shifted, and then a heavy body filled its vacancy.

When my eyes flicked upward, they landed on the man I'd been hunting. With blue eyes that matched the summer sky and a hard jaw that looked like it'd been carved with a knife, the beautiful man I'd been watching from afar sat in front of me.

He didn't greet me with that handsome smile I'd seen him flash to his women. Instead, his eyes were hostile and his lips were slightly pressed in amusement. He wasn't wearing a suit and tie like he usually did when he frequented this spot. Today, he was dressed in jeans and an olive green t-shirt, a V in the front so his chest muscles were unmistakable. At this close distance, I could clearly see the tight cords in his neck, the obvious tension of the muscles of his physique. His sunglasses hung from the vee in his shirt, and he rested his forearms on the armrests of the chair. They were flanked with the same veins that matched his neck, and he was the tightest and fittest man I'd seen. It seemed like he only worked out and ate protein. No wonder he could get three different women in a row to make out with him without even making an intro-duction.

He'd caught me off guard and he knew it, judging by the hint of arrogance in his eyes, but I refused to acknowl-edge it. My table was scattered with images of a living room and I was looking up artwork online, so it was clear I was actually working on something. I never allowed fear to enter my expression, so I remained as calm as ever. "Hello." That was the only response I would give him. Saying the least amount possible was the smartest thing to do in this situation. Maybe he'd figured out I'd been following him. Or maybe he was making a pass at me.

There was no real way to know until he stated his intentions.

"My stalkers aren't usually young and beautiful women. This is a nice surprise." He sat forward and moved his forearms to the top of the table. His hands rested on my paperwork, but he didn't look down to examine my project. His eyes were glued to me and focused, like there was nothing else more important in the world than watching me. He didn't blink as he took me in, and it seemed like I was sitting across from him in a business meeting. I wouldn't be able to leave until I gave him what he wanted.

I kept my eyes on him as I shut my laptop. "Thank you. But I'm not a stalker."

His eyes narrowed slightly as he examined me. "Don't insult me. There's nothing that goes on around me that I don't notice." His voice complemented his appearance perfectly. It was deep and sharp, just like the edge of a knife.

Even though his assumption was totally accurate, I didn't like his arrogance. He was the conceited playboy I'd assumed he was. The whole world revolved around him—and him alone. Maybe I was just jealous that he could have hot sex every night of his life when I hadn't gotten action in over a month. Or maybe I hated men who thought they were better than everyone else. I used to be rich once upon a time. I knew how rich people thought—that they were above everyone. "Maybe if you weren't so cocky, you would realize it's just a coincidence. Not everyone wants your balls."

The corner of his mouth ticked slightly, like he wanted

to smile but stopped himself from doing it. "If you don't want my balls, then why are you following me?" Within the short time he sat there with me, he'd drawn attention from the other tables. Women turned around to look at him, aware that the sexiest bachelor in Italy had spotted a random woman he liked.

What a wrong assumption that was. "Coincidence."

"Really?" He cocked his head slightly, his blue eyes taking me in aggressively. His wide shoulders looked broad in the cotton on his shirt, and the veins on his forearms moved all the way up to his biceps. "If you don't want my balls and this really is a coincidence, then I should never see you again." He rose to his feet and pushed the chair back at the same time. He walked off, turning his back on me and walking down the sidewalk. His ass looked snug in his jeans, and all the women in my vicinity noticed the exact same thing.

There was no mistaking the subtle threat in his tone. He let me off the hook because his formidable power was enough to chase anyone away. Unless I acted like I wanted to fuck him, he wanted nothing to do with me. If I had an ulterior motive, then I should stay the hell away from him.

But there was a problem with that.

I couldn't stay away—not if I wanted my father to live.

4

Siena

I'D DISLIKED CATO THROUGH MY OBSERVATIONS, BUT after our short conversation, I liked him even less. He was exactly what I assumed he would be—an arrogant son of a bitch. There was no need to feel guilty for my intentions of handing him over to Micah, not when he was that much of an ass.

So cocky, Jesus Christ.

I wanted to call the whole thing off because I didn't want to deal with him, but when I remembered that my father's life depended on me, I realized giving up wasn't an option. Besides, I didn't want Damien to rape me either. This was the best way out of this mess—for my father and me.

It looked like sleeping with Cato was my only option.

I didn't want to do it, regardless of how hot he was. He was an arrogant douchebag, and that wasn't sexy to me. I liked a sexy man as much as the next woman, but I needed other qualities too—like humility.

But I wasn't given the luxury of choice in the matter.

———

I RETURNED to his favorite club a few nights later, this time intending to be noticed. There were no further observations I could make in these conditions. I'd failed to uncover new information, other than the fact that he was the most arrogant man on the planet.

But I didn't know how to use that to my advantage.

I wore one of my older cocktail dresses that I'd stashed away in my closet. I wore it to a special dinner my father had hosted, and there had been five hundred people there to celebrate his newly designed cigar. The dress was black and backless, hugging my body right above my ass. The halter top front was skintight and outlined the shape of my tits and my flat stomach. It was short, even shorter in the sky-high heels I wore. Up until this point, I'd never dressed to impress, but now I had to step up my game. Diamonds were in my ears, and my hair was pinned into an elegant updo so my bare back was more noticeable.

I hoped Cato would take the bait.

I assumed he would notice me whether he was impressed or not, simply because I'd seen him at that bakery just days ago.

I couldn't believe I was doing this.

I would get on my back to achieve my goals.

If only there were another way.

An hour later, Cato and another man walked inside. Both dressed in jeans and t-shirts, they ignored the collared shirt dress code and helped themselves to the leather couches in their favorite area. The man with Cato hadn't accompanied him last time, but his striking blue eyes and solid build told me they were related.

Probably brothers.

The waitress waited on them instantly, and then their groupies arrived. All beautiful and tall, they filled the empty spaces on the couch and rubbed their palms against his thighs. Like last time, kisses were shared.

His brother was getting the same level of action.

I rolled my eyes so hard it actually hurt my head a little. "Pigs."

Fifteen minutes later, Cato's attention on his fans started to wane. His eyes scanned the bar, like he wasn't entirely happy with his catch for the day and was looking for something else. It only took a few seconds for his eyes to land on me.

Then we stared at each other for what seemed like an eternity.

He didn't show a hint of surprise. He didn't seem angry. Instead, he just seemed intense, his unblinking eyes focused on me like a target. His arms were around the two women that were still lavishing him with affection, but his eyes were reserved for me.

I looked away first, not in admission of defeat, but indifference. I picked up my scotch and took a drink. There was no way in hell I would walk over there and start a conversation with those women clawing his thighs. My only option was to get him alone—and that meant he had to join me.

I set my glass down and continued to look away, hoping Cato would take the bait.

My brilliant plan was sabotaged when a handsome man came to my table with a scotch in his hand. "Looks like you're getting low."

Really? This guy had to make his move now? A smile emerged, and I kept up my calm façade, pretending this guy hadn't just ruined an opportunity I'd worked so hard to set up. "Thank you. That was kind—"

"Leave." Cato appeared at the table, towering over my guest with a few extra inches of height. His deep voice was as sharp as ever, slicing the poor guy with his razor edge. He threatened him with his gaze and size, spooking him like a frightened dog.

The guy didn't put up a fight. He disappeared into the crowd—and took the scotch with him.

"There goes my free drink." My legs were crossed under the table, and I rested my arms on the surface. My shoulders were back and my posture was poised, commanding the situation with my silent confidence.

Instead of taking the seat across from me, he sat right beside me, his thigh touching mine and his arm pressed against my shoulder. With his eyes trained on me, he subtly lifted his hand and beckoned to someone watching us.

The waitress appeared instantly.

"Two scotches," he said, still looking at me. "One ice cube."

She walked away without saying a word.

He was even more intense than the last time I saw him. I turned my gaze to meet his, showing the same fear-lessness that he possessed in his own eyes. As far as I knew, this man was rich, but he was honest. He wasn't a criminal who sold drugs or weapons. He made an honest living—so he couldn't be too dangerous.

The waitress was back in a flash—along with the two glasses.

I grabbed mine and took a drink. "Thank you."

He continued his relentless stare. "You've successfully claimed my attention. Now, what are you going to do with it?" His eyes flicked away from mine, traveling down my dress until he spotted my bare thighs under the table.

"I wasn't trying to get your attention." I took another drink, the booze calming my nerves.

"Really?" His blue eyes were chilly, like the arctic. "In a dress like that?"

"What's wrong with my dress?" I countered, the drink in my hand.

He slid his hand over the back of the chair, his muscular arm pressing right against my shoulder blades. His skin was searing hot, a nice relief from the cold leather. He tilted his face nearer to me, our bodies so close together it didn't seem like we were strangers. "You're still wearing it."

I shivered as the smooth words rolled off his tongue. He said it with such confidence, in a way no other man could pull off. I'd been with good men, but I'd never been with a man who possessed such raw masculinity. Cato was definitely a different breed of man. His arrogance could be attractive—once in a while.

I took another drink just to mask the heat that flushed into my face. "I'm not the kind of woman to straddle your hips and make out with you in a bar."

The backs of his fingers moved to my cheek, and he

gently grazed them toward my hairline. His skin was warm, innately inviting. "But you're the kind of woman to stalk a man for two weeks?"

I turned to him, the ferocity entering my gaze.

A slow smile formed on his lips, the look so handsome and so arrogant that it was undeniably sexy. "Has anyone ever told you how gorgeous you look when you're pissed?"

Damien popped into my mind. "Actually, yes."

His smile widened even more. "I get under your skin, don't I?"

"I think you're a bit arrogant."

"If you think I'm bad, you should meet my brother."

"You're more than enough."

His smile continued, but his gaze sharpened. "You've got a quick mouth on you."

"Thank you."

"I wonder what else your mouth can do." His smile faded away, but the intensity remained in his eyes. He made his moves one after another, seducing me without even trying. Maybe he was an excellent entrepreneur, but making panties drop was his next best skill set.

"You'll never know." I finished my glass then took a drink of his.

He watched my movements, not protesting when I helped myself to his booze. When the glass was back on the table, he moved his fingers under my chin and slowly forced my gaze toward his.

I easily could have fought it—but I didn't even try.

"Yes, I will." He moved his hand into my hair as he pulled me in for a kiss. He cradled my head against his palm then kissed me softly on the lips, giving me a tender embrace that was nothing like what he gave the other women. This was purposeful, soft, and so slow that it made my legs shake.

I'd just watched him kiss those other women minutes ago, and instead of being disgusted by being the third in line, all I could think about was how good his mouth tasted. His cologne was purely masculine, and when I felt his hard muscles brush against me, I wanted to sink my nails into his skin. My thighs tightened, and I breathed into his mouth as my hand gripped his thigh under the table. He was a solid rock under my fingertips, pure muscle stretching denim. My mouth naturally matched his cadence, moving past his and receiving his tongue with vigor. I sucked his bottom lip before I gave him mine. There was nothing I liked about this man besides his looks, and I never thought I could have such an incredible kiss with a man I could barely tolerate. I had never experienced lust quite like this, where physical attraction was more important than anything else.

His kiss slowed to a gradual halt. His final embrace was a gentle suck on my bottom lip. Just like an intense workout, he gave me a nice cooldown before he ended it altogether. He pulled his face away while his eyes were still glued to my lips. "Let's go." He took my hand and guided me out of the booth.

I didn't appreciate being told what to do. I didn't appreciate the assumption that I would go to bed with him just because he kissed me. But my eyes stayed on the prize, and I focused on why I was there in the first place.

To save my father.

————

WE WALKED into the building and took the elevator to the top floor. There was no one in the lobby and the side-walk was deserted, so I assumed he owned the entire building. A multibillionaire probably protected his privacy above all else—even if he had to drop millions on an entire building.

The doors opened to a luxurious living room and the sound of classical music in the background.

But I didn't have a chance to look around for clues before I was yanked into his arms for a kiss. His hand gripped the hair tie that kept my hair in place then he yanked out the remaining pins hidden in my brown hair. His mouth continued to move with mine, and he was much more aggressive than he'd been at the club. He gripped my ass then scooped me up before he carried me down the hallway.

My arms circled his neck, and I continued to kiss him, feeling my arousal seep into my panties. It'd been over a month since I'd had a man in my bed, and the sex hadn't been all that great. There was no doubt in my mind this man knew how to fuck—so I decided to enjoy it.

I explored his shoulders and back through the cotton shirt and imagined how he would look in nothing but his birthday suit. He would be just as gorgeous, but even better because his package was probably impressive. A man couldn't be so arrogant unless he was packing a big dick in his pants.

He lowered me onto the bed and kissed me for a few more seconds before he rose to his feet and pulled his shirt over his head. He was carved out of marble, the lines separating his muscles so deep he looked like a statue. His pecs were hard and wide, and his narrow waist was a complex display of rivers and mountains of muscle.

Now it was no surprise he could get laid whenever he wanted.

"Christina." He undid his jeans and dropped them to the floor so he was in only his boxers.

I didn't focus on the outline of his erection through the material because I was stunned by what he said. "Christina?"

His knees hit the bed, and then he leaned down to a kiss woman beside me.

A woman I hadn't noticed because I'd been too focused on him.

He kissed her hard on the mouth then pulled her panties down her long legs.

I was in too much shock to move.

This asshole brought me here for a threeway?

After he finished kissing her, he moved over me and grabbed one of my heels to slip it off.

I yanked my foot out of his grasp. "Are you kidding me right now?"

He stilled on top of me, his eyes narrowing on my face.

I'd already had to talk myself into sleeping with him in the first place, but there was no way in hell I could talk myself into a threeway. It would do nothing to further my agenda anyway. I was just another body in a bed to fulfill his fantasies. There was no intimate connection that would allow me to manipulate him. I would be kicked out first thing in the morning, or I wouldn't even make it through the night. He wouldn't pay any attention to me ever again. I would be another notch on his belt before he moved on to the next. He probably wouldn't even remember this night in a few weeks.

I pushed him hard in the shoulder so he rolled over onto his back. "You're such a pig. The biggest fucking pig I've ever met." I got to my feet and stormed out of the bedroom, furious that my plan was going to shit. If I couldn't sleep with him to get my way, and I didn't have another trick up my sleeve, that meant I was completely out of ideas. I moved through the living room and headed to the elevator, not expecting him to stop me.

His loud footsteps sounded behind me, his bare feet hitting the hardwood. "What the fuck was that?"

I jammed my finger into the button before I turned around. "You bring me home to a threeway? Call me old-fashioned, but you should at least ask a woman first before you throw her into bed with another woman."

"You've been following me for weeks. When am I ever with just one woman?"

I saw him make out with several, but I didn't know he fucked multiple women at a time. "You're disgusting." I turned back to the elevator when the doors opened.

He snatched me by the arm and yanked me back.

I spun my wrist out of his grasp quickly then slapped down his hand before he could grab me again. "Don't touch me." I stepped inside the elevator.

He followed me and placed his body in between the doors so I couldn't go anywhere. In just his boxers, he stared me down with ferocity, like my tantrum was pissing him the hell off. "I know what I like, and I'm not ashamed of it. Every man in the world wishes they could have what I have, but they aren't man enough to make it happen. Just remember that the next time you screw someone. He may enjoy fucking you, but he would be much happier if there were two of you."

I shook my head slightly, my disgust growing by the second. "Trust me, he wouldn't be thinking that. Because I'm the kind of woman a man can barely handle on his own. I'm the kind of woman who doesn't share. I'm the kind of woman who keeps his attention until I'm finally done with him. If you need two women in your bed every night, then you obviously haven't met a single woman who can hold her own. That could have been me—but now you'll never know."

5

Cato

I LAY BETWEEN CHRISTINA AND STEPHANIE, THE FLOOR-to-ceiling windows showing the bright lights of Florence. The Catholic church down the street was lit up every night, a guiding star to all the lost souls of this city—including me.

I didn't stop that woman from walking out of my home.

No one talked to me that way.

But once the rage had passed and I'd fucked two beautiful women in my bed, I reflected on everything she'd said.

If you need two women in your bed every night, then you obviously haven't met a single woman who can hold her own. That could have been me—but now you'll never know. She successfully planted a seed of doubt, a hint of regret. I wondered if I had spent the night with just her, would the sex have been as marvelous as she promised.

I guess it didn't matter anymore. I would never see her again.

Didn't even know her name.

She was too beautiful to be one of those stupid obsessed women who thought they could change me, who thought they had something special that would make me settle down and marry them.

I would never marry.

I was way too rich to get married.

Women wanted to be in my bed because I was good at fucking. But they agreed to threesomes in the hope they would mean something to me, that I would see them as adventurous and exciting enough to be my wife.

There hadn't been a single woman who'd turned me down—until now.

My phone vibrated on the nightstand with a call, so I carefully reached over Stephanie to answer it. No one called me at this hour unless it was an emergency.

And it better be an emergency.

I saw the name on the screen. *Mother.*

I jumped out of bed and walked into the living room to answer it. "Mother, what's wrong?" Buck naked, I stood in my living room with my hand on my hip. Slowly, I paced, fearing the worst. "Are you alright?"

"I'm so sorry to bother you right now, Cato." She sighed into the phone, but her tone didn't hint at any distress. My mother had always been that way, eerily calm even in the most dangerous situations. It made her impossible to read.

"You never bother me. Now tell me." I stood in front

of the window and looked across the city, holding my breath as I waited for an answer.

She sighed before she answered. "He's here...and I can't get him to leave."

I knew exactly who he was. "Why the fuck did you let him in?"

"Said he wanted to talk."

"He had plenty of time to talk to you twenty-five years ago." With a clenched jaw and flexed biceps, I started to pace through the living room again. "That was his chance —he blew it."

Calm like always, she didn't rise to my anger. "Are you coming, Cato?"

She never had to ask that question. "You know I am."

————

SINCE THIS WAS PERSONAL, I drove myself. I took my Bugatti west to the countryside, while my team followed behind me. They accompanied me everywhere I went. In this instance, I didn't need them at all, but if someone wanted me dead, this was a perfect opportunity to catch me alone.

I didn't take risks.

I called my brother on the drive since this was his business as much as mine. "Bates."

He sounded wide awake despite the hour. "This should be good..."

"Mother just called me. That piece of shit is at her house right now."

Bates knew exactly who I was talking about without

asking. "What the hell is he doing there at two in the morning?"

"I don't like it either." I drove with one hand on the wheel and saw the headlights from the brigade of men behind me. "I'm five minutes away. You can join me if you want, but I've got this handled."

"By the time I make it out there, he'll already be dead."

"Yeah, you're probably right." I thought of my pistol sitting in the glove compartment. It was fully loaded and ready to go, but not all men deserved the mercy of a bullet. In this case, a clean bullet was way too good for him.

"Let me know what happens."

"Alright."

He hung up.

I pulled up to the house, a two-story Tuscan home surrounded by vineyards. In the darkness, the beauty was difficult to see. She had several acres of land, a fountain in the center of a circular driveway, and a gorgeous home I'd bought for her. She preferred the Italian countryside to the city so she could keep up her garden and enjoy the sound of the birds in the morning. I always worried she was too far away—especially during times like this.

A beat-up black car was in the roundabout, and I parked my Bugatti right behind it.

Pissed off, I stormed the front door and shoved it open. "Where the fuck is he?" Whether I was dressed in jeans and a t-shirt or a full suit, I was equally formidable. If someone crossed a member of my family, they wouldn't live long enough to cross anyone else. I moved past the entryway and the staircase into the living room that faced the back patio.

The second he looked at me, he flinched.

Like a pussy.

He turned to me and held up both hands. "We were just talking—"

I punched him so hard in the face he was on the floor instantly. And he didn't get up again.

Mother covered her mouth with her hand and silenced her gasp. "Cato, you could kill him."

I watched his motionless body on the floor. "That's what I'm going for."

After a few seconds of immobility, he slowly lifted his weight with his arms and stumbled to his feet. Blood poured from his nose, and his skin was already becoming discolored. With my height and a similar build, he wasn't a weak man—but I was definitely stronger. "Cato—"

"Come near my mother again, and I'll kill you next time." I never made threats I didn't mean, and I definitely meant this one. "No one will come looking for you. No one will file a police report. I own everything in this country—and I can make you disappear without a trace. Don't call my bluff, asshole." I took a step toward him, tempted to give him a black eye to complement that broken nose.

The asshole was stupid enough to speak again. "I just want—"

"You turned your back on my mother and left her alone to raise two sons. She had no job and no money, and you fucking left anyway. You're the definition of a coward. Now you show up on her doorstep asking for a handout—

because you're pathetic." I moved even closer to him. "I'm the man who takes care of her now. I'm a bigger man than you'll ever be—because my mother knew how to raise a man. We didn't need you then, and we don't need you now. Get the fuck out."

He held my gaze as he breathed hard, the blood dripping down his lips. His facial structure was similar to mine, and it was clear from whom I'd inherited so many of my features. But he didn't possess a spine, and he didn't possess honor. "I'm not looking for a handout—"

"Bullshit. I'm a thirty-year-old man. I don't need a father anymore. You're twenty years too late. My mother doesn't need a man without balls. You serve no purpose to either one of us. You stopped being a part of this family when you turned your back on us. That door has been shut and locked. There's no going back." I pointed to the front door. "Now get the fuck out."

He held my gaze a moment longer before he finally made his way toward the door. He wiped his nose on the sleeve of his collared shirt before he crossed the threshold and disappeared. Some of my men would escort him off the premises and follow him to see where he went.

I turned back to my mother. "Are you alright?"

A silk robe was tied across her body, and despite the late hour, her hair was still elegantly styled. A life of luxury suited her, and she kept up her classy appearance constantly. She stepped closer to me, the fatigue in the bags under her eyes. "I'm fine, Cato. Thank you for coming."

"There should be security guarding the perimeter." I'd offered it to her before, but she never took it. I had men watching me all the time because I had a lot of enemies—known and unknown. Any man who had my wealth was always a target.

"I don't want to live that way," she said dismissively.

"And I don't want to worry about you."

"Then don't." She looked up at me, her blue eyes identical to mine. "He says he regrets leaving…"

"Because we're rich, Mother." Sometimes my mother was naïve, despite the way she'd been betrayed. She wanted to see the good in people even when there was none there. "Of course, he regrets it. His two sons have founded the most lucrative banking company in the world."

"You're probably right…but he does seem sincere."

"He'll seem sincere until he gets a check." I was tempted to pay him off. Give him a million-dollar check just so he would leave us alone. That was just pennies to me, and he would never bother us again. But I had too much pride to give him anything, not after he hurt my mother. I couldn't care less there wasn't a father figure in my life when I was growing up. My mother was more than enough. But my loyalty to her fueled my rage.

"Maybe." She tucked a loose strand of hair behind her ear. "You should get going, son. I know you have work in the morning."

"Alright. Good night."

She walked me to the door. "I really appreciate you taking care of me, Cato. Not all sons would be so generous."

I turned my gaze on her before I walked out the door, examining the petite woman who had somehow given birth to two behemoth sons. She worked around the clock to put a roof over our heads and food on the table, and somehow, we always had a nice Christmas. When Bates and I found our success, we didn't even need to have a conversation about our mother. We took care of her because it was the right thing to do. "It's the least I can do, Mother."

————

I HAD a three-story home on forty acres of land in Tuscany. The drive branched off the main road and entered a forest of trees that hid the house from view. After nearly a mile, the drive finally reached the black gates with my surname fashioned in iron. A wall made of cobblestone surrounded the entire property, covering the forty acres and making it a hidden gem in the middle of the countryside. Men were stationed all along the wall—whether I was home or not.

It was the perfect meeting place for my biggest clients.

Because it couldn't be more private.

Clients could slip in and out without being spotted by another living soul. Transactions could be made with fifty men on duty. It was a place where men could loosen their ties and refresh their drink as many times as they wished.

Also, not all my transactions were legal. I made money in a lot of ways, and I broke the law in many ways to make that happen. I hid money from various governments for tax purposes and made a profit off those investments. Any powerful person in this world came to me if they wanted to keep their money safe—and make more money.

Bates and I just finished a meeting with clients from China. They were chauffeured out to the roundabout near the fountain and then guided to the end of the driveway and the iron gate. Photographers and journalists couldn't follow them here, and my clients were always pleased and comforted by the extreme privacy—along with all the security that combed the property.

Nothing happened under my watch.

I sat in the leather chair near the window, my legs crossed and my fingers resting under my chin. It was a bright summer day in Tuscany, and the brilliant rays penetrated through the glass and shone across my thigh. My callused fingertips brushed against my chin, soft from shaving that morning.

Bates sat in the comfortable armchair with his empty glass of scotch on the table. He was looking through the paperwork we'd just discussed with our clients. We were being given a great deal of money for safekeeping, which would be disguised as international investments in America. We evaded foreign detection and took advantage of the interest rates. He licked his thumb before he turned the page.

I kept my gaze out the window, thinking about nothing but also everything. "Bates."

"Hmm?" Wearing jeans and a t-shirt, he'd ditched a classic suit because we didn't need fancy clothes for meetings at this place. The estate spoke for itself.

"Doesn't it feel like the same shit over and over again?" From the third story, I could see over the cobblestone wall and to my neighbor's property. Vineyards backed up all the way to my property line, but his actual residence was too far away to be seen.

Bates lifted his gaze from the documents in his lap. "You could say that—not that I'm complaining."

Every day felt like déjà vu. My routine was almost always the same. I was referred to new clients from happy clients, and then I made new deals that increased my institutional holdings. More money was thrown on the table, but the pile was always so big I couldn't see it grow anymore. As a thirty-year-old man, I'd accomplished everything a sixty-year-old man could only dream of. It used to be exciting. Now it seemed repetitive.

Bates lifted his gaze again, his eyes narrowing on me. "We just scored a huge deal. Don't sit there and tell me you're bored."

I slowly turned in my chair and faced him, forcing my gaze away from the window and the landscape around my property.

Bates watched me with powerful eyes, regarding me like an opponent rather than a brother. The folder was open across his crossed legs, the signatures collected.

My glass was empty, and my mind was dead. Throughout the entire meeting, my heart rate didn't rise once. It was the same meeting I'd had a million times, just with different faces. It was the same conversation I'd had a million times, the same handshake. "Yes. I'm bored."

Bates slowly raised his right eyebrow, regarding me like I was losing my mind. He shut the folder without taking his eyes off me and tossed it on the large wooden table where the men had been gathered just twenty minutes ago. Their empty glasses still remained because the maids knew better than to interrupt us. "You have everything any man could ever want. How the hell could you be bored?"

"Good question."

Bates turned silent as he waited for me to elaborate. When I didn't speak, he pressed forward. "The women are boring you?"

There was nothing wrong with the women in my bed. Beautiful, sexy, and adventurous, they were exactly what I fantasized about. I always fucked two women at once. Made it carnal and animalistic. A single woman seemed too intimate now. I couldn't remember the last time I'd been with just a single woman. It must have been years ago. "I suppose."

"Jesus, I hope this isn't going where I think it is…"

"And where do you think that is?"

"You want a wife?"

If being with different women every single night was boring, then a marriage would be even worse. My head would explode from mundane repetitiveness. "No. It's the last thing on my mind."

Bates released an audible sigh of relief.

Marriage wasn't in the cards for either of us. It was too complicated. There wasn't a single woman in the world who wouldn't be tempted by our wealth. The second she got her hands on it, it would destroy her. It would complicate our business relationship, even if we drafted all the legal paperwork to keep her hands off the company in the event of divorce. It was something we'd agreed on a long time ago. So far, neither one of us struggled to keep our promise. After so many years of fucking around, women were all the same.

"Then what's your problem, Cato?"

I didn't have a single thing to complain about, and it would be childish to be ungrateful. My family struggled when I was young, and I would forever be humbled by my years of being poor. But now my life lacked purpose. "Wish I knew."

"Does this have anything to do with what happened to Mother the other night?"

"No." I made sure that asshole stayed away from her. This time, I put a team of security on her premises—even though she wasn't happy about it.

"Then where is this coming from?"

Those green eyes popped into my mind, brilliant like emeralds and highlighted by the sternness of her eyebrows. She had the most elegant neck, long and slender with gorgeous skin. Her lips were soft like pillows, and her small tongue was both timid and inviting. The desire in her eyes had flickered away when she'd seen Christina beside her—and that longing never returned. She told me off before she marched out of my home, taking me to task like I wasn't the most powerful man in this country. It was the most interesting conversation I'd had in a year. "No idea."

6

Siena

I SAT AT THE KITCHEN TABLE IN MY HOUSE, information and photographs of Cato spread out everywhere. There was an open bag of candy I was munching on, along with my third cup of coffee. Fresh out of ideas, I sat there and tried to think of a plan.

I had nothing.

Cato was too much of a pig to seduce. He was too strong to take down. And he was too guarded for me to intercept him.

I had a greater chance of flying to the moon than making this work.

The last memory I had of him floated in my mind. He stood outside the elevator in his black boxers, his muscled chest heaving with rage. Everything about him was sexy, from his narrow hips to his muscular thighs. He looked at me like I was the biggest pain in the ass—but he was still sexy.

Such a damn pig.

I'd had my fair share of playboys and assholes, but Cato Marino was a whole new level.

The man thought he was God.

He thought he could do whatever he wanted without explanation. It was so selfish that he didn't even consider what his date might want. The second I walked out of there, he probably called another woman to replace me. Then he fucked them both and forgot about me altogether.

Pig.

My phone rang, and someone I didn't want to talk to was on the other line. "Yes, Damien?"

His smile was audible over the line. "Sweetheart, I love the happiness in your voice."

"You call it happiness. I call it disgust. So what do you want?"

"Right to the point," he said with a chuckle.

I cut to the chase before he could drag it out. "I'm still working on it. I've interacted with Cato a few times but haven't figured out a way to make this work."

"So you did decide to sleep with him."

"No. Never said that."

"Whatever you say, sweetheart. When do you think this is gonna happen?"

"I really don't know," I snapped. "You've given me a task that's impossible to complete."

"That doesn't bode well for your father…"

Instead of pitying my father for being locked away, I was livid with him. If only he had listened to me, all of this wouldn't be happening. He cared more about money than protecting his family—now I was the one fixing everything. I despised money with every fiber of my being. I didn't miss a life of luxury, not when it came with so much hardship. My little house outside of Florence was perfect. I had enough money for everything I needed on a budget—and that was more than enough. "I'll figure it out, Damien."

"Alright. Just don't take too long." Click.

I set the phone down and shoved my hand back into the candy bag. I got a fistful of sugar then stuffed it into my mouth, not caring about the impact on my waistline. It wasn't like I still needed to seduce Cato.

My phone started to ring again, this time with a number I didn't recognize. I answered. "Siena."

"Hello, Siena. How are you?" The deep voice over the line was inherently familiar, filled with a fatherly affection.

The image of Crow Barsetti popped into my mind, but that was ridiculous considering I hardly knew him. Our interactions had only lasted a handful of minutes. I'd had an immediate draw to him the last time I saw him, feeling that same sensation in my chest that I felt toward my own father. "Crow?"

"Yes." He spoke with affection. "I have a distinctive voice, don't I?"

"Yeah, I guess you do." I was just threatened by Damien minutes ago, but that seemed so long ago now. Crow's warmth washed away Damien's coldness. "How can I help you?"

"I've been thinking about our conversation a lot."

Had he decided to help me?

"I haven't changed my position on the matter. I've got

a large family to think about. But I was able to make some calls and get some information for you."

"Really?" I asked, gasping slightly. "Oh my god, thank you so much. I don't even know what to say…"

"Well, it's not a lot to work with, but Cato is looking for an art buyer to decorate his home in Tuscany. That's what you do for a living, correct?"

"Yes." I didn't ask how he knew that.

"I put in a good word for you. Said you were the best."

He'd really stuck out his neck for me. "Wow…"

"It's a way into his home and a way to get his attention. It's not the kind of job his assistant can handle. Art is very personal, so he'll have to approve of everything you find for him. It's the closest you're going to get."

I already got pretty close to his bed…but that didn't work out. "Thank you so much, Crow. Really…it means a lot to me. I'll never forget your kindness."

He was quiet for a long time, letting the silence dangle between us. "I know how important family is. So do you."

———

I WAS at the gallery a few days later when the phone rang on the desk. It was a Tuesday afternoon, and business was slow. Few people were looking for a professional art buyer in the middle of the day.

I answered. "The Rosa Gallery. This is Siena." I had a list of clients I met through the gallery, and my job was to find the perfect pieces for them. I had a few high-profile clients who commissioned me to decorate their homes or offices, but most of the time, people were just looking for one single painting.

"Siena Russo?" the man asked bluntly.

"Yes, this is she. How can I help you?"

"My boss is looking for someone to decorate his home with specific pieces of art. He has very particular taste and a very large budget. I've done my research, and it seems like you've made quite a reputation for yourself."

Thank you, Crow. "I'm flattered."

"Are you interested in the project?"

A normal person would ask a million questions, but since I already knew this was for Cato, I didn't. "Very much so. Just let me know when you would like to get started. I should probably meet your boss to garner what he likes."

"I'll see if he has the time. He's very busy."

Yes. Busy being a pig. "You know where to find me."

———

I DROVE into western Tuscany and approached the large cobblestone wall that surrounded the property. It was a private piece of land, and I couldn't see any neighbors on either side of the road. The foliage was dense and green despite the merciless heat, and like always, there was a scent of grapes in the air.

I pulled up to the black iron gate and watched the security detail examine me. One came to my window and asked for my identification before they opened the doors and allowed me through.

My heart fell into my stomach. This man was guarded

at all times. I would need a hundred armed men if I had any chance of accomplishing anything, and even then, the odds weren't in my favor.

I drove up the road and onto his property, seeing the acres of lush landscape enclosed within the walls. Cato's security team seemed to stay along the perimeter because his actual home was peaceful and quiet. Three stories tall, it was a mansion big enough for twenty people.

Hard to imagine he lived there alone.

Even though he certainly didn't sleep alone.

I parked in the roundabout, gathered my things, and prepared to come face-to-face with the man I blew off. The angry look in his eyes was still fresh in my mind. I insulted him and stormed off, something he probably wasn't used to. Everyone bowed down to him like he was some kind of king.

He might not even hire me.

He might take one look at me and order me off his property.

I knocked on the door and was greeted by a man in slacks and a polo shirt. "You must be Siena." A man in his late fifties with salt-and-pepper hair smiled and showed his nice grin. His skin was distinctly tanned, like he attended to the needs outside the house as well as inside. "Please come in."

"Thank you." I wore a black dress with a black cardigan, a string of pearls around my neck. Whenever I worked, I always wore those two shades. It complemented the artwork I showed and made me seem neutral in comparison. My heels were higher than usual, giving me an extra three inches of height. They clacked against the wood as I carried myself inside. "I'm excited to be here."

"We're excited to have you. It's a beautiful home, but it needs to lighten up a bit." He placed his hand between my shoulder blades then guided me into a private room. The entryway had two staircases on opposite sides, and the space in between was big enough to fit a cocktail party. Hardwood floors and beautiful moldings made it the most beautiful house I'd ever set eyes on.

The sitting room had two couches with a coffee table, along with other chairs and a large window that showed the rest of his property in the rear. It smelled clean and fresh, but it looked like a room that was never touched. It was probably one of the many rooms reserved for private conversation, but not quite a business meeting.

"Coffee or tea?" he asked. "Or are you prepared for something stronger?"

"I'll have whatever Mr. Marino enjoys."

"Well, Mr. Marino is a scotch fan."

I already knew that. "What a coincidence. So am I."

He gave a slight nod. "You two will get along just fine. I'm Giovanni, by the way."

"Nice to meet you, Giovanni."

He walked out and left the door open.

I organized my papers and readied my notes, my heart hammering in my chest. Even if I didn't have ulterior motives, this would still be my dream job. This place was enormous, and judging by how elegantly it was already decorated, only the most beautiful pieces of art should hang on these walls. It would be an honor to work on something like this—and get paid for it.

But I wondered what his reaction would be once he saw me.

Giovanni returned a few minutes later. He set down a tray with a decanter of scotch, two glasses with a single cube of ice in each, and assorted cheese and grapes. "Mr. Marino is just finishing up with his mother. He'll be in shortly."

"Thank you."

After Giovanni left, I sat still and felt the nerves get to me. There was no reason to let his intimidation affect me, not when I had a mission to fulfill. My father's life was on the line, so even if he were a good person, it wouldn't change the way I felt about the task.

I heard his voice a moment later. "I'll see you later, Mother." His heavy footsteps echoed in the entryway.

The sound of her heels accompanied his. "Thank you for making time for me, son. I know how busy you are." She spoke like a queen, retaining so much elegance that I imagined her wearing a tiara.

A door shut a moment later.

Then I heard his footsteps get closer as he approached. Louder and louder they grew until his presence filled the air. Rigid with power and authority, he owned the room the second he stepped into it.

My back was to him, so I couldn't see his face.

He couldn't see mine.

He didn't apologize for making me wait, and he didn't introduce himself either, like announcing his name was simply redundant. He carried himself like a king, like every single one of his subjects should know exactly who he was and never turn their backs on him.

I rose to my feet and faced him, keeping my poise as if his undeniable power had no effect on me.

He didn't pause when he recognized my face, but there was a flash of surprise that moved across the surface of his eyes. He stopped near the couch like he was about to shake my hand, but he never extended the greeting. His blue eyes were even brighter than before, probably because of the sunlight coming through the large window. He was in dark jeans and a gray t-shirt, the kind of clothes that fit his frame beautifully.

He continued to stare, his eyes unblinking and his gaze intense. It was the same stare we'd shared across the room in quiet moments, an entire conversation passing between our expressions. Maybe he was thinking about our kiss in the bar. Maybe he was thinking about the way my ankle felt under his fingertips. Or maybe he was thinking of throwing me out of his house right then and there.

It didn't feel right to say hello or ask how he was doing. It didn't feel right to say anything at all. So I didn't.

He moved to the other couch and sat down, slowly lowering his large build across from me. Without taking his eyes off me, he poured two glasses of scotch and took a sip from one.

It was so quiet in the room I could hear every little sound. I could hear the ice cube tap against the glass, the sound of the decanter as he returned it to the tray. I could hear the scotch swirl around his mouth, right over his tongue.

He set the glass down and looked at me again, his hands coming together between his knees. "Siena. Beautiful name."

That was the last thing I expected him to say. "Thanks."

"Are you from Siena?"

"No. I was born here."

He grabbed my glass and handed it to me.

I accepted his offer and took a drink.

He watched every second of my movements, his eyes focused on my mouth and throat.

I returned the glass to the table and didn't start discussing the job. There was a good possibility he wouldn't want me in his home much longer. "Do you want me to leave?"

His pretty eyes were the only soft feature he possessed. The rest of him was hard and cold, like a man thawed from ice. He was impossible to read, his expression always stern. Whether he was that way intentionally or not was a mystery. "Why would I want you to leave?"

"Because I called you a pig." There was no way the memory of that night wasn't as fresh in his mind as it was in mine.

He tilted his head slightly. "I am a pig."

I couldn't stop the slight look of surprise from entering my face.

The corner of his mouth tugged up into a smile, but it happened so quickly I wasn't sure if it really happened at all. "And I like being a pig."

My smile didn't mirror his, but I didn't despise him like I did before. At least he was honest about who he was —even if he sprung it on you without warning. "Yeah, I can tell." I grabbed my folder and clicked the end of my pen. "I can discuss my qualifications for the job, or you can ask me whatever you want to know."

"Alright." He brought his hands together, his fingers massaging his knuckles. "Was this what you were after the entire time?"

I held his gaze as my heart leaped into my throat. Scrutinized, I felt like a specimen under the microscope. It was a question I couldn't dodge, and I had to answer it carefully. He knew I'd been following him. He knew I didn't want to sleep with him. What other explanation did I have to give? It seemed to be a strange coincidence that I was there now—asking for a dream job.

When I didn't answer, he pressed me again. "Answer me."

"Your team reached out to me."

"Too big of a coincidence."

I still didn't give an answer.

He continued to massage his knuckles. "I've got all day."

Cato Marino was far too suspicious of a man to sneak by. If I didn't admit to this, he would just keep digging until he found my purpose. And my real purpose was much worse than my fake purpose. That was something he couldn't uncover. "Yes. I wanted this job. I wanted to study you to find out what kind of artwork you might like. I wanted to get to know you to understand your soul. That way, when I pitched myself to you, I would have more to offer than anyone else."

He held my gaze and listened to every syllable coming out of my mouth. His reaction wasn't obvious because he kept his intimate thoughts too close to his mind. "That's dedication."

"I take my job seriously." Along with my father's life.

"Very seriously, if you're willing to sleep with a man for it."

It was an insult that I deserved because that was exactly what I was doing. I didn't want anything to do with this man. If our fates weren't so intertwined, I never would have bothered. He was way too complicated for me. But I didn't want him to perceive me that way, like I was really that ambitious. "That wasn't the only reason I wanted to sleep with you."

He watched me for a long time, his eyes hooked to mine without flinching. He didn't seem pleased or annoyed by that response. Like I hadn't said anything at all, he changed the subject. "It's a big project. Hope you can handle it."

"I can handle anything."

He rose to his feet and left his scotch behind. It seemed like the conversation was over because he headed to the door. "Then you're hired."

7

Cato

JUST LIKE EVERYONE ELSE, SHE WANTED SOMETHING from me.

Most women wanted a good lay. Most women wanted the opportunity to make me fall in love with them. Most women wanted to get their hands on my money.

But no woman had ever wanted a job from me.

I should be annoyed with Siena, but in actuality, I was impressed. Just like me, when she wanted something, she went out and seized it. Most people wouldn't have that kind of drive and patience. She did all her research before she finally made her move.

I'd done the same thing at the beginning of my career. I studied all my targets before I moved in. Tried to learn what they liked and didn't like. From their religious beliefs down to their economic standpoints, I knew every little thing.

She'd been on my radar since the first time I'd spotted her, so I didn't feel fooled by her ploy. My guard had always been up because it was a permanent fortress that surrounded my hard exterior. Maybe if she really had fooled me, I would be angry with her. But I couldn't be angry with a woman who worked so hard to get what she wanted.

I didn't know shit about the art industry, but I knew this was a multimillion-dollar project.

Anyone would kill for the opportunity.

If she were a man, anyone would call her ruthless and ambitious.

That was exactly how I saw her.

My Tuscan home was relatively new. I'd purchased it last summer and had the interior designer take care of all the changes I wanted. It was a long project, and now that it was completed, it needed the finishing touches. My home wasn't just the residence where I spent my summers, but it was also the place where I invited my special clients and threw my cocktail parties. Having stunning pieces of art on the walls was an essential part of that experience. I wasn't an art aficionado by any means, but I could appreciate it—to a certain degree.

Bates and I had just finished work in the main office when Giovanni stepped inside.

"Miss Siena is waiting for you in the drawing room, sir." Instead of having him wear a butler's outfit, I allowed him to dress casually like the rest of the staff. I only wore suits for special occasions, so I didn't see why he needed to vacuum in three layers of clothing.

I gave him a slight wave in understanding.

Giovanni walked out.

Bates shut his laptop then stuffed it into his brown leather bag. "Who's Siena?"

"The art buyer." I stood up and finished the rest of my glass before I left it behind.

"Good. She'll liven up the place." Bates pulled the strap over his shoulder, a slight smile on his face. "Or at least your bedroom."

I hadn't told my brother about my previous experience with her. "I don't think I'll get the honor."

"Wow. Didn't realize there was a woman out of your league."

I walked him to the door. "I just think we have different preferences." My cock needed two pussies every night, two mouths, and two assholes. Regardless of how stunning Siena was, I suspected a lay with her would be disappointing.

"Then that means she's fair game." Bates walked out and entered the entryway. The second we were out in the open, he stopped discussing her, knowing she might be able to hear our conversation.

Which was why I didn't speak further on the matter.

Bates invited himself into the drawing room and found Siena sitting on the couch like last time, a glass of scotch in front of her. He turned to me, wore a smug smile, and then kept walking. "The art buyer."

Siena turned around at the sound of his voice. She must have realized we were related because our features were so similar. Anyone with eyes could figure it out. She stood up and gave him an effortless smile, one that wasn't genuine but still undeniably beautiful. Whether she was smiling or frowning, she still had the exact same appeal. It was something I'd noticed after watching her from across the room. "Hello." She shook his hand. "You must be Bates. Pleasure to meet you."

Bates reciprocated, but he had a sinister look in his eyes. It was the same expression he wore when we were out on the town. He liked what he saw and wanted more of it. His hand squeezed her wrist a little too long, and he took his time withdrawing. "The pleasure is mine." He slid his hands into his pockets and continued to stare at her.

My brother and I were both predators, stalking our prey in the open. We'd shared women before, so he wouldn't hesitate to do it again if I were interested.

But I knew Siena would never go for that.

I gently clapped my brother on the back, silently excusing him. "I'll see you tomorrow, Bates."

"Alright." He kept his gaze on Siena before finally turning away and walking out.

He shut the door behind himself, so it was just the two of us.

The second he was gone, Siena dropped her smile. She regarded me seriously, turning into the cold professional she'd been just a few days ago. Today, she was in a black pencil skirt that hugged her hourglass frame phenomenally and a white blouse. Pearls hung around her neck. She also wore pearl earrings. Her hair was pulled back like usual, showing the contours of her feminine face. I preferred it when women left their hair down, long and luscious around their shoulders. My fingers liked to grab on to something while I pinned a woman underneath me. But her elegant updo enticed me anyway. She commanded respect in her silence. It must have been her posture or her natural confidence. She'd turned me down and called me a pig, but I still found her fascinating.

My hands rested by my sides as I gazed into her face. Her tall stilettos still couldn't make her match my height— not even close. But her poise made her confidence rival mine. Most women couldn't tolerate my intensity. They fidgeted in place and looked visibly nervous, waiting for me to take the reins and guide them. But just as she'd warned, Siena seemed like a woman who could hold her own.

"Let's get started, Mr. Marino." She sat down and crossed her ankles, sitting like a princess wearing an invisible tiara.

I stared down at her, imagining her on her knees instead of her ass. "Cato is fine." I lowered myself onto the couch across from her.

"I prefer Mr. Marino." She opened her folder and examined her notes.

I liked the way she referred to me with respect, but I didn't like the way she challenged me. "Cato." When she referred to me by my surname, it seemed like she was just another person in the crowd. But when she said my first name, it was easy for me to imagine how differently that night would have gone if she hadn't stormed out.

She lifted her gaze to meet mine, looking at me through the thickness of her lashes. Coy but confident, she was alluring.

Fuckable.

When I'd looked at her initially, I'd thought she was beautiful like most other women. Nothing too special about her. But her smartass mouth and strong opinions made her far more interesting than I'd anticipated.

She finally yielded to me. "Cato."

Yes, I definitely liked the way she said my name.

"Is there a specific artist you like? A certain period you want me to explore? Perhaps each room or floor is different?"

"You're the one who's been studying me. You tell me." What had she gleaned from me after studying me for so many weeks? She'd seen my home in Florence. She'd kissed me in a dark room. She'd even seen me near naked, seen the bed where my fantasies came true.

She held my gaze for several seconds, thinking of what her response would be. "I do have some ideas for you. But I think a tour of your home would give me a better idea of where everything should go. I brought my measuring tape. I hope you don't mind if I make some notes."

"No."

She rose to her feet with the folder held to her chest. "I can have Giovanni show me around. I'm sure you're busy."

I did have other things to do. I had people to call, emails to write, but staying with her seemed more appealing than all of that. "I'm only busy when I want to be busy." I led the way out of the room and back into the entryway.

She followed behind me with her pen and tape measure in hand. "I've been thinking about this room a lot since it's the only one I've really seen. It's the first thing guests see when they walk in the door, and you have so much space on this wall that the crown jewel should go here." She walked to the left side of the room and looked at the blank wall over the staircase. "I can get a ladder and get the dimensions later."

"Giovanni can help you with that." I stood behind her with my hands in the pockets of my jeans. Instead of staring at the available wall with the same fascination she had, I tilted my eyes down to her ass. I never got to see her dress on the floor that night. The closest I got to getting her naked was slipping off one of her heels. Now that I was staring at her in the light of day, there was no denying just how sexy she was, from her long legs, perky ass, and those soft shoulders.

"Thanks." She scribbled a few notes before she turned back to me. "I'm ready to see the next room whenever you are."

———

MY PRIVATE OFFICE was on the third floor, along with my bedroom. I didn't use it very often, and most of the time, I just used it to drink and gather my thoughts. It had a large fireplace, one almost as big as the enormous one in the entryway. On a winter night, the raging fire seemed to extinguish the bitterness in my thoughts.

I opened the door and allowed her to examine the mahogany wood of my desk. It was a beautiful, deep color, an example of fine Italian craftsmanship. There were two leather sofas near the fire along with a table. Cabinets were placed on either side of the fireplace, mostly full of booze. There was only a single window in this room right behind the desk. It didn't have a great view like the other rooms in the house, but that was how I preferred it.

She took her time as she absorbed the mood of the room. "This room is different from all the others. At least, the other offices."

I leaned against the fireplace and continued to study her, study her the way she studied my environment.

"It's dark. Moody."

"I'm a dark and moody man." I'd always been that way since I was a boy. A therapist could blame it on my father's abandonment, but I didn't think that was the only culprit. Ever since I was born, I was a quiet child. During adolescence, I became even quieter, choosing my friends wisely and avoiding romance because it required too much talking. Bates and I were the same in that regard. That was probably why we got along so well.

"You don't show this room to many people, right?" She turned back around to look at me, her green eyes complementing the wood of my desk and floor.

Bates had been in here a few times. Giovanni and the cleaners stopped by to keep it tidy. Other than that, I seemed to be the only visitor. "No."

"Then perhaps this room doesn't need anything. It already has so much character." She returned to me by the door, holding my gaze steadily. She gripped her folder and mastered her confidence even though I was standing right in front of her. Like a real soldier, she didn't cower easily. Actually, she didn't cower at all.

"Your call."

I stared at the pearls encircling her throat and yearned to grip them hard. I wanted to yank her necklace free and shatter it, making the pearls drop to the floor with quiet thuds on impact. Then I wanted to smother that slender neck with my lips, kissing and sucking the flawless skin until it was bruised with my marks everywhere.

She waited patiently for an answer.

As if I hadn't just experienced a vivid fantasy, I answered her. "Leave it as it is." I left the office and guided her to the last room in my home—my bedroom. It took up half of the third floor, having an Alaskan king bed, a private living room, a balcony that overlooked the back-yard, and a bathroom that was big enough for a gym.

It was the only time she'd slightly cowered on the tour. She stepped inside my room and looked at the bed for a long moment before she appraised the barren walls around it. The bed was custom-made and shipped across the pond. It was nine feet by nine feet, perfect for more than two guests at a time.

It was the exact reason I had it.

Siena must have pieced that information together, but she didn't comment on it. She moved through the rooms and examined the other spots. She scribbled notes then came back to me. "You have a beautiful home, Cato. Decorating it should be no problem, especially when it'll look amazing no matter what hangs on the walls."

"Thank you." I stood near the foot of the bed, reflecting on the last kiss we'd shared. We'd stepped off the elevator, and then my lips were on hers. I smothered her with hot kisses as I guided her back to the bed. I'd kissed a lot of women, but she was exceptional.

She'd said she didn't want to sleep with me just for the job, and I believed her. If that were the case, she would have gone through with it—including Christina. But she was sincerely offended at the thought of sharing, and that drove her away.

I could slip my hand into her hair and kiss her then and there. I could rumple the sheets with our sweaty bodies. I could make her come just the way I fantasized about. But being with one woman hadn't been my taste in a long time. It became too boring to be exciting. Now I always had two women at once—and even that was becoming tedious.

Siena wouldn't be any different.

She scribbled some notes then came back to me. "Since this room is primarily just for you, I thought we could go with dark and sultry images, of women and historic landscapes, unless there was something you specifically had in mind. I have a few clients who prefer to decorate entire rooms inspired by a single artist."

I heard everything she said, but I didn't really take it in. I watched her lips move and focused on the way her sexy mouth opened and closed. Glimpses of her tongue reminded me of the way it felt in my mouth. "Whatever you think is best."

———

BATES JOINED me at the bar. Instead of going to the club right away, we met up for a drink in Florence. I left Tuscany because I had work to do in one of our offices in the city. Bates was managing another just down the road. The trouble with having a big company was two people weren't enough to keep it running. Neither one of us trusted anyone else to delegate any high-profile work, so it always fell to us two.

Bates clinked his glass against mine. "How'd it go with Siena?"

She'd been on my mind a lot lately. It surprised me how she could walk into my home and remain professional, when our initial meeting had been anything of the sort. Maybe she was just trying to get a job at the time, but no woman kissed like that unless she enjoyed it. The fact that I had no idea what she was thinking or what she wanted was a turn-on in itself. Women were so brazen with me, throwing themselves at me with little respect for themselves.

Siena was different.

"Took her on a tour of the house. She already has a lot of ideas." I stared at the TV in the corner and ignored the woman who was staring at me from across the bar. I had a whole phone book of women I could contact for a dirty night. There wasn't much excitement in the chase anymore. Like an animal that already had a carcass by its side, there was no reason to go out and keep hunting.

"Married?"

"No idea." I never asked because I didn't care if a woman was married. Her husband could hate me all he wanted, but there was nothing he could do about it. If he didn't want his woman to hook up with someone else, he should be a better husband.

"Boyfriend?"

I took another drink. "Does it matter?"

"I suppose not." He rested both of his arms on the table as he fisted his glass.

I still wanted to fuck this woman, but I didn't have any claim on her. I'd never made a claim on any woman in my life. It would be strange to start now. "But since she works for me, lay off."

"Her job won't last forever, so that's fine."

Even when she was finished, I didn't like the idea of her screwing my brother. Bates would be down for a one-on-one, so he could give her exactly what she wanted. "Let this one go, Bates."

Instead of taking a drink, he lowered his glass and looked at me.

I felt his stare on my face but ignored it.

He kept up the look. "If you want her, why haven't you done something about it?"

"Already did."

He ignored his drink altogether, far more interested in our conversation than booze—which was a first. "So, she really did turn you down. That's a first—and Cato doesn't like it."

"That's not what happened."

"Well, what did happen?" He turned on his stool so he could look at me better, ignoring the TV I was looking at along with the pretty women in the bar.

"Saw her in a club. Kissed her. Took her back to my place—but she bolted when she saw Christina."

"So she's *that* kind of girl." He nodded slightly. "Not the adventurous type."

"I suppose." I took a drink.

"How did she end up being your art buyer?"

"One of my men said she was the best."

Bates, the most paranoid person on the planet,

simmered with hostility. "You don't think that's an odd coincidence?"

"Yes. I asked her the same thing. I noticed she'd been following me for a while."

"How long?"

"A few weeks. She was at the bakery outside one of our offices, watching me. I caught her off guard and confronted her about it."

"Interesting."

"In the end, it seemed like all she wanted was this job. Claimed to be researching me so she could figure out exactly what I liked and didn't like." I wasn't the kind of man who believed people so easily, but her story fit. She was clearly passionate about her job, and she'd been at the gallery for many years. "She's ambitious and driven—and was willing to do anything to get the job."

"Except a threeway."

I shrugged and took another drink.

"I don't know about her, man." Bates turned sinister, the anger slowly coming into his eyes. "We can never be too careful."

"I agree. But I think she's harmless."

"You just think she's harmless because she's beautiful."

"No." The more beautiful they were, the more dangerous they became.

"I'll keep an eye on her. Don't trust her."

"Fine with me." As long as he wasn't fucking her, I didn't care.

"If you want this woman, why haven't you made it happen? She was just at your place a few days ago." When the tension in the conversation faded away, he turned back to the TV and scanned the people in the bar.

"I'm not a one-on-one kinda guy."

"Not even for one night?"

I shook my head. "If I'm bored with two women, you don't think I'll be bored with one?"

He clinked his glass against mine again. "Touché."

"And she won't change her mind."

"Must be a good girl."

It seemed that way. She had the kind of beauty that could capture the soul of almost any man. The curves of her waist and lips weren't the only sexy things about her. Her eyes drew me in the deepest. So bright and intelligent. And the way she strutted into every room like she owned it made me respect her. Instead of jumping into a threeway she didn't want, she decided to walk out and find a better alternative. She wasn't the kind of woman to make a sacrifice for someone else.

And I wasn't the kind of man to make a sacrifice for anyone else.

Maybe the sex would be incredible. But we were just too stubborn to find out.

8

Siena

BONES SAT ACROSS FROM ME AT THE TABLE IN THE BAR, looking furious from the second he took his seat. Covered in tattoos and awash imminent threat as he was, not even his pretty eyes could make him seem harmless. His muscles stretched his t-shirt, and his broad shoulders looked like a solid wall. A glass of scotch sat in front of him, and he downed it quickly before he ordered another.

"Thanks for coming." Now that I'd had a tour of Cato's home, I realized it would be impossible for me to pull any kind of stunt—at least with my skill set. I could win a shootout and fight off a grown man, but to kidnap someone so protected was impossible.

"You aren't welcome." Both of his elbows rested on the table, and he sighed as he glared at me. "I'm only here as a favor to Crow. Make it quick."

"How do you know him?" The Barsettis seemed to have a connection to everyone in Italy, from the Skull Kings, to the mob, and even politicians.

"He's my father-in-law."

It took a moment to process his confession. "You're married to his daughter?" Bones seemed too dangerous to be part of the simple life Crow described. He was hostile and aggressive, a man with a reputation for blood lust.

"Yes."

"Oh…I didn't know that."

"Don't blame him for being ashamed. Now get on with it. My wife has a Barsetti attitude, so if I'm out too late, she'll raise hell."

"Yeah, of course." I pulled out the rough drawing I'd made of Cato's home in Tuscany. The dimensions weren't perfect, but I had a good schematic of the place. "I got a good look at the house. It seems like there're five staff members at all times, and the outside wall is protected by a security detail of at least thirty men."

Bones didn't even glance at the schematic. He kept staring at me, his hostility rising. "You're kidding me with this bullshit, right?"

"Bullshit?" The only way I was going to pull this off was by collecting every ounce of information possible. Maybe Cato's home in Tuscany wasn't the best location, but his building in Florence was even worse.

Bones pressed his finger into the page, his eyes still focused on me. "You think you're gonna overpower him and somehow sneak him past all these people?"

"Overpowering him will be the easy part." Nothing a syringe couldn't handle.

"So, your plan is to drag a 200-pound man out the front door?" His jaw tensed noticeably, filled with rage.

"No. I'm asking you for advice, which is why you're here."

"I already gave you my advice." He pushed the paper toward me. "You want this guy? You need to fuck him."

"And what will that accomplish? He'll screw me then forget about me like all the others."

"Then make sure he doesn't forget you."

The last time, just when things got hot and heavy, Cato threw a curveball and expected me to share his bed with another woman. Regardless of how open-minded I was, that wasn't a course of action I would take. "Even if I could pull that off, what then? If I get him to like sleeping with me, how does that get me closer to saving my father?"

"When a man is obsessed with a woman, he can't think straight. It's the only situation where he can be manipulated or misled. Get him wrapped around your finger and deep in your pussy, and you can get whatever you want."

I didn't appreciate the crass way he spoke to me, but I liked his candor. He didn't seem like the kind of man who could speak any other way. Brutal honesty was the only way of life he knew about. "I'm an experienced woman, but if Cato is obsessed with threeways, I don't think there's anything special I can offer him." Even in lingerie with a kinky trick up my sleeve, there was nothing that could surprise him.

Bones took a long drink from his glass then wiped his mouth with the back of his forearm. With the same irritation in his eyes, he looked at me. "I remember the moment I fell in love with my wife, even though I didn't realize what was happening at the time. She was just some woman I wanted to murder for revenge. But the second I fucked her, it was game over. She took all the power—and I surrendered."

I cocked an eyebrow. "Wait, you wanted to murder your wife?"

"Yeah, long story." He brushed it off with a wave of his hand. "But my point is, I was thinking clearly before I got between her legs. The second I was there, all my ambitions were destroyed. She became my biggest obsession. Like she was a drug, I couldn't stop until I got the next hit...and then the next."

"How romantic..."

His hard expression didn't change. "That's what you need to do with Cato."

"You're simplifying it. Were you screwing lots of women before her?"

He took another drink. "Yes. And I was into kinky shit too."

"Well, I can't control Cato's reaction to me. The idea of him becoming obsessed with me seems unlikely. This guy gets more ass than he knows what to do with. I'm a talented lady, but there's nothing I can do to impress him."

"My wife just lay there—and that was more than enough." An evil grin stretched across his face.

"Well, maybe she's your soul mate."

His smile dropped, but the intensity in his eyes deepened. "I don't believe in that bullshit."

"Then what other explanation is there?" I didn't believe in true love or soul mates either. My own father wouldn't protect my mother, and now I was being threatened with rape and death by his enemies. If he'd spent more time loving us instead of trying to gain more power, I would be living a normal life right now.

He shrugged. "Till this day, I still don't know."

"Well, that definitely won't happen with Cato. He's not my type. I'm not his either."

"All women are his type," he said. "Has he tried getting you into bed since?"

Cato didn't say much when we were together, but I could definitely feel the tension in the room. His eyes always scanned my body, and he blinked so little, sometimes I wondered if he needed to blink at all. "No."

"Cato is the kind of man who always gets what he wants. Maybe defying him is your ticket."

"I just said he hasn't tried to hit on me."

"That doesn't mean anything. He wanted you before, and you took off. It's unfinished business for him."

"Maybe."

"The best way to stand out is to be different. Denying him definitely makes you different."

I tried to follow his logic, but I came to a dead end. "You said I needed to fuck him, but now you're telling me not to?"

"I'm telling you to play hard to get. When I met my wife, she wasn't afraid to tell me off. She wasn't afraid to shoot me. She stood her ground when other women would have melted. It was that spark that captured my obsession to begin with—because she didn't need me."

What kind of relationship was this? "Your wife shot you?"

His grin returned to his face, full of sincerity. "Yeah."

He rubbed his left shoulder, like he was remembering the pain from the wound. There was no denying the pride in his eyes, like that memory was holy to him.

"Alright…" I didn't understand how a relationship based on such violence turned into a marriage, but asking more questions wouldn't make me understand it better. "Well, I'm not gonna shoot Cato."

"Then keep him on your line—and slowly reel him in."

"And then fuck him and hope it goes well?" I asked incredulously, despising myself for sinking so low. No one would judge me for sleeping with a man to save my father's life, but I wished there was a better way to do this.

"You have no other option, Siena. Even if you had a team of thirty trained men, getting him away from his guard and making the handoff would be impossible. Not only would your father die, but you would die too. It would accomplish nothing."

"So if I make this happen, then what?"

"You'll have to gain his trust. Then the two of you go off somewhere together—alone. You have Damien wait for you there."

"I never see Cato go anywhere alone."

"I know." Bones nodded in agreement. "Which is why he'll need to trust you. Have him take you away for a romantic evening or something. All you need is a thirty-minute window. You guys make the trade, and then you run for it."

That was the only plan that seemed feasible. Plotting an escape from one of his residences would be futile. There was no way I could pull this off under these circumstances. Getting him alone and away from his men was the only possibility, and for that to happen, he would need a reason to want to be alone with me. Sleeping with him really was the only way this would work.

Bones watched me from across the table, examining my expression as I gripped the glass in front of me. "Your father is an asshole. No one would blame you if you left him to his fate. It's his fault he's in this situation —not yours."

I stared at my glass as my fingers felt the condensation on the outside.

"He had his chance to walk away—but he didn't."

Crow had given me the same advice. I lifted my gaze to look at Bones again. "As much as I don't want to do this, I couldn't live with myself if I didn't try. He's my father...my blood. Loyalty is the most important thing in this life."

Bones opened his mouth like he was going to argue with me, but then he closed it again as if he'd changed his mind. He gave a slight nod instead. "I understand."

"I don't know how Cato is mixed up in all of this, but I'm beginning to feel bad for what I'm about to do to him." He wasn't the kind of man who trusted anyone. He didn't even seem that warm to his own brother. If I successfully tricked him, it would destroy him. Was he innocent the way I was innocent?

"Don't feel bad for him. He's not a good man."

"He's not?" I whispered.

Bones shook his head. "His money isn't clean. He's the richest banker for a reason—because he uses blood money."

"What's blood money?"

"He acts as the treasurer for all organized crime. When the mob needs cash, they call him. When the Skull Kings need to hide their cash, they call him. When they need to borrow money for a weapons deal, they call him. Cato Marino knows about all the crimes against humanity because he funds most of them—and makes a profit each time. He doesn't hesitate to kill anyone who gets in his way. His finger doesn't stay on the trigger for long."

I felt a tremor move down my body when I realized who I was dealing with. This man was pretty on the outside but murderous on the inside. He had more power than anyone I'd ever heard of. "No wonder Damien wants him gone."

"I'm sure Cato is funding competition. If they can get rid of him, the nucleus binding all the organizations together, it would be chaos. A free-for-all. There're just as many people who want him dead that want him living."

And I would be the one to make it happen.

"So, don't feel bad. Cato Marino is just as evil as I am."

After listening to Bones speak so highly of his wife, I didn't feel afraid of him. "You don't seem so bad."

He finished his drink then turned the glass upside down on the table. "Trust me, I am."

9

Cato

I HADN'T TOUCHED MY GLASS SINCE THE MOMENT I SAT down. It was my favorite drink—scotch. A single ice cube sat at the bottom, slowly melting and mixing with the booze that burned my throat with every sip. Four of my men stood behind me, all packing under their jackets.

Claw sat across from me, a large scar down his left cheek. It looked like someone had tried to skin him alive—but he managed to escape. He wore a blue blazer with a gray V-neck underneath, and while he sat with grace, he didn't possess a hint of dignity the way I did. He was a thug, a criminal, and a pawn.

I was the king. "Twenty percent."

He cocked his head slightly, his eyes narrowed in revulsion. "You can go lower than that."

"I can go as low or high as I wish." Every room I stepped inside had a temperature. It rose and fell depending on the mood of the inhabitants. But I was the thermostat. I was the one who controlled everything.

Claw clenched his jaw slightly. "Ten."

I chuckled. "It's twenty-five now."

A glimmer of rage sparked in his eyes, but he kept the rest bottled inside his body. "You gave a much more generous offer last week."

"That was for Kevin—who asked for a much smaller loan. You expect me to give you two hundred and fifty million without something in return? You're asking me to front the costs for enough military weapons to provision all the soldiers of an entire country. Yes, asshole. It's twenty-five percent interest. Take it or leave it." My biggest profits came from my connections to organized crime. I got high interest on my investments, and since criminals cared more about their reputation than innocent people, they always paid their debts.

Claw shook his head slightly, furious with the terms but unable to protest. If they wanted to make this happen, they needed me. All the assholes of the underworld needed me in one way or another. "I'll take it."

———

I SAT in the back seat of the armored car as I was escorted back into Tuscany. It was three in the morning, but I had clients visiting the estate the next day, so I'd rather make the drive now than later.

Bates called me. "How'd it go?"

"Twenty-five percent."

Bates paused as he let the number sink into his skin like water into a sponge. "They couldn't have been happy with that."

"No." The Skull Kings didn't like it at all, but since their balls were in my hand, there was nothing they could do about it.

"Shit. That was easy."

"Too easy." I'd been in the game for a long time, and my reputation was doing all the heavy lifting. Deals were made for me with little work, and getting incredible deals in business negotiations wasn't even hard anymore. I looked out the window as I mulled over a word in my head. Bored.

"We'll talk about it tomorrow after the meeting."

"Alright." I hung up then looked out the window into the darkness. Once Florence was behind me, it was nothing but black on the way to the house. Some homes were lit up from a distance, but since the countryside was asleep, it was just me and the stars.

I arrived at my home fifteen minutes later, then stepped inside the house.

Regardless of the hour, Giovanni was awake and ready to greet me. "How'd it go, sir?"

"Fine." I slipped off my jacket and handed it to him.

"Anything I can get you? Or are you straight off to bed?"

I was going to bed, but not to sleep. "No. Go to sleep, Giovanni. It's been a long day." Giovanni served me all hours of the day, and even when I tried to give him time off, he never wanted to take it. Keeping up my home seemed to keep him sane.

"Alright, sir."

I turned to the staircase on the right.

"Sir?"

I looked at Giovanni again, knowing he wouldn't disrupt me unless it was important.

"I wasn't sure if I should notify you now or in the morning, but…there's been a situation with one of the men on the team."

Survival was about keeping two eyes in front of you and two eyes behind you—at all times. Even with so many men guarding me, I never truly felt safe. As long as I possessed this kind of power, the rest of the world would want to take it away from me. No one could be trusted—not even my butler. "Yes?"

"They think he's been planted by the Russians."

The best way to get to me was through my security team. It was my strongest asset but also my greatest vulnerability. I paid my men the kind of salaries that would make them loyal to their last breath. If any of them were suspicious of anyone else, they were encouraged to come forward. "Which one?"

"Jeremy. They found unauthorized wiring in his uniform. He's also made unrecorded calls during his shift. The location of his calls can't be traced. He's clearly communicating with someone he shouldn't be."

Any suspicious activity was guilty activity in my eyes. I made it clear to my men I would execute them myself if I ever suspected any foul play. There was no such thing as a trial or an opportunity to make a case for freedom. I just didn't have time for that. "I'll take care of it in the morning."

10

Siena

"LET ME GIVE YOU A HAND WITH THAT." GIOVANNI appeared out of thin air and picked up the painting carefully wrapped in plastic sheathing. "Are these for Mr. Marino?"

"Yes. I wanted him to see them in person before he made his decision." I picked up the next biggest one and carried it into the drawing room. One by one, we stacked them against the walls near the window so the natural light hit the colors on the canvas.

I walked back outside to gather my things from the passenger seat when another car pulled up. With black windows and a black exterior, it resembled a tank more than a car. Bates got out of the back seat, dressed in a black suit with a hostile expression on his face.

He didn't look at me once.

There was bad blood brewing. I could sense it in the air, smell it on my nose. It didn't seem to have anything to do with me, but whatever was about to boil over was very near. I was tempted to get back into the car and drive away, but now the passage was blocked.

By two men dragging another in front of the fountain. They pushed him to his knees and stepped back.

What the hell was going on?

Bates stood off to the side and crossed his arms over his chest, his eyes reserved for the man sitting on his knees on the concrete.

Giovanni came back to my side. "Miss Siena, you should go inside." He gently touched me by the elbow and escorted me up the steps. "This isn't any of our business."

"What's going to happen?" It looked like an execution was about to take place.

Giovanni never answered me.

At that moment, Cato stepped out of the house—a pistol in his hand. He was dressed in dark jeans and a black t-shirt, and his muscled frame looked even thicker today—because he was clearly pissed. Blood lust was in his eyes, and his finger was already on the trigger.

Oh no.

He didn't look at me as he passed and made his way down the steps.

Giovanni led me inside.

The man about to be executed started to beg for his life. "Cato, please—"

A gunshot went off.

The sound of a falling body came a second later.

My back was to the door so I didn't see the execution happen, but I could picture it vividly in my mind.

Cato didn't hesitate. He didn't let the man beg. He just pulled the trigger and got it over with.

I controlled my breathing, but I felt the adrenaline sear my veins. Bones warned me this man was dangerous —and that warning wasn't an exaggeration. Cato shot that man for whatever reason, and he didn't hesitate. When he realized I was a fraud, what would he do to me?

"Clean this up," Cato ordered. "And burn the body."

———

I WAITED in the drawing room for fifteen minutes before Cato appeared.

Perfectly calm, like he hadn't just executed someone, he stepped inside and glanced at the paintings I had unwrapped. His eyes took in each one for only a few seconds before he sat down and looked at me. "Yes."

Just when my heart had slowed down, it sped up again. The palpitations had nothing to do with his good looks, but rather the memory of what happened on his doorstep not even twenty minutes ago. He knew I'd witnessed the entire thing because he'd walked past me with the gun in his hand. "Yes, what?"

"Yes on the paintings." He was in the same clothes as before, but his gun was missing.

I'd been around guns my whole life and even stashed a few in my own home. They didn't make me uncomfortable. But being in the presence of someone who could wield one so mercilessly certainly made me uncomfortable. "Great." I'd been expecting a lengthier discussion, but after the execution, it seemed strange to discuss something as frivolous as artwork.

He must have detected the unease in my gaze. "Trust me, he deserved it."

"What did he do?" I asked, not expecting him to actually answer me. None of it was my business.

"He's a spy."

"Oh…" Just as I was a spy. "How did you figure that out?"

He held my gaze for a long time, like he might not answer. "Because I know everything. Nothing goes on under my nose that I don't know about. And if I don't know about it, I will very soon. I run a dictatorship, not a democracy."

Should I be terrified he was telling me all of this? "Do you want me to sign an NDA or something?"

A charming smile came across his face, like I'd just told a joke. "Why would I do that? If you told anyone, they would believe you. But no one would be dumb enough to repeat it or print it."

I was a confident woman, but I'd never underestimated my targets—until now. My father's life was in the balance, but now it didn't seem like he had a prayer. Cato Marino was an opponent I had no chance against. None whatsoever.

"Don't be afraid of me."

My eyes moved back to his, seeing the sincerity in his gaze. "I was never afraid of you."

"Your eyes say otherwise."

"Well, they just watched an execution. Can't exactly blame them."

The corner of his mouth rose once more. "I only kill

people who are stupid enough to cross me. Don't cross me, and you'll never have anything to be afraid of."

Was it my paranoia, or did it seem like he was threatening me? What if he already suspected me and he was waiting for me to make a definitive move? Or perhaps I was reading between the lines too much. I kept up a blank façade even though that was nearly impossible to do. "You shouldn't cross me either."

His smile slowly faded, and he regarded me with his cold stare. His arms rested on his thighs, and his expansive shoulders looked broad and powerful. Even without a weapon, he was a terrifying man. His beauty was a bullet, and his body was the barrel. "I wouldn't dare." His hands came together, and he massaged his knuckles as he continued to watch me.

I could definitely feel the intensity between us, feel the potent lust and hostility swirl around us. I was both aroused by him and afraid of him, feeling two powerfully conflicting emotions at the exact same time.

"You should give me a chance. I think you'll enjoy it." He said it with such confidence, the kind of assertiveness another man couldn't reproduce. He clearly viewed himself as untouchable, like there was nothing he couldn't ask for.

He'd dropped the subject the last few times I saw him, but now he was circling again. I considered what Bones said and kept Cato at a distance. "I like men."

"I'll be there." He leaned forward a bit more, bringing us closer together on the two couches. His thick arms stretched his sleeves, and his beautiful tanned skin looked as delicious as caramel candy. His cologne filled the room as he sat there, casting a spell that spread into every corner.

"I *only* like men."

"Are you sure? Have you ever tried it? A lot of women I've bedded weren't excited about it at first…but now they enjoy it."

I couldn't believe there was ever a moment when I felt guilty for tricking him. This guy was a murderous pig. He was so stubborn and conceited that he continued to pester me for what he wanted instead of just giving in. That was a whole new level of arrogance. "Alright. I'm in."

His eyes shifted noticeably, the color draining from his face as the excitement rushed into his eyes.

"You. Me. And a man of my choosing."

Instantly, the excitement disappeared. His jaw clenched slightly, as if I'd seriously offended him.

"What?" I mocked. "How will you know unless you try it?"

Cato kept up his hostile stare but said nothing in retaliation. It didn't seem like words could match the rage in his eyes, so it was easier to remain quiet. He definitely got his point across that way.

I shut my folder and set it on the table. "I'll hang these up for you. I'll be back next week with a new set of paintings and pottery I'd like you to see." I stepped away from the table and grabbed the first painting on the ground. I had my tools, so I could take care of the labor for him.

He came up behind me then gently placed his hand on my elbow.

My initial impulse was to fight him, to twist out of his grasp because no man could touch me whenever he felt like it. But instead, I let the touch linger, let his fingertips slowly dig into my soft skin. "Yes?"

He slowly pulled me toward him, making me turn on the spot so I would face him again. He looked down into my face with his bright eyes, his hard jaw chiseled from marble. His fingers still gripped my elbow, the same fingers that had pulled that trigger. "You're teasing me."

His lips were dangerously close to mine, and I didn't let them get any closer. "You teased me first." He was the one who gave me the greatest kiss of my life before he threw me into bed with another woman. He'd moved his hand up my thigh under my dress and made me think I was the only one on his mind.

His eyes shifted back and forth slightly as they looked into mine. When he was this close, I could really smell his cologne, really feel his presence. There was a distinct warmth to him, like he was the sun in his own solar system. His fingers gradually dug into my skin harder as he kept his grip on me. "You're an enigma."

"Me?" I asked, our faces still close together. "I'm pretty easy to read—because I say what I want. You just don't like it because what I want isn't what you want."

"And what do I want?" His hand left my elbow and snaked up my back. His large palm pressed hard against my body, his fingers burning through the thin fabric of my black dress. He moved farther up until he reached the back of my hair. He gripped the strands like reins, securing me in place so I wouldn't go anywhere.

Now I wasn't thinking about my plan anymore. I wasn't thinking about anything anymore. "Me."

He controlled my neck and moved my face until my

lips were upturned to his. He had ideal access to my mouth, for a perfect kiss that would rival the last one we shared. His arms were comfortable around my body, and his hands actually felt like a safe haven.

It would be easy to succumb to my hormones, especially when this man would give me the best sex of my life, but I had to focus on the prize. A good lay wouldn't be enough. He'd stop thinking about me the second we were finished. I had to keep him at bay, to make sure his interest didn't burn out too quickly.

I finally found my footing and pulled away, stopping the moment before his lips could press against mine. I turned away and cleared my throat, breaking eye contact with him. "Since I'm working for you, this should stay professional."

He didn't reach for me again, but his eyes shone like two hostile beacons. "You want me."

"No, I *wanted* you. That moment has come and gone." I turned back to him, doing my best to seem sincere. "When I kissed you in that bar, I wanted to go home with you. I wanted an amazing night of sex to get me through a few weeks until I found my next fix. But you're into some things I'm not into, so that was the end of the story. Now I work for you—and it should stay professional."

"I just killed someone in my driveway. Not exactly professional."

I swallowed the lump in my throat, afraid that might be me in the future. "All the more reason we should forget about this."

"I don't think either one of us can forget something we can't stop thinking about."

It would be pointless to pretend I didn't want him, so I stopped saying otherwise. Instead, I picked up the painting and stepped away from him so he couldn't reach me again. "I need to get back to work. I have to return to Florence for my date tonight."

He tensed on the spot, the muscles of his frame tightening slightly before thickening. There wasn't a possibility that this man could get jealous, but there was definitely a flare of his nostrils. He was used to getting what he wanted, and the second he didn't, he lost his mind. "You have a date?"

"Yes." I grabbed my level and a couple of nails. "Have a good evening, Cato."

He ignored everything I said. "You're going to waste your time with some random guy instead of me?"

"Well, I'm pretty sure this guy doesn't kill people. And I don't think he's going to throw me into a threeway either." I headed to the door before Cato could say anything else. "You don't know me very well, but I'm not the kind of girl who's expecting anything out of a man. I'm at a point in my life when I'm just looking to get laid and focus on my career. I'm not in the market for anything complicated, but you made it complicated the second this turned into a sick power play. You have your rules, and that's fine—but I also have mine."

11

Cato

I SAT IN MY STUDY ON THE TOP FLOOR AND PUFFED ON my cigar. I wasn't a big smoker, but every once in a while, I allowed myself the luxury. It gave my throat a break from the burn of the booze I downed all the time.

I stared out the window and kept thinking about the same woman I always thought about.

Siena.

She told me off like no one else. She threw me away like she had nothing to lose. She treated me like I was nobody, not the handsome billionaire every woman wanted in their bed. To her, I was just another guy in the crowd. All she wanted from me was a job, and now that she had it, she didn't want anything else.

Why did that make me admire her?

Why did that make me obsess over her?

No idea.

When my cigar burned out, I had nothing else to look forward to. Lighting another was tempting, but having

Siena in bed tonight was even more tempting. I didn't want to bend my rules for anyone, but I bent them for her already.

If not, I would be fucking two women right now.

I didn't think twice before I'd pumped a bullet into that traitor's skull. My hand didn't shake, and my finger didn't feel hot after pulling the trigger. But now I kept replaying my final conversation with Siena like I was filled with regret.

She had a date tonight.

Because she would rather do that than bend over backward for me.

I wasn't used to that.

I stared at my cold cigar for a few minutes before I rose out of my chair, suffocated by my thoughts. I'd never been the kind of man to sit back and do nothing when something bothered me. If someone crossed me, I hunted them down and killed them. If there was someone I wanted, I didn't stop until I had them.

So why wasn't I doing something now?

———

WHEN NEARLY THE entire country was at my disposal, I could find a needle in a haystack instantly.

I found Siena in five minutes. She was having dinner at a bistro in Florence. Her date was an accountant. His background was squeaky clean, so clean that it was dirty. Only pussies had nothing to hide. Real men had skeletons to be proud of.

It would be easy for me to have her date dragged out

of the restaurant. Or I could just drop an envelope of cash in front of him. He would take the bait just like anyone else. But Siena wouldn't be impressed by any of that. She would probably slap me.

Might slap me anyway.

I spotted them together at a table in the corner. She looked beautiful in a red dress with a single strap. It was short with a slit up her thigh. Her hair was pulled back the way it was when we worked together, and the entire look made her the most beautiful woman in the room.

I took a moment to stare at her before I looked at her date.

He was a good-looking guy. Solid build with masculine features. He had a light beard and bright eyes. His t-shirt fit his ripped arms, and he had a muscular back that suggested he hit the weights hard. She definitely didn't struggle to pick up handsome men for the night.

Maybe she really didn't need me, after all.

I approached their table and pulled a chair with me, putting it in between them before I sat down.

Siena turned to me, and her look of terror was undeniably sexy.

Her date stared at me blankly before he looked at her again, clearly seeking an explanation.

I leaned back in the chair and crossed one leg, letting my ankle rest on the opposite knee. My hands came together in my lap, and I kept my attention on her, even though her date's look of bewilderment was probably entertaining. "You look beautiful tonight, Siena." I liked the dark tones she wore at my estate, but the vibrance of that dress really complemented her coloring.

Her eyes narrowed in ferocity. "What are you doing here, Cato?"

"Getting a drink." I placed my hand in the air, and instantly, the waitress arrived and took my order. "Scotch, one ice cube." I kept my eyes on Siena because no one else in the room was important.

Her date was obviously a pussy because he hadn't said a word to me.

Her beauty was even more apparent when she was pissed. Her eyes lightened noticeably, her cheekbones became more pronounced because she pursed her lips so tightly. Her thick lashes opened and closed quicker with her frustration. "I'm in the middle of a date, Cato. You don't belong here."

The waitress returned with my drink, and I brought the glass to my lips. "The more, the merrier, right?"

"No." Siena's eyes flashed with threat. "How would you feel if I crashed one of your dates?"

I grinned. "I would love that, actually."

Quick like a snake, she pulled her hand back and slapped me across the face.

Slapped. Me.

The hit didn't hurt, but the shock slowly circulated in my veins until my adrenaline boiled over. No one had ever pulled a stunt like that besides my mother—and that was twenty-five years ago.

I set my glass down and examined her harder, pissed off and aroused at the same time.

Her date was still like a statue.

"I just killed someone." My words escaped as a soft whisper. "Are you sure you want to do that?"

"Yes." Just to prove her point, she slapped me again. "You think you own the world, but you'll never own me, asshole. Now leave so Aaron and I can have dinner then have sex. Good night."

The thought of her screwing this guy when she should be screwing me only tested my resolve even more. Without turning to her date, I commanded him. "Leave."

He stayed put.

Siena didn't look at him. "Don't listen to him."

This time, I turned in my chair and made direct eye contact with him. I gave him the same look I gave all my enemies, scaring him to death with only a subtle expression. My men were all over the place, and I could kill him with a flick of my fingers.

"You're Cato Marino…" He seemed to be saying it to himself more than to Siena and me.

I snapped my fingers in his face. "Beat it."

This time, he listened. He pushed his chair back and left the restaurant.

When I turned back to Siena, I couldn't keep the smug look off my face.

Now she looked like she wanted to murder me. Hatred burned in her eyes, and her palm was getting ready for the next hit.

"Make it good, baby." No one else would get an opportunity the way she did. No one else would survive such a strike. The only reason she did was because I allowed it to happen.

She snatched my drink and prepared to throw it in my face.

I didn't appreciate booze on my face and clothes, so I

swatted the glass across the table before she could do anything.

But she got her palm in my face, striking me just as hard as last time. "You're such a—"

I fisted my hand in her hair, and I yanked her into me for a kiss. My cheek burned from the hits she planted on me, but it aroused me even more. I clenched her hair in my fingers and gripped her around the waist with my other arm. I pulled her tight against me and kissed her stubborn mouth.

She didn't fight me. Instead, she kissed me back with revulsion, as if she hated herself for what she was doing but couldn't stop herself. Her mouth wasn't pliant like it was during our first kiss. It was harsh and aggressive, conveying all her animosity for me in a single embrace. But then her hatred softened, and her lips turned apologetic. With lips full of remorse, she kissed me, felt my mouth with hers the way she had in the bar.

The restaurant was full of people, but that didn't seem to matter.

I'd dare them to say something.

When she pulled away, her eyes were full of self-loathing, like she hated herself for allowing that to happen. She hated herself for enjoying that kiss. She hated herself for being relieved that her pussy date was gone.

My cheek must be red from the way she'd struck me so hard, but the burn felt so good. I could feel the outline of her hand against my cheek like she'd just hit me. If I focused, I could replay it in my mind over and over. Every single flashback made my cock just a little bit harder. All the women in my life bent over backward for me, pushed away other men's advances just in case I might notice them instead. They made out with me in clubs and shared me with strangers. They were willing to drop everything just for the mere opportunity to be with Cato Marino.

This woman did no such thing.

She didn't give a damn who I was.

That was the sexiest thing I'd ever seen.

I dropped money on the table, grabbed her hand, and pulled her out of the restaurant, ignoring all the customers watching us make our exit. We'd just put on a sexy production no one could ignore. My cheek was red, and if only everyone were a little braver, they might have snapped a picture and put it online.

I took her outside, and my car pulled up to the curb. Bulletproof with pitch-black tinted windows, it was the safest vehicle on the planet. Even a tank would struggle to take it down. With a large back seat, it provided ample room for my long legs—and my dates.

She pulled her hand away from mine when we reached the sidewalk.

I let her pull away only because I was interested in whatever she had to say. My cheek was still throbbing after being her punching bag, and my dick was so hard it was about to rip through my fly. This woman needed to be stuffed full of my dick, to be satisfied the way she deserved. Now I didn't care she would be the only woman in my bed tonight. I didn't worry I would be bored. My knuckles ached with excitement because I couldn't wait to have her legs spread in my bed.

Her hair was a mess from the way I'd fisted it, so she

pulled out the pins she had set in place and let her brown hair fall around her shoulders. It immediately framed her face perfectly, like she planned for it to look so beautiful. After a slight shake of her head, she scolded me. "You're such an asshole, you know that?" She didn't possess the same rage as she had before, but there was no doubt she meant her words.

"Yes. I do know." I stepped closer to her and focused on her top lip, the soft pillow I wanted to kiss again and again. I wanted to brush the backs of my fingers along that soft bow then feel the rest of her cheek. I wanted to explore this woman everywhere, to see her gorgeous curves under that skintight dress. When I spotted her across the bar on that unforgettable night, I forgot about the women who were already at my beck and call. None of them compared to this hostile woman.

"You can't just sabotage people's dates like that."

"He could have fought for you."

"Really?" She crossed her arms over her chest. "Against Cato Marino?"

I shrugged. "You do it all the time."

"That's different."

"I don't think so." She was the only person in the entire world who had the balls to stand up to me. Sure, my brother gave me shit, but not so adamantly. She spoke her mind without fear of repercussions, and when I was a dick during her date, she slapped me like I deserved. "The only person who's ever slapped me is my mother—and I was five."

Her eyes stared at the red mark on my cheek, the

product of the powerful strikes from her small hand. "Don't expect me to apologize for it."

"I wouldn't like you so much if you did." I snapped my fingers at one of my men, and they opened the back door. "Let's go."

"Where are we going?"

My look said it all.

"You chase off my date, and now you think you get to fuck me?" She cocked her head slightly, her hair swaying with her motions. Any other woman in the world would be thrilled to score my intimate attention. This was a dream come true, a fairy tale. But unlike the rest of the world, Siena didn't care.

"You get to fuck me too."

She rolled her eyes. "Just when I think you can't be a bigger pig, you somehow manage it."

My hands rested in my pockets as I stared at her in the light from the lamppost. With messy hair and angry eyes, she was the most alluring thing in the world. I could walk into my bedroom and see three naked women on my bed, but the image wouldn't be nearly as arousing as the look on her face. "You could go home alone. Or you could go home with me."

She shook her head slightly. "I could walk into a bar and pick up someone else." She had the kind of confidence that rivaled my own. She knew exactly what she was worth, and she owned it.

"As could I. But neither one of us wants that." I stepped closer to her, noting the way she didn't step back. I moved farther in until our faces were close together in the dark. A couple left the restaurant and walked down the sidewalk, the woman's heels clacking against the concrete. Cars sounded in the distance. But all I could think about was the soft sound of her breathing, the way her eyes held mine with a mixture of desire and uncertainty.

My hand moved around her neck, cupping it right in the front. Her pulse thudded against my skin, slow and steady like she wasn't the least bit afraid of me. That controlled response was arousing, the way she held her own against an opponent like me. My fingers moved to her soft jawline before I pressed my mouth to hers. I kissed her softly, the way I did in that bar all those weeks ago. I took my time because there was no need to rush to the ending. This story would end exactly how I wanted it to end—with her digging her heels into my ass as she came.

There was no hesitation on her part. Her lips parted for mine just the way her legs would soon. Her warm breath greeted me along with her tongue. Her hand snaked to my bicep, and she kneaded my muscle as she kissed me, as she dropped her dislike and enjoyed the undeniable chemistry between us.

I'd never had a kiss quite like this. I'd never taken the time to slow down and cherish an embrace with a woman. I preferred to be sucked off in the back seat on the way back to my place while another woman sucked on my neck.

But this was better.

My dick became uncomfortable in my pants the harder it pressed against my jeans. The only thing my dick should be pressing against was a soft, wet pussy. The fantasy of sinking deep into her beautiful cunt aroused me to the point of insanity, so I ended the kiss and turned to the door. "Get in."

She usually protested my commands, but this time, the lazy look in her eyes said it all. She didn't want to argue anymore. She wanted to be on her back in my enormous bed, a real man giving her the best sex of her life. She gave me a final glance before she ducked her head and got inside. "Don't make me regret this."

I narrowed my eyes at the challenge. "Never."

12

Siena

WE STEPPED INSIDE THE DOOR OF HIS TUSCAN ESTATE, and Giovanni appeared out of the shadows to serve him. "Sir, I—"

"It can wait until tomorrow." Cato ignored his most loyal servant and guided me to the staircase. The trip back to the house had been spent in quiet tension, his hand squeezing my thigh and his eyes staring deeply into mine. He didn't kiss me, as if he was waiting for the right moment to drop his restraint.

Giovanni disappeared again, obeying Cato's orders.

He unexpectedly scooped his arms underneath my body then lifted me to his chest. Like I weighed nothing and he could move a mountain, he carried me up the three flights of stairs to his bedroom on the top floor.

I circled my arms around his neck, and I stared at his handsome expression, the pretty color of his eyes and the way they contrasted against the hardness of his jaw. If any other man pulled a stunt like he did, I would kick him in the crotch and storm off. No man had the right to control my life, to sabotage my evening just because he didn't like it. There were so many things I disliked about Cato—and his arrogance was at the top of the list. But he was the sexiest man on the planet, with those good looks and perfectly chiseled body. His power and wealth weren't necessary to make him irresistible because he already was. If he weren't so attractive and confident, this would be a million times harder. I could sleep with someone I disliked —if he were this beautiful.

He carried me into his bedroom without effort and then set me down on his enormous bed, the bed where he often had several women at once. Sweaty and kinky sex happened here on a nightly basis. The women were willing to do anything, dirty things I would never compromise on. So, would fucking me be enough? Or would he be finished with me in the morning? There was only one way to find out.

He kneeled on the floor in front of me and held my gaze as he slipped off each of my heels. He handled me delicately, his fingers gently rubbing against the softness of my skin. His blue eyes were focused on my face, like it was impossible to pull his gaze away for even a moment.

I liked seeing Cato beneath me, a strong man on his knees to assist me. When he wasn't being an arrogant prick, he was a sexy gentleman. I studied him as he took his time with the straps before both my heels were off. Then I watched him press a kiss to the inside of my ankle.

I closed my eyes automatically, loving the way those soft lips felt against my skin.

He did the same to the other foot before he trailed

kisses up my legs and to the inside of my knees. He kept going, moving higher and higher until he was between my thighs.

My breathing escalated, and I slowly lay back on the bed as he tilted me backward. My eyes closed for long periods of time as I waited for that mouth to reach the area that ached the most. Maybe I disliked Cato Marino, but there was no doubt I wanted him—bad.

He kept moving until his lips pressed against my black thong. He kissed me gently, my dress bunched up to my hips. He kissed me a little harder for the friction then took a deep breath, inhaling the scent of my arousal through my lacy thong.

He pulled back then raised his head level with mine, a look of arousal on his face so intense he seemed angry. He gripped my hips with his hands, and he stared at me without fear, as if he was struggling not to fuck me so hard he might break the bed.

I'd been the focus of a man's desire before, but a man had never looked at me the way Cato did now. This was just sex, a conquest he was obsessed with completing, but it still made me feel like the most beautiful woman in the world. It was more fulfilling than making love to a man I cared about. It was more fulfilling than a booty call with a man who could make me come. I was prey to this man— and it was the first time I enjoyed feeling that way.

He rose to his full height then pulled his t-shirt over his head. Like last time, he was nothing but man, nothing but pure sex. His strong pecs led to the valley of rivers and grooves in his abdomen. Near his hips were two thick veins that led up from the top of his jeans. He was in perfect physical shape, with the strength to kill a man with his bare knuckles.

I couldn't take my eyes off him. My panties felt wetter by the second, and any uncertainty I had about what I was doing was gone. My thighs ached to open, and my pussy screamed to feel every inch of him inside me. This started off as a task, but now it was the only thing in the world I wanted to do.

He undid his belt then took care of his jeans, pushing them down along with his boxers.

I stared at his long dick, my eyes focused and wide. Dicks were nothing special, nothing to get particularly aroused by, but damn, it was the most beautiful dick I'd ever seen. He wasn't just long, but also thick. His crown was prominent, and even his balls were beautiful. Perfectly manicured for a fuck or a suck, it was the kind of dick I would be happy to choke on. "Jesus Christ..." I couldn't take my eyes off the monster cock that stood so erect and proud. My tongue ached to feel the vein along the shaft, and my belly yearned for a taste of him. Sucking dick wasn't one of my fetishes, but when one looked like that, I'd be happy to hit my gag reflex over and over. "That is one beautiful dick." My eyes finally flicked back up to his.

Flames burned in his eyes, not from anger, but from ecstasy. Now he looked like he wanted to fuck me even harder, to slam his dick so deep inside me it made me explode. His hands reached up my thighs until he gripped the lace of my panties. Then he slowly pulled them down until they were free of my ankles. His eyes locked on to my pussy, staring at it with the same obsession I felt for his cock.

He lowered himself to his knees again then pressed his mouth right between my legs. He immediately smothered my clit with his tongue and kissed it harder than he'd kissed my mouth. He inhaled deeply then blew his warm breath across my most sensitive area. He ate my pussy like he was starving and there was nothing else on the menu he wanted more.

I screamed right away, just because it felt so unbelievably good. My head rolled back, and I looked at the ceiling as my vision began to blur. Men had eaten me out before, but not at this caliber. I fisted his hair with my fingers, and I wondered if leaving his place that night had been a mistake. Even with another woman there, the sex still would have been incredible.

He sucked my clit a little harder before he pulled away. He opened his nightstand and pulled out a foil packet before he came back to me on the bed.

I was about to come when his mouth was pleasing me, so having his enormous girth inside me was exactly what I wanted. But now all I could think about was that cock inside my mouth. I'd never wanted to give head so much, to explore something so big. "Wait." I rose to my feet and unzipped the back of my dress so it could fall to the floor. I wasn't wearing a bra, so now I was completely naked.

Cato's eyes went to my tits.

"I really—" I lowered myself to my knees in front of him "—really want to suck your dick first." I ignored the man who possessed the dick and gripped his muscular thighs. He had tanned skin everywhere, along with packed muscles underneath. He was such a pretty man that even his feet were sexy. I flattened my tongue and opened my mouth wide before I pressed him inside me. Then I moaned. As a woman, I appreciated every single inch of his perfection. I appreciated his length and his thickness. I appreciated the way he tasted, the way he could keep his hardness with no effort. His dick was perfect and deserved to be worshiped.

Cato's expression hardened as he stared down at me. He watched me move his length deep inside my mouth before I slowly pulled it out. Getting head was enjoyable regardless, but he probably got off on how much I wanted to do it, how much I wanted his dick against my tongue. He fisted the back of my hair, and his deep breaths slowly escalated the longer I went to town on his length.

I never imagined I would be so thrilled to be on my knees. Just thirty minutes ago, I thought he was an arrogant pig. I'd seen him make out with random women in bars, one right after another. But now that I was enjoying this man, I couldn't judge him. Even without his fortune, he was the most desirable man on the planet. Those women probably didn't even want him for his money. They just wanted this—a night with a real man.

My tongue coated more saliva onto his length, and I pushed him as deep as I could. I only made it halfway because he wasn't just long but wide. Giving head was about making your partner feel good, but right now, my actions were completely selfish. I was sucking his dick because I enjoyed every second of it. In fact, I felt the same burn between my legs that I felt when his mouth was pressed to my clit. I was so aroused by his dick that I felt an explosion on the horizon. Just his dick turned me on more than sex with any other guy had. My fingers moved between my legs, and I rubbed myself as I continued to suck him off, knowing I was about to explode with a dick in my mouth.

Cato inhaled a deep breath between his teeth before he yanked on the back of my hair. "No."

His dick left my mouth, but I pressed a kiss to the crown, my eyes on him.

"Up."

My sight was blurry from arousal, and I had to rely on his powerful legs to make my way back to my feet.

"On your back." He grabbed the condom then proceeded to put it on. He rolled it down his length to the base, keeping a large pocket at the end to hold the come he would release for me.

I moved onto his Alaskan king-size bed and lay my head on one of his pillows. I expected kinkier sex, something not missionary. I didn't even mind skipping sex as long as his dick was in my mouth. But I was excited to feel his thick length deep inside me. I'd never taken a bigger man, and now I was afraid I would never be able to go back once we were finished.

He climbed on top of me, his heavy weight shifting the mattress as he moved. His enormous cock hung at the ready, pointing at my entrance like he couldn't wait to be inside me. His arms immediately hooked behind my knees, and he stretched me apart, as if I would need to be open as wide as possible if I was going to take that behemoth between his legs. "Notice anything about my bed?"

My hands clawed at his chest because I was so anxious for sex. I'd never wanted a man to fuck me more. I'd hated him that morning, but now he was my ultimate fantasy.

My hands moved into the back of his hair, and I brought his lips to mine for a kiss. "Shut up and fuck me." I could taste my pussy on his lips, and the sensation only aroused me more.

He kissed me back but only for a few seconds. "You're the only one in it."

I rested my face against his and felt my pussy tighten. Unlike everyone else, I got to enjoy him exclusively for the night. I got all his attention, all his affection, and all of his dick. "Good. Because I don't like to share." I grabbed his length and pointed his crown at my entrance.

He pressed his dick inside me and ignored the resistance. His cock was way too big for my small size, but he wouldn't accept the denial. He pushed again until he got past the barrier and met the pool of moisture that was practically dripping between my thighs. Then he sank the rest of the way, sheathing more and more until most of his length was deep inside me.

A cock had never felt so good. "Cato…" My hands left his hair and glided down his back. My nails sliced him with my enthusiasm, but it couldn't be controlled. Now I was just a woman lost to her hormones, a woman who just wanted to be with a man. "Fuck, you feel good." If I'd known it would be this good, I would have fucked him in the back of his car on the way here.

He moaned as he started to thrust, his eyes locked on mine as he tapped his headboard against the wall. "Damn, this is good pussy."

I grabbed his ass and yanked him deeper into me, feeling the climax hit me right away. I didn't need more than ten thrusts to come apart. I'd been ready for a climax for the last fifteen minutes. It was surprising that I didn't explode the second he was inside me. "God…" My head relaxed into the pillow, and I watched him continue to thrust into me, continue to give me his enormous dick at the perfect pace. "Yes…yes." My nails clawed down his arms, and my hips bucked back into him. I bit my bottom lip as I came undone. This man had accomplished something no other man ever could. He made me come so hard, I didn't think that intensity was possible—and he didn't even try. Maybe his arrogance was appropriate, after all.

He went still as he kept his entire length inside me. With my legs still pinned back and his eyes glued to mine, he wore the same look of arousal he started with, but now it was accompanied by a hint of torture. "You better not be done. I haven't even gotten started yet."

———

ORGASMS later and early in the morning, I lay in bed beside him, listening to his deep, even breathing. He was fast asleep, fully satisfied after making me come for him so many times.

I opened my eyes and spotted the time on the clock.

It was six in the morning.

That was the greatest night of sex I'd ever had, and I could easily lie there forever and just enjoy it. I couldn't remember the last time I'd been so well pleased. No man had ever stepped up to the plate and hit a home run like that. Cato Marino wasn't just the most successful banker in the world—but he was the most successful lover.

I'd enjoyed screwing a criminal mastermind who murdered someone in his driveway, and the sex was so good I forgot just how much danger I was in. My task was to manipulate him and somehow isolate him from the herd of his security detail, but that operation seemed impossible. Last night, the sex was amazing for me, but it was probably average for him. It didn't matter how wet or eager I was, his threesomes and wild nights would always triumph over anything I could offer.

Maybe this was a bad idea.

Maybe I should give up while I still had the chance.

I pulled back the sheets and carefully slid to the edge of the bed. My plan was to slip out before he woke up. Maybe he didn't even expect me to spend the night in the first place. He probably would have kicked me out if he wanted me gone, but maybe he'd been too tired. I grabbed my dress from the floor and started to put it on.

"Did I say you could leave?" His masculine voice filled the bedroom, not raspy like it should have been since he'd been sleeping for hours. He didn't move from his position in bed, the sheets bunched around his waist.

My attitude fired up at the insinuation. "No. But I didn't ask." This man might be incredible between the sheets, but he was still an asshole at the end of the day. That big beautiful dick wouldn't change that.

"Get back here." He didn't open his eyes, as if he just expected me to listen.

I wasn't the kind of woman to listen. Not now and not ever. I zipped the dress.

He sprang out of bed quickly and came right toward me, over 200 pounds of hostile muscle. It was dark in his bedroom because all the curtains were closed, but he didn't struggle to find me at the foot of his bed. He snatched me by the back of the hair and threw me onto the bed, my face hitting the sheets and my ass rising in the air. His hand gripped the back of my neck, and he pinned me down with his weight. "Lesson learned. Never make me ask you twice." He grabbed a condom from his night-stand, rolled it on, and then he fucked me like an animal, keeping my face pressed against his sheets while his enormous dick slammed into me over and over.

My initial impulse was to fight him, but once that cock stretched me wide, I did nothing in retaliation—except enjoy it.

He grabbed both of my wrists and pinned them against my back as he kept his hold on my neck. His thrusts were deep and hard, not sensual and gentle like they were last night. He seemed more angry than lustful, like my disobedience infuriated him and turned him on at the same time.

"Fuck you, asshole." I bit my lip as my face pressed into the mattress, feeling that perfect cock hit me in the right spot over and over. I despised him as a human being, but I loved being taken like this, screwed in a way I'd never been before.

"I am fucking you, baby." He gripped the back of my hair and forced me up, arching my back and treating me like a horse being controlled by reins. "And I will fuck you as long as I want." His hand moved to my neck, and he squeezed me hard as he slammed into me, his grip almost choking me.

I closed my eyes and bit my bottom lip, feeling my

body betray me instantly. He hadn't been inside me for long, and I wasn't even aroused before he threw himself at me. Now my cunt was soaking wet, and it was tightening on him with every passing second.

"So fucking tight." He leaned over me and pressed his chest against my back, his lips near my ear. "Come, baby. I know you want to."

I wanted to fight the feeling because I was a proud woman, but when he felt so good between my legs, that seemed impossible. It didn't matter how arrogant he was. It didn't matter if he was a pompous asshole. He made me come better than any other man. "God…"

"Say my name."

In the throes of passion, I couldn't hesitate. "Cato."

"Good, baby," he breathed against my ear as he kept fucking me, kept driving his huge cock deep inside me.

My face moved into the mattress as I finished, the sheets swallowing my final moans.

He held his weight on top of me and finished with a masculine groan, his satisfaction audible in his deep voice. He hovered for a moment as he enjoyed every single second before the feeling wore off. Then he pulled his softening dick out of me and walked to the bathroom. "I'm taking a shower."

I listened to the door shut behind him then heard the water run a second later. I stayed in the same position as my heart rate began to slow. That was the kind of morning sex I'd never had in my entire life. It was the perfect way to start a morning, even if my lover was a pompous and controlling asshole.

Now that he was gone, I picked up my dress and got

ready. I didn't know if he wanted me to stay or not, but I should leave as soon as possible. Cato Marino was a serious opponent that I couldn't overpower, and now I feared my talents wouldn't be enough. Even if I could lure him into trusting me, that only put me in more danger. Because the second he realized I was fooling him…he would shoot me in the head in his driveway.

———

AFTER WORKING at the gallery all day, I went home to my place outside of Florence. There was a black car in the driveway, and the front door was unlocked. Someone else would immediately call the cops, but I knew exactly who'd broken in to my home and trespassed on my property.

"A phone call would suffice." I shut the door behind me and stepped into the house, knowing I would come face-to-face with Damien in just a few seconds.

"I'd rather see your pretty face, sweetheart." Even when Damien was being civil, he sounded evil. He was a creepy goon, a vulture just waiting for me to be murdered so he could pick me apart.

I stepped into the kitchen and spotted him at my dining table. He'd helped himself to a glass of wine and had his feet resting on the other chair. He'd made himself at home—even though I would kill him if I ever got the opportunity. "Yes?" I snatched the bottle of wine off the table and poured myself a glass. "Does the little bitch have a message?"

His smile remained plastered on his face, but his eyes displayed a slight look of annoyance. He was second-incommand to Micah—and he didn't like it one bit. He was the man who did the dirty work, much like a janitor in a school. "You're the little bitch in this situation."

"I disagree." I took a drink then licked my lips. "What do you want, Damien? I'm busy."

"You aren't busy enough because we don't have Cato."

"You expect me to take down the richest man in Italy in a few weeks?" I stood at the counter with the glass in my hand, tilting my head slightly as I examined him. "Something you and Micah can't even do? Don't be ridiculous."

He pulled a knife from his pocket and set it on the table in front of him. It was a subtle warning, a threat to slit my throat if I became difficult. "Between you and me, I want you to fail. Then you'll be all mine. I'll fuck you in the ass with this blade pressed right against that beautiful artery in your neck."

Regardless of the danger, it was unacceptable to give in to fear. I refused to be afraid, to let this twisted man get under my skin. The second I did, he would have the upper hand. I sipped my wine like he hadn't just threatened to rape and murder me. "I'd chop off your dick before you ever got the chance."

His grin widened, because he was a sick son of a bitch that got off on this stuff. "I wonder if your cunt is as sweet as that mouth of yours."

"You'll never know."

His smile dropped, just for an instant. "Are you going to make this happen or not?"

I'd slept with Cato, but I was no closer to accomplishing anything. That man was far more terrifying than

Damien ever could hope to be. Not only was Cato cold, but he was controlling and domineering. He didn't give second chances to anyone. The second he figured out my plan, I would be executed liked a prisoner of war. "You're asking me to accomplish the impossible."

"Then we won't bother keeping your father alive."

No matter how many times I reminded myself that my father deserved his fate, knowing he was locked up broke my heart. I wanted my father to be free, not tortured by Micah. He probably knew I was trying to save him, and that just made him feel worse. "I can give you all the information I have about Cato. That's still worth something."

"What information? Access to bank accounts? Security measures? Codes into his residence?"

"Well…no."

"Then what?" he asked, laughing slightly. "What valuable information do you have?"

In that moment, I understood I knew nothing. The man was a quiet enigma who hardly spoke. His thoughts were a mystery. The only part of him I was acquainted with was his dick. I knew that pretty well.

Damien looked away and sipped his wine. "You have nothing to offer."

"You're giving me nothing to work with."

"You have a pussy, don't you? Look at you. How hard is it to get this guy pussy-whipped?"

I was the one who was dick-whipped. Cato was the most amazing hunk I'd ever been with. I was just another woman in a very long line of beautiful women to him. "This guy is too smart for that. There's no way he could become so successful by ever being stupid. You picked the wrong guy to cross. I saw him execute someone right in his driveway. You should pick a different target."

Damien shook his head. "It's gotta be him."

"Why?"

"Because if we take him down, we'll own everything— and not just the drug trade."

"You're forgetting his brother." Bates was clearly just as shrewd as Cato.

"He'll be easy to take down once we have Cato."

I'd been out of the game for a long time, but I knew Damien was oversimplifying this task.

"Are you going to deliver or not? I should know now. It costs money to keep feeding your father. And if I can start fucking you now, I'll stop wasting my time with this wine." He pushed the glass away and looked me up and down.

I didn't have a trick up my sleeve or any idea how I was going to accomplish this. Cato was too smart to fall for something so dumb. I let him conquer me in bed, but it seemed like he'd gotten me under his thumb instead of the other way around. But the thought of my father reminded me what I was fighting for. "Give me more time."

————

I HADN'T SPOKEN to Cato since I'd slipped out of his house a few days ago. Maybe he was pissed I left. Maybe he didn't care. I had no idea. Sleeping with him might have brought us closer together, but more than likely, it had turned me into another conquest he could forget about.

If that was the case, I was screwed.

When I got off work at the gallery, I walked to the grocery store to pick up a few things to make dinner. I usually made a few meals and then brought the leftovers to work to save money—and to keep the inches off my waistline. Walking to the store was good too, since I usually sat around at the gallery all day.

I was in the canned food section when someone appeared beside me, a tall man with midnight-black hair. He was in jeans and a black t-shirt, his head tilted down like he was trying to hide his face. He came close to me, too close for someone just browsing.

"Why don't you back up, buddy?" I pivoted my body toward him and kept my basket between us just in case I needed to hit him with it.

He turned my way slightly, an enormous grin on his face.

I recognized that grin. "Landon?"

He kept scanning the cans of beans on the rack. "Keep your voice down."

The shock hadn't worn off, and the warmest feeling spread throughout my chest. Hot summer days with freshly mowed grass came to mind, along with the small bikes we would leave in the roundabout. I thought of fresh cookies out of the oven at Christmas time, thought of all the times he would hide my dolls and force me to search for them. "I don't care." I set the basket on the ground then moved into his side for a hug. I buried my face into his chest, and I smelled his cologne, immediately recognizing it. "I can't believe it's you."

Landon didn't push me off, but he hardly gave me a

pat on the back. "Pull yourself together, Siena. People are looking for me, and I know people are watching you. So get off."

I pulled away reluctantly, heartbroken I couldn't give my brother a proper hug. We'd never been particularly close, but blood was blood. With Father gone, he was all I had left in the world. "I'm sorry... I'm just so happy to see you."

He grabbed a can off the rack and pretended to read the label. "I know what happened to Father, and I know what Micah and Damien are expecting you to do. You need to forget about it. Take off and run."

That was the last thing I expected Landon to say. "And leave Father to his fate?"

"I'll figure it out," he whispered. "It's not your problem, Siena. You didn't want anything to do with this life, and you shouldn't have to get your hands dirty now. I'm sorry you got involved in the first place."

Even if I wanted to run, I couldn't. There was nowhere to go. "Can we meet somewhere? You know, so I can actually look at you when I talk to you? So I can actually hug you?"

He put the can back on the shelf and sighed, his height towering over mine. "Where? We can't meet at your house."

"A bar," I suggested. "Somewhere in the back."

"Alright. I'll meet you at Baron's at ten." He walked away without another word.

I wanted to watch him go, but I focused on looking straight ahead. Just when my world had become so bleak and dark, a ray of sunshine popped through. My brother was on the run because the business had been dismantled, and I was working for the enemies that took everything from us. But at least if we had each other…we had something.

————

LANDON WAS ALREADY THERE when I walked inside. A glass of booze sat in front of him, and judging by his track record, it was probably his third or fourth glass.

I sat across from him at the table in the back, my eyes taking him in with a slight film. My brother and I had drifted apart over the last few years, and now that I was looking at him, I couldn't understand why I'd allowed that to happen.

He showed a cold stare, the same one my father wore most of the time. Landon's fingers rested around his glass, and he glanced around us every few minutes, checking for unfriendly eyes. His beard was gone, and his green eyes were bright despite his obvious sadness. "Don't fuck with Cato Marino. That guy is a monster."

Yes, I'd seen it firsthand. "I know." Cato was cold as ice and so pragmatic he didn't seem human. All he cared about was sex, booze, and money. Without a heart, he didn't hesitate before he ended someone's life forever. He traveled in a huge caravan everywhere he went because he knew the world was full of his enemies.

"If he suspects you, he'll wring your neck."

"I know that too."

He glanced around the bar before he looked at me, the hostility in his eyes. "Then you need to leave. Grab your things and take off." He reached inside his blazer and pulled out a thick envelope stuffed with cash. He set it on the table between us. "That should be more than enough for whatever you need."

It was sweet my brother wanted to take care of me, but I didn't need his support. I pushed the money back toward him. "I don't need it. But thank you."

A sigh escaped his lips. "Now isn't the time to be stubborn."

"I'm not being stubborn. I'm not leaving Father behind. He doesn't deserve my loyalty, but I can't just leave him like that."

Landon bowed his head slightly and looked into his glass. "You have absolutely no chance of tricking Cato. You're just going to get yourself killed."

"And if I get killed, so be it."

Landon's eyes narrowed in hostility, like that was the worst thing I could have said. "I don't want this. Father doesn't want this."

"But we're family—and we're in this together."

He ran his hand through his short black hair, his jaw still clenched with ferocity. We always bumped heads because we were equally stubborn. Landon wanted to be the alpha, but I'd been the alpha since the day I was born. I'd never been the push-over type. Instead of wearing a pretty dress and keeping my mouth shut at a party, I was the one who spoke the loudest. He respected me for it, but during times like these, he also hated me for it. "It's a suicide mission. Cato is at the top of the food chain for a reason. You think you're going to outsmart him?"

"I don't know what I think right now. I'm feeling him out."

Landon didn't directly ask about my relationship with Cato. He knew I was sleeping with him to get what I wanted, but that was such an awkward subject that he didn't want to open it for discussion. "Father didn't make the sacrifices he should have made for our family. It doesn't make sense for you to make any now."

"I agree. But if I can make this work, I can get Father back and we can start over. Maybe we can move to France and open a wine shop or something. At least we'll be together…" I hadn't felt whole ever since our mother passed away and our family disbanded. There had always been a piece of my heart missing, a void no one could ever fill.

He gave me a look full of pity. "Even if we could rescue Father, that's unlikely. They'll hunt us down until we're all annihilated. That's why I'm telling you this plan is stupid. Even if you save Father, what then?"

"And you can really sleep at night letting him die?" I challenged, refusing to believe my brother would be that much of a coward.

He held my gaze but didn't answer.

"I'm not leaving Father behind. I admit my plan with Cato isn't the best—"

"He will kill you." Landon squeezed his glass with his fingertips. "Siena, you don't know this world the way I do. You don't understand what these men are capable of. Just because you're a beautiful woman doesn't mean he won't torture and kill you. It doesn't mean he won't give you the greatest agony before he finally puts a bullet in your brain.

You have a strong confidence that gives you an unrealistic belief that you can accomplish anything. Siena, it doesn't matter how good you fuck him, he will see right through you. He's the smartest, most cunning man in the world. I say you drop this approach and we figure something else out."

I'd be lying if I said I wasn't scared. Any time I was in that fortress, I knew I was outnumbered. Anytime I was alone with Cato, I knew he could do whatever he wanted to me. "What other option do we have?"

"We'll figure it out."

"Even if I wanted to walk away, I'm working for him now."

"Then finish the job and disappear."

"It's not that simple."

"Then resign. Get someone else to replace you."

"Don't you think that would draw more suspicion?" I asked. "Not to mention, piss him off? I already slept with him, so the damage is done."

If Landon was uncomfortable, he didn't show it. "And what is his attitude toward you?"

I shrugged. "We haven't spoken."

Landon took a long drink from his glass. "Then your plan failed. He's the same womanizer he was before. No surprise there."

"Yeah, I guess."

"So maybe you can get out of this unscathed. Just finish the job and leave. Keep Damien on the hook. Maybe we can figure out a different plan in the meantime."

"What kind of plan?" I asked. "They have hundreds

of men working for them. What do we have?" Our business, our reputation, and our money had been stripped away from us. Now we were both victims without protection. Our men had abandoned us, and now we were just two lone wolves.

He shrugged. "We have each other—it's a start."

13

Cato

When I got out of the shower, Siena had already left. She did the walk of shame and asked one of my men to take her back to Florence. I expected her to still be in bed when I walked out with the towel around my waist. I expected her to stay for a few hours.

But she disappeared the second the opportunity presented itself.

She couldn't sit still.

I didn't have to wonder if the sex was good for her because I could feel it anytime I was inside of her. She was so wet the condom didn't experience any friction. She was so wet I could get my fat dick inside without issue. And she sucked my dick like nothing in the world would make her happier.

But when she got her fix, she disappeared.

I'd never seen that before.

Bates and I had a meeting with our Chinese clients at the estate, and after several hours of crunching numbers, they finally departed the property. More money was in our accounts, hiding in plain sight from their government. Some of it would be used to fund the Skull Kings and their weapons project. Money was taken from some piles and dropped into others. It was the nature of the business.

Bates helped himself to the decanter of scotch then relaxed in his leather chair around the conference table.

I shut the folder in front of me, partially thinking about the money I'd just made and partially thinking about the woman I'd fucked two days ago. Still hadn't heard a word from her. She hadn't come to the estate to continue decorating it.

She just disappeared.

"What's on your mind?" Bates asked. "Money or pussy?"

"What if it's neither?"

He chuckled before he took another drink. "It's never neither. Which is it?"

I'd been thinking about pussy a lot more than money lately. "Siena."

"And what's new with her? Haven't seen her around lately."

"Neither have I." I ignored my scotch because I wasn't in the mood for booze. A cigar would be nice, but I didn't have the energy to get up and fetch one. Giovanni was always two seconds away, but I was too proud to have the man wait on me hand and foot.

"Really?" he asked. "That's interesting."

I didn't do much kissing and telling. Bates knew about my rendezvous because he usually witnessed them directly, but I rarely mentioned them out of context. I'd finally had

Siena and assumed I would forget about her now that her name was carved into my bedpost. But I was even more confused than I had been before. "She stayed over the other night."

Bates watched me, his hostility slowly filling the room. "How'd that go?"

I skipped the details. "I haven't stopped thinking about her."

"Then it went really well. You're usually bored by the time you get into the shower."

I definitely wasn't bored this time. She was the only woman in my bed, and that seemed to be perfect for me. My fingers drummed against the table as I pictured the way she looked underneath me. With her ass in the air and her face pressed into the sheets, she was the sexiest thing in the world.

Bates studied me for a moment longer. "I was hoping this interest would burn out like all the others."

I knew my brother was suspicious of her, but I believed she was harmless. If she really had negative intentions, she wouldn't be so cold and distant. It seemed like she genuinely hated me, but her attraction to me kept her in place. She wasn't like the others, the ones who threw themselves at me in the hope something would stick. "She's harmless, man."

Just like every other time he made a speech, he sighed before he spoke. "I did some digging. I didn't like what I found."

"How many parking tickets does she have?"

Bates didn't laugh. "I'm serious, Cato. She's Siena Russo."

Was that name supposed to mean something to me? "Russo is a common surname, Bates."

"She's the daughter of Stefan Russo."

Now that name did mean something to me. Stefan had a drug enterprise. He smuggled his goods in cigars. He'd asked me for money on many occasions, but I always turned him down because we could never agree on a mutually beneficial interest rate.

Bates held my gaze, knowing this information was important. "You don't think it's a strange coincidence that she follows you around and gets a job working where you sleep almost every night?"

I was the most paranoid man on the planet. I didn't trust anyone—except my own brother. Even then, that was difficult to do sometimes. "You think this woman is here to take me down? What's she going to do, Bates? She can't get a gun past security, and she certainly couldn't fight me off. Even if she did, how is she going to get me out of here? I admit it's a weird coincidence, but that doesn't mean she's guilty of anything."

Bates tensed visibly like a snake, as if he wanted to lunge at me with a knife raised. "I know you like pussy, but come on. How stupid are you?"

"I'm not stupid. I'm just not afraid of a woman who's a little over five feet tall. She's been working at that gallery for five years, so it's not like this was all some setup. If it is, then she and her father have been plotting this for a long time."

"Actually, she hasn't spoken to her father in five years. When her mother passed away, they stopped speaking."

I hardly knew this woman so I shouldn't care about

her feelings, but sympathy immediately tugged on my heart. Not only did she lose her mother, but she also lost her father. "Why?"

He shrugged. "From what I can gather, Siena blamed him for her mother's death. She wanted him to walk away from the business because it wasn't safe. Her mother was taken as a hostage and then murdered. That's when Siena turned her back."

Again, I shouldn't care. But I did care. "She didn't want anything to do with the business."

"I guess not."

"Which is why she got a job at the gallery."

Bates shrugged again.

"She's not a threat, Bates. She's just a woman trying to get by. Everyone in Italy has ties to the criminal underworld. It's impossible to meet someone who doesn't."

"I still think it's too much of a coincidence. If she wants nothing to do with the underworld, why is she working for you?"

"She wants to decorate my house with artwork, not work in one of our offices. She's still sticking to her own discipline."

He shook his head. "Maybe I'm being paranoid, but I don't think I am. The last thing I want to say is I told you so."

"If she has no connection to her family, then what's the harm?" I questioned. "It's not like she has a group of men she's reporting to. She's completely on her own, and even though she's got a serious attitude, one woman is no threat to us."

Bates dropped the argument because he knew he

didn't have a case. "I just wanted you to know. Do whatever you want with the information."

I was glad my brother told me all of that, but not because I thought she was a serious threat. Now it all made sense. She didn't want anything to do with me because she knew what kind of lifestyle I led. She knew I was at the top of the hierarchy of the underworld. She knew I was dangerous, and being associated with me for too long would put her right back where she didn't want to be.

Now it was no wonder she was nothing like the other women.

Because she really didn't want me.

———

THE MORE SHE distanced herself from me, the more interested I became.

Four days had come and gone, and I hadn't heard from her once.

All I got was a shipment of paintings I had already approved of. She didn't even deliver them in person. There was just a note for Giovanni and instructions where the paintings were to be hung.

Was she avoiding me?

I got her address from my security team and stopped by for a visit. She had a quaint little house just outside Florence. It was a two-bedroom Mediterranean-style home with a small garden and driveway. It wasn't ideal for a family, but for a single person, it was the right size. I left my Bugatti out front then knocked on her door.

It took her a few minutes to answer, and when she did, she didn't look happy to see me. "What are you doing here?" The annoyance was bright in her green eyes, like she couldn't stand the thought of my stopping by unannounced. The signs of arousal that she showed the last time I saw her were long gone. Now I was just a nuisance to her.

My hands slid into the pockets of my jeans. I admired the way her blouse clung to her curves so snugly. Her black jeans fit her long legs perfectly, catching the perkiness of her ass and the tightness of her legs. "Came to see you."

"Well, a phone call would have been more appropriate." She stepped outside and shut the door behind her, as if she was trying to hide something from me. Or she was hiding me from someone else.

I glanced at her closed door before I looked at her again. "Got company?"

She kept her hand on the doorknob, like standing in my way would really stop me from getting inside if I wanted to. "I'm on a date right now."

The last thing I should be was angry. We only had one night together, and that was the most time I extended to any woman. After that, they were just a memory. There was no attachment or interest. By the following night, I was usually with another woman anyway. But I'd never been the recipient of such indifference, of a woman so unaffected by me that she looked for someone else the second we were finished.

It reminded me of myself—which annoyed me. "Then tell him to leave."

"Why would I do that?" She stood her ground when everyone else would crumble. "I'm not going to let you ruin a second date."

"Do you regret how the last one went?"

Her rage slowly died away when she remembered our night together—and how she loved sucking my dick as much as she enjoyed fucking it.

"Why would you want him when you could have me?" I didn't need to see what this guy looked like to know he was no match for me. I didn't need to remember our last rendezvous in absolute detail to know I was a better lay than he would ever be. Never in my life had I chased a woman who couldn't be conquered. I constantly had to remind Siena of my qualities, like they were so easy for her to forget.

"That's a bit arrogant, isn't it?"

"It's a serious question."

She rested her back against the door, giving herself extra space between the two of us. "I thought that was a one-time thing. We had fun, but it's over. You're my boss."

"And as your boss, it's smart not to piss me off." I stepped closer to her and pressed my hands against the door, blocking her in so she had nowhere to run. I tilted my head toward her and brought my lips close to hers, remembering exactly how that mouth felt against mine—and my cock. "So get rid of your date and invite me inside."

She showed subtle signs of melting, but she was also annoyed by my orders. "If you want to come by tomorrow, I'm free. But I'm not blowing off my date just because you don't like it. I don't owe you anything, and you don't owe me anything."

My hands moved to her hips, and I squeezed her gently, my thumbs digging into her waist. "No."

"You really think I would march up to you in a bar when you were with someone else and demand you ignore them?" she asked incredulously. "Demand that you go home with me instead?"

"I would love it if you did." I pressed my forehead to hers and smelled her perfume. I remembered how it smelled against my sheets after she left. I loved the way she smelled when she was coated with her sweat as well as mine. I'd never been a man obsessed with the chase, but the more she evaded me, the more I wanted her.

"Leave—"

I pressed my mouth to hers and kissed her against the door. It was quiet being so far away from the city, so I could hear her breaths as they entered my mouth. Every time our lips moved together, they made the sweetest sound. Her breath of arousal was the best noise of all, so subtle and sexy. My hand moved into her hair, and I kissed her deeper, wishing she was naked with her legs spread. I didn't want to leave knowing she would be fucked by some other guy. I wanted to be the one to do the fucking. "You know you want me to fuck you tonight. Not him." I kissed the corner of her mouth then her neck. "Get rid of him. Or I will." I was the kind of man who shouldn't have to ask more than once. People didn't dare defy me, not if they wanted to live a long and happy life.

She tilted her chin up to look at me, her eyes a deep green like the Tuscan hillside in the height of summer.

Her gaze shifted back and forth slightly as she debated her next move. Even though she wanted me, she might continue to be stubborn out of principle. Or she might drop this charade altogether and ditch the loser who would never please her the way I could. "Give me a minute." She walked back inside and shut the door.

Minutes later, her date walked out. Tall and handsome like the last date, he seemed worthy of a beautiful woman like Siena. She certainly didn't struggle to replace the men she used. Just like me, she could be entertained by a new man every night because she was magnetic. He got in his car and drove away.

Siena opened the door again but didn't invite me inside. She walked back into her home and headed into the kitchen. "All I've got is wine. Red okay?"

I walked down the hallway and examined her cozy home. With wooden floors and historic architecture, it was clear the house could easily be a hundred years old. The windows were blurry from age, and the hallways were smaller than homes built in the modern age. "Yes." I rounded the corner and arrived in her small kitchen. There was a dining table that could seat four people, so I took a seat. Paintings of flowers were on the walls, along with family portraits on the mantel. One that stuck out to me the most was a picture of her and her mother. At least, I assumed it was her mother—because they looked like sisters.

Siena placed the glass in front of me before she took a seat, the bottle in hand. She swirled the contents before she brought it to her lips. Lipstick was already smeared across the glass because she'd been drinking out of it with her other date.

"When did you meet him?"

"You really want to talk about the guy I just got rid of?" With her elbow resting on the table, she held the glass near her lips. She licked her lips slightly, collecting the last hint of taste before she took another drink. Her actions were so smooth it didn't seem like she was making them on purpose. It was natural.

She was naturally sexy. "Just curious. You seem to have a new guy every time I see you."

"I could say the same about you," she countered. "Except, in your case, you always seemed to have several new women every time I spotted you."

I was a magnet for beautiful women. They could feel the pull from my wallet and crotch. "When did you meet him?"

"He came by the gallery the other day. We made small talk before he asked me to dinner."

"And how did you end up here?"

"I invited him." She didn't possess a hint of shame whatsoever. This woman wasn't afraid to be herself at all. She couldn't care less about my opinion. She lived a life similar to mine, and she enjoyed every second of it.

If I didn't want her all to myself, I would actually respect it. "I'm just a phone call away."

She set her glass down before a ghost of a smile stretched across her lips. "I never pinned you for the jealous type."

"I'm not jealous."

"Really?" She swirled her glass again. "You usually

sabotage dates? Show up on a woman's doorstep without an invitation? Demand for her to get rid of her date? If you aren't jealous, then what are you?"

I didn't have an answer. None whatsoever.

She set her glass down then shifted her gaze out her back door. The sun was setting, and the heat was slowly dissipating. A gentle glow from the sunset still filled the room and blanketed her skin in the most beautiful color. "I'm not looking for anything serious right now. I told you I'm just interested in good sex and my career. And even if I were looking to settle down, you aren't my type."

It took me time to process a response because her words caught me off guard. Like she threw a pitcher of cold water in my face, I was stunned. No woman had ever said anything like that to me. Even when I was just a man with a dream, women wanted me for more than the night. It made all the muscles in my torso tense in both offense and curiosity. This woman was completely unaffected by my charm, and it drove me crazy. "Then what's your type?"

"Not a murderer, for one."

"Then you're going to end up with a pussy."

She ignored the insult. "An average man with average means."

All women wanted was a rich man who could buy them the world. They wanted nice cars, a beautiful mansion, and a necklace covered in a wealth of diamonds. They wanted to feel like a queen and be married to a king. "Bullshit."

Her eyes moved to mine, full of hostility.

"All women want security. All women want a powerful man who can protect them."

"Only women who can't provide for and protect themselves." Her fingers wrapped around the stem of her glass, and she fidgeted with it as she kept her eyes on me. "I've been doing it for a long time, and I'm pretty good at it. That's not what I'm looking for in a man. And money is the root of all evil. When you have too much of it, everyone wants it. It's impossible to tell who really likes you for you...and who wants to screw you over. People will do anything to get their hands on it...even murder innocent people."

I had a few asshole comments in retaliation, but I didn't say them because I understood the context of her words. Her mother had been murdered because of her father's empire. Being associated with a life of crime had only ripped her family apart. Now she lived on her own and hadn't spoken to her family in many years.

"So, you aren't my type, Cato."

I hadn't touched my wine since I walked inside. I was far more interested in drinking her in than letting the alcohol touch my lips. Bates's paranoia seemed like overkill now that I'd heard her confession. This woman didn't have a trick up her sleeve at all. She really just wanted a job from me—and that was all. If anything, she was a lesser threat than anyone else I dealt with. "You aren't wrong. But you aren't right either."

She placed her hand under her chin as she examined me. Her thick lashes made her eyes even more beautiful, hypnotic. They shone with ecstasy when I was deep inside her, and the effect was absolutely stunning.

"With great power comes great responsibility. If you're a man worthy of that power, you will rule without consequence. I'm the biggest shark in the ocean, the top of the hierarchy. I control this world, down to every last detail. Men look over my shoulder for me, but my power is untouchable. I'm the most powerful man in this world—and no one can ever take that away from me. Perhaps my station makes me a target, but it also makes me untouchable. If a woman were ever by my side, she would never have to be afraid of anything—because the world serves me." Her father had a respectable empire with plenty of men, but he was still no match for me. She thought she understood wealth and privilege, but the others were penniless compared to me. She had no idea what real luxury was like. "I can make all problems go away."

She hung on every word without blinking, but she still didn't seem impressed by what I said. "You can make problems go away, but I prefer not to have problems to begin with." She grabbed the bottle and refilled her glass. "I inherited this house from my grandmother. It's small and quaint, but it's perfect for me. I don't owe anything on it, and the money I make from the gallery is enough for a comfortable life. There's nothing else I need or want."

I wasn't envious of her attitude, but I respected her for it. It gave her the ultimate level of power. If there was nothing else she needed, then she didn't need to bend over backward for anything or anyone. She was in control of her life, and she wasn't looking for a man to make her life easier. She didn't need anyone for anything.

She drank her wine, licking her lips in between tastes.

It was the first time in my life when I'd wanted a

woman who was borderline indifferent toward me. She wanted to sleep with me, but not enough to blow up my phone with texts or to show up at one of my favorite clubs. She didn't have an ulterior motive, a fantasy that she could become the richest woman in this country. She didn't need anything from me—so I meant nothing to her. It was pretty sexy.

She met my gaze and didn't blink for several heart-beats. "What?"

"You're sexy."

"Me?" She tilted her head sideways slightly.

"Yes. You."

A smile formed on her lips, and this time, it was genuine. "You like an independent woman?"

"I don't have a type." As long as she was beautiful and subservient, I didn't care. Her personality, religion, and beliefs were irrelevant. I'd never paid enough attention to a woman to learn anything about her. "But I was raised by a single mother. She worked as many hours as she could to provide for Bates and me. Not once did she complain or seem weak. So I do have a soft spot for a woman who takes care of herself."

Her eyes slowly softened, and the smile on her lips faded away. Her fingers rested against the rim of her glass, and the playfulness she'd shown just seconds ago was gone. "I didn't know that."

"You're not a very good stalker."

"I guess I didn't think your childhood mattered."

"Every boy becomes a man. But the man never forgets who that boy was." It didn't matter how rich I was now. I could never forget what it meant to struggle. I could never forget the winter nights we couldn't afford heat and the summers we couldn't afford air conditioning. I could never forget picking up food at the homeless center when Mom got laid off from the cannery. My suits were as expensive as cars, but underneath my skin, muscle, and bone was the memory of where I came from.

"Your mother must be proud of you."

"Yes." It didn't matter how old I was, my mother seemed to relish any opportunity to compliment me. "My father took off when Bates and I were young. Being a father and a provider was just too difficult for him. My mother had to be two parents and two incomes. But she made it work and always made us feel loved. She's a badass...and there're not many women out there like her."

Siena's eyes filled with emotion, like that story was as touching to her as it was to me. "That's sweet. I'm guessing you take care of your mother now."

"Of course."

"That's even sweeter." She didn't seem interested in her wine anymore, only focused on the conversation we were having. "I lost my mom a few years ago. We were really close, and it's never been the same without her. She was always so strong and driven. She was a homemaker, but that didn't stop her from being my role model. I've been trying to pick up the pieces since she left, but I feel like I never make any progress. Anytime the holidays roll around, I have to start over."

I could see the devastation in her eyes the second she mentioned her mother. Without a father and brother in the picture, she was really on her own. Bates and I didn't exchange heart-to-hearts, but he was still a prominent figure in my life. I had him and my mother. It seemed like she had no one. "I'm sorry."

"Thank you. She's the reason I want my own family. I want to be a mom the way she was my mom."

I didn't know her well, but I could easily picture her surrounded by three kids. I could picture her making dinner for an imaginary family, all living under this small roof. It would be cramped, but they would still be happy. My future didn't involve a wife or kids. Bates and I knew we could never marry, not when it was impossible to trust anyone besides each other. So Siena was right—I could never be her type.

I grabbed the glass and took a drink, keeping my eyes on that deep brown hair. Her fair skin contrasted against the darkness of her hair, creating a captivating beauty that was impossible to ignore. The only reason I'd noticed she'd been following me was because she was the most stunning woman in the room. I'd have to be blind not to notice her.

"What brought you here tonight, Cato?" Her eyes followed my movements as I lifted the glass and returned it to the table. "What exactly do you want?"

I rested my arm on the table and felt my watch tap against the wooden surface. "You." I could have gone out with Bates and found someone to occupy my bed for the night. I could have called up one of my regular girls for entertainment. Instead, I'd been fixated on one woman.

She held my gaze with her usual look of bravery. She must have been expecting that response because she didn't have a perceptible reaction. This was the second time I'd shown up unannounced, tracking down her location because I had the power to do whatever I wanted. "You might own the world, but you don't own me. I don't appreciate being followed on my date or you showing up on my property like this. You have my number—you can always call me."

I couldn't stop the smile from entering my lips. "So you can follow me around, but I can't do the same to you?"

"I followed you in public spaces. I never encroached on your love life or showed up on your property."

"Because you would have been shot if you did so."

"Whatever," she said. "If you want me, you need to respect me. That's the only way this works."

I had all the power, but she was calling the shots. It was cute. No one else would have the balls to make a request like that. "Alright." I grabbed my glass of wine along with hers and carried them to the sink. Her date's glass sat at the bottom, drops of wine dripping down the drain. Just the thought of her getting naked with some other guy made me livid, so I walked back to the table and stared down at her.

She held my gaze, unafraid. Sitting there with her head held high, she was a queen without a throne or a crown, but she possessed such dignity and grace it was impossible not to respect her. I could be out with any other woman, but I was standing in her kitchen, her cheap wine still flavorful on my lips.

Maybe her coldness burned me. Maybe her indifference thrilled me. Maybe the only reason I was there was because I wasn't bored, because this relationship had unfolded much differently from all the others. "I could leave now. I could bring another woman to my bed—preferably two. Or I could stay here—with you. What will it be?" I slid my hands into my pockets and stood near her dining table. My hand ached to grab her by the back of the neck and bend her over the table. Or better yet, throw her on top of it and ram my dick deep and hard. The last thing I wanted was to go out and find pussy elsewhere. It was uninteresting and boring, the same thing over and over. The only remotely interesting woman I'd ever had was sitting right in front of me, defiant and beautiful. Since she didn't want anything I could offer her, there was no reason for her to be impressed with me. It only made me want to prove her wrong.

"If I asked you to leave, would you actually do it?"

I didn't do anything anyone asked me to do. "Not sure. I've never actually listened to someone before. But we both know you don't want me to leave, so let's stop pretending." Arrogant as it made me seem, I didn't stop the words from coming out of my mouth.

She stared at me for several heartbeats, her poker face impenetrable. Maybe she didn't like me as a person, but she certainly liked the way I made her feel. She'd been coming around my dick all night, so enthused it was like she'd never had such good sex in her life. She needed me for a good time, needed me to make up for all the boys who wasted her time.

She rose to her feet then slowly sauntered toward me, her presence drawing the air right out of the room. With eyes glued to mine, she approached me until her hands touched my muscular arms. Her fingers felt the corded veins and bulging muscles. Then she slowly slid up to my shoulders while she eyed my lips. "I want you gone before I wake up in the morning."

She pushed me away before we even began. It was the same attitude I took with my lovers, but coming from her, it still surprised me. I was disposable, worthless. It only made me want her more, made me want to conquer this cold woman and turn her red-hot. "We'll see." My hands helped themselves underneath her blouse, and I felt the soft skin of her tummy. My thumbs caressed her abs through her skin as I pressed my face closer to hers. The longer I held her stare, the more I felt her strength wane. She was a spitfire when she was in control, but the second my hands were on her, she was easily defeated. My mouth teased hers, coming close to her lips but never kissing her. I backed her up to the table then pulled my shirt over my head.

Her eyes immediately worshiped my body, her desire burning hot. Her palms planted against my pecs, and she slowly dragged her fingertips down, feeling the grooves of muscle in the valleys of my stomach. That fiery attitude was long gone, and all that remained was a woman full of ache. Just like the last time we were together, she quickly slipped into a different person, like there was no other man in the world she would rather be with. Maybe her attitude fooled other people, but it certainly didn't fool me.

I angled my neck toward hers but still didn't kiss her, purposely teasing her.

She leaned in to take my mouth, her fingers clawing at my chest.

I refused to give her my lips. "Tell me you want me."

"You know I want you."

"Say it." I would punish her for teasing me, punish her for making me want her so much that I marched over here like a possessive jackass.

Her hands clutched my shoulders. "I want you, Cato."

"No more other men. Only me." I'd never made that request of another woman. They seemed to drop everything in their lives to focus solely on me. But with this woman, she had more suitors lined up every time I turned my back. She was the kind of woman who didn't wait for a man—and that made her incredibly sexy.

The arousal in her eyes died away at my demand. "You can't be serious."

"Am I ever not serious?" My life was centered around work and booze. I had a piss-poor sense of humor.

"I just told you I'm not looking for a relationship."

"Neither am I. But I want you when I want you. I'm not getting in the back of the line every time I want a turn." I pressed my forehead to hers as I held her against the table. My fingers explored her hips underneath her top, feeling that silky soft skin I wanted to kiss everywhere.

"You don't seem like a monogamist."

"Because I'm not." I rubbed my nose against hers then stared at her lips. "But I can make an exception—for a short period of time."

A grin stretched across her face, a knowing look in her eyes accompanying it.

"What?"

She shook her head slightly. "I was right."

"About what?"

"I told you I could handle my own. I told you I was

the kind of lover a man could barely handle on his own. I told you I didn't share—a man would never want to share me."

It had seemed like an empty threat at the time, but her words had haunted me ever since she'd spoken them. Every time I was with a woman, I wondered if Siena would have been better. I wondered if I'd made a mistake bringing her home with the expectation of a threeway. Now that I'd had her, I realized her threat had been real. She was a special kind of woman—one I'd never met before. "Congratulations. You're the first person to prove me wrong."

Her hands started below my pecs and slowly snaked upward. "I like the taste of victory."

"I like the taste of you." My fingers played with the top of her jeans, and I discreetly unfastened the top button. My eyes moved to those plump lips, but I still didn't take them into my grasp. The idea of being with a single woman didn't sound like a sacrifice. It sounded like an opportunity I'd never explored before. The repetitiveness of my life had become mundane, and ever since meeting Siena, everything seemed to be more interesting.

"So, I don't date other men. That means you don't date other women."

"I never dated to begin with."

"You know what I mean." Her hands trailed to my jeans, and she slowly unfastened them. The button popped open then she worked the zipper. Slowly, she dragged it down, along my hard outline which was noticeable in my boxers. Whether it was intentional or accidental, her eyes flicked down and she licked her lips, like seeing my dick was exactly what she'd been looking forward to the most. "Just you and me for a few weeks. When my project is complete, so are we." She pushed my jeans past my hips so they slid to the floor. She was getting me naked, and she was also establishing a deadline without hesitation. A long-term commitment really was the last thing she wanted from me.

Made me want her more.

She hooked her fingers into my boxers and slowly dragged them down, pulling them over my thickness and then down my thighs. Every inch was revealed slowly, showing the deep vein in my shaft, along with the thickness of my crown. Like a woman who could appreciate the fine things in life, she looked at my cock as if it was a work of art. "I don't say this often…but you have a beautiful dick." She looked down at it while her fingers still gripped the fabric of my boxers. Her fingers twisted it in place, her tongue swiping across her bottom lip in the sexiest way.

My hand moved to her neck, and I slowly guided her to her knees on the tile. I'd gotten a good blow job in the back seat of my car or in a bathroom stall, but I'd never gotten head quite so spectacular as I did from her. She had an enthusiasm that couldn't be replicated or faked. She was a woman who got off on enjoying me, on pleasing me.

She opened her mouth wide and got to work, using that slender neck to take my length in and out. She flattened her tongue and kept her mouth wide as she pushed me deep inside her. Her hands gripped my boxers and yanked them farther down until they were gathered around my ankles. She closed her eyes and slathered me with saliva, soaked me so much, drops sprinkled on her dining room floor. Instead of giving me a quick round of foreplay so we could skip to the good part, she slowed down and took her time. She enjoyed it even more than I did.

And that made it the sexiest thing in the world.

Women wanted to please me to get my attention. Siena sucked my dick because she liked it, had nearly climaxed the last time she did it. Her nails dug into my muscled thighs, and she moaned even when my dick was so deep it might choke her.

Best head I'd ever received.

My hand dug into her hair, and I stared down at the woman beneath me, watched her ignore the discomfort of her knees because my dick was just so good. I'd fucked a lot of throats, but I'd never fucked one so amazing.

"You love my dick, baby?"

She pulled her mouth free and stroked me with her hand. A drop of saliva dripped from the corner of her mouth and fell to the floor. "Yes. So much." Her fingers caressed my balls, and she pushed my length back inside her throat.

It would be so easy for me to come inside her, to release my hot seed in the back of her throat so it could drip down into her belly. There was nothing I loved more than a good suck, gripping the back of their neck as I kept them in place to finish. But this woman was so good at everything that I wanted more. I wanted to come in her mouth, her pussy, and her ass all at the same time.

Too bad that wasn't possible.

I pulled my dick out of her mouth and tried not to shove it back in when she made that disappointed face. "Up."

She used my thighs as a ladder to pull herself up. Her jeans were undone, and her top was slightly bunched up from the way I'd gripped it earlier. When she was on her feet, she pulled her top over her head and stood in a lacy black bra, a push-up that highlighted the beauty of her naturally perky tits.

I'd seen a lot of tits in my life—but nothing compared to hers.

She pushed her jeans down and let them fall to the ground. What was left behind was a matching black thong.

I knew she wore the lingerie for her other date—but now I was the one who got to see it.

My hand slid up her back, and I undid her bra with a snap of my fingers. I yanked her thong down next, pushing it over her sexy hips so it could fall down to her ankles. Now that she was naked and painfully beautiful, I wanted to fuck her so hard it was a punishment. I wanted to reprimand her for bringing another man to the house. I wanted to torture her, thinking another man could fuck her as well as I could.

My body was eager to speed things up, but my lips slowed everything way down. My hands palmed her perfect tits, and I kissed her. My mouth moved achingly slowly, treasuring the softness of her lips and the way they gently moved against mine. Our breathing filled the quiet room, and the sun slowly disappeared over the horizon until we were left in the darkness. Only a few lights in the house kept the room illuminated.

I lifted her onto the dining table and dragged her ass over the edge. Her nipples were so hard they could sharpen a knife. Her voluptuous tits were paired with a slender rib cage, an hourglass frame that could put her on the cover of a dirty magazine. Her flat stomach led to a perfectly manicured pussy, nicely waxed and gorgeous. I'd already tasted her before, but now my cock just wanted to fuck her.

Fuck her so good.

I gathered her legs in my arms then pressed my cock inside her entrance, my large crown pressing through the tightness of her beautiful lips. My head could feel the moisture that was there, and that told me she'd wanted me to fuck her long before my dick was even in her mouth.

"What are you doing?" She propped herself on her elbow and pressed her hand against my stomach, her fingers hitting the thick grooves of muscle. "You aren't fucking me without a condom."

"If I'm not fucking anyone else, then I'm definitely fucking you without a condom." I'd never been bare with a woman, knowing they would take the first opportunity to get knocked up. But this woman didn't want anything to do with me, so I wasn't worried about that.

She kept her hand on my stomach. "Show me your papers, and I'll show you mine. Until then, put one on."

The head of my cock could feel how wet she was, how much she wanted to take my cock deep inside her over and over. Just feeling that single inch was enough to make me ignore her and do it anyway. But once I turned over my papers, she would be mine and I could fuck her as much as I wanted.

I pulled out then rolled a condom on.

"Thank you."

I yanked her to the edge of the table and gave a violent thrust as I shoved myself inside her. I pushed through her tightness and wetness and claimed her pussy as mine. That other guy only wished he were me. He was probably at home beating off that very moment, wishing he were fucking her instead of me.

But I was the one fucking her.

She rolled her head back sexily, her long hair catching the drops of wine that had spilled from the glasses. With her lips wide apart and a beautiful zest for life in her eyes, she was a woman being thoroughly fucked the way she liked. She didn't miss her old date, not when she was being fucked by a dick as big as mine. "Cato...I love your dick." She grabbed on to my hips and pulled herself into me, meeting my thrusts by dragging her body closer. Her head rolled back, she bit her lip, and then she said it again. "Such a good dick."

My hand gripped her neck, and I pulled her into me that way, controlling her completely as I slammed my entire length inside her. I hit her over and over again, claiming this pussy as mine. Soon enough, the condom wouldn't separate us, and I would dump all my come deep inside her, making her the first woman to have the honor.

Couldn't wait for that moment.

She held herself on one elbow and then tugged my neck down to hers so she could kiss me. She cupped my face as she gave me a hot kiss, her legs still separated so she could keep taking my length. "Keep fucking me…just like that."

Nothing sexier than a woman saying what she wanted. Unashamed of her sexuality, she used me the way I used her. She used me to get off, to drive herself into a scorching climax that made her toes curl.

"Right there…" She stopped kissing me so she could scream, right in my face. "Cato…yes." She rested her forehead against mine and closed her eyes as she finished, her perfect pussy squeezing my dick like a python. She came hard and fast, drenching me with another wave of arousal. "Do it again." She opened her eyes and shot me a fearless expression, like my disobedience wouldn't be tolerated.

My cock had already thickened because I wanted to explode after her performance. Watching a woman take the lead while being on her back was a rare sight. All they usually did was moan and compliment me. This woman pushed me a little harder, told me how she wanted me to make her come. "I can make you come as many times as you want."

She gave a gentle kiss to my lips, a subtle apology for her aggression. "I'll hold you to that."

––––––––

WE ENDED up in her bed upstairs. It was a small queen in a cramped room. The window overlooked the backyard and the hillsides in the distance. She had a mighty oak just outside her window, the leaves rustling with the nighttime wind.

A behemoth like me couldn't be comfortable in a bed

barely big enough for a single woman, but we made it work by placing her on top of me. She was lighter than a feather, so I hardly noticed she was there in the first place. My hand rested in the deep curve of her back and caught a few strands of hair at the same time. I watched the shadows dance on the ceiling as I held this woman, the most confusing woman on the planet.

I'd never stayed at a woman's house before, but there I was, about to break her mattress with my weight. I'd never ambushed someone without notice, never asked a woman to stop seeing other men. I turned into a completely different man overnight—and I had no idea why.

She eventually drifted off to sleep on top of me, her even breathing possessing the same beautiful cadence as a waterfall. She was so small and beautiful, but her magnetic presence rivaled my own. It would have been easy for another man to take my place that night, and that somehow made me feel special.

Even though special wasn't in my vocabulary.

She took a deep breath then stirred, something in her thoughts waking her up. She moved off my chest then ran her fingers through her hair, getting the long strands out of her face to reveal her smeared mascara. With heavy lids and a distinct look of exhaustion, she seemed ready to sleep for days. Instead, she got off my chest and yawned. "You should go. I have a long day tomorrow."

Frozen in place, I couldn't believe the simple way she kicked me out of her house.

Cato Marino.

I owned everything, and she was kicking me out?

When I didn't speak or move, she turned to look at

me, sexy with the covers barely covering her perky tits. With that sleepy look in her eyes, she looked even more beautiful tired than wide awake. The hour I spent pleasing her had drained her completely. "Did you hear me?"

"Yes. Doesn't mean I'll listen to you."

"This bed isn't big enough for the both of us."

"You can just sleep on me."

She propped herself up on her elbow. "Do you always try to sleep over when a woman asks you to leave?"

No. Because I'd never tried to stay. I kicked the sheets back and rose to my feet.

She stayed in bed and pulled the sheets to her shoulder. "Good night."

I stood naked at her bedside, shocked once again. "You aren't going to walk me out?"

"You know where the front door is."

I always thought I was an asshole, but it looked like I met my match. "You need to lock the door after I leave."

"I'm not scared of anyone. I have a gun, and I'm not afraid to use it."

I lingered at her bedside, having no reason to stay and not a word to utter. Her indifference confounded me. Her coldness seared me. Any woman would kill for my attention, but it didn't mean a damn thing to her.

I left her bedroom and grabbed my clothes downstairs. I pulled everything on then checked my phone. Of course, there were ten missed calls from various people. One of them was Bates.

I walked out the door and got into my Bugatti, my security team spread out around the perimeter over the course of a mile. I drove away and called my brother back.

"Where are you?" he asked the second he picked up.

It was pitch black outside, and I headed back to Tuscany instead of my place in Florence. I didn't get to drive as much as I wanted, so it was a rare treat. With no music, I could hear the sound of the powerful engine as it carried me across the beautiful landscape. "What do you want?"

"Whenever you don't answer me, that means you're doing something you shouldn't—or doing *someone* you shouldn't."

"Don't worry about my dick, and I won't worry about yours."

"You don't need to worry about mine—because it's not stupid."

"That's debatable."

"Anyway, rumor has it the Beck Brothers are going bankrupt. Their adventures in oil reservoirs have gone belly up. Information isn't public, but I always have one man on the inside."

I'd loaned them half a billion dollars to fund the project with a hefty interest rate in return. Their agenda seemed so simple that I was dumbfounded they could screw it up. "Hopefully, your informant is wrong."

"He's not, Cato. They've spent half the investment, and apparently, it's gone. We'll be lucky to get the second half back."

"They'll recoup what they lost—one way or another."

"That's a lot of money, Cato—even for us."

I drove with one hand on the steering wheel and

noticed the lights from the cars behind me. It was easy to spot me in the middle of nowhere because a dozen cars packed with men and weapons accompanied me everywhere I went. Even when I was alone, I was never really alone. "People trust our money because we always make our clients pay. It keeps us liquid. We will get that money back one way or another. I'll see to it."

"Or we could execute them."

"Killing them is too easy. Putting them to work is more practical."

"But we've got to kill them anyway."

Everyone knew that was a risk once they borrowed money from me. I had the cash to make their investments come true, but they were bartering with their lives. If they failed to make good on their promises, they would face torture and death. There were no exceptions. "Yes. I'll do it myself." I'd killed so many people it didn't faze me. I didn't lose a moment of sleep over it. Most of my business associates were criminals anyway, so it wasn't like I murdered innocent people. I did business with the rest of the world, families that needed a loan to buy their first home, but that was a completely separate side of my business. That was the public version, the one that was written about in the newspapers. The underworld was where I made my real money. I was a glorified gangster in a pretty suit.

"I'll do some more digging and let you know."

"Alright." The phone call seemed finished, so I was about to hang up.

"Were you with the art buyer?"

My finger hovered over the button. "I'm not sharing her, so stop asking."

He chuckled. "I'm not interested in sharing. I'm interested in getting rid of her. If she turns out to be the worm I think she is——"

"I'll put a bullet in her brain myself."

————

I SAT in the conference room alone and took my time enjoying my cigar. The smoke filled my lungs with pleasurable electricity before it slowly filtered out of my nose. I'd finished paperwork, emails, and phone calls, but I was in no rush to leave. Time passed slowly, and I sat there, thinking about nothing.

I wasn't just the richest man in this country, but I was also the youngest to accomplish the feat. My mother never had to worry about money ever again, and my brother and I would never have to struggle for the rest of our lives. Sitting at the top of the world should give me a beautiful view, a climax that never faded.

But it felt bland, boring, and artificial.

Was this depression? Was this hopelessness? I didn't have a single complaint to make, but yet, I felt empty inside.

Why?

Giovanni knocked before he opened the door. "Miss Siena is here to see you, sir."

I kept smoking my cigar. "Send her in." I'd forgotten she was stopping by that afternoon. Decorating my home was a large task that would take her at least a month, and every time she moved on from one room to the next, she needed my approval.

She stepped inside a moment later, dressed in black with white pearls. Her elegance was respectable, but anytime I looked at her, I pictured that hourglass shape, those luscious tits, and that wet pussy that could service my dick like a pro. Her folder was under her arm, and she helped herself to the seat on my left, remaining as professional as ever.

I didn't put out my cigar like a gentleman. I continued to draw the smoke into my lungs as I stared at her, admired the woman who was so indifferent to me it was a miracle she remembered my name.

She crossed her legs then opened the folder on the table.

I waited for her to tell me to put out the cigar.

"You seem moody today." She flipped to the correct page then clicked the top of her pen.

"I'm always moody."

Today, her hair wasn't pulled back in the rigid librarian look. It was curled and thick, framing her face and reaching past her shoulders. Pearl earrings were in her lobes, and her bright red lipstick was the perfect shade for her skin tone. She was a gorgeous woman whether her hair was up or down. She could be dressed in a potato sack with no makeup, and I would still find her fascinating. Something about this woman drove me wild, but I hadn't figured out what that quality was.

She watched me bring the cigar to my lips and puff the smoke into the air.

I waited for her to tell me to put it out.

"You're being awfully rude."

"Am I?" I set it in the ashtray, letting the smoke rise to the ceiling.

"You don't offer me a cigar?"

I did my best to hide the surprise from my face, but I couldn't. Instead of nagging me to be healthier, she wanted to join in on the fun. I grabbed another cigar and placed it in my mouth to light it. Then I handed it over.

She held it between her fingers and took a deep breath, the smoke dancing around her slightly open mouth.

I'd never seen anything so sexy.

She slowly let the white smoke escape from her mouth and nostrils before it rose to the ceiling. She took another drag, closing her eyes like she was really treasuring it. Then she set it in the ashtray and turned to her notes.

"Most women would ask me to stop."

"Most women have never enjoyed a good cigar." She turned her papers toward me and showed me pictures of the new paintings she wanted to hang on my walls. "I visited Milan the other day, and I found these. Since you host important clients in this room, I thought we should put our most stunning pieces here."

I looked at the pictures she'd taken with her phone, but the flash and poor quality didn't do the work justice. "Bring them here like the others so I can see in person." The paintings weren't that important to me, but seeing them with the naked guy was a much better way to judge the impression.

"I can't do that with these. They're being housed at the museum. You never gave me a budget, so I wasn't sure what price range you were looking for. But these are also some of the most expensive pieces in the world."

The arrogant asshole inside me wanted to laugh. "Money is no object, baby."

"This one alone is ten million euros." She pointed to the Monet. "It's been at this museum for twenty years, and they aren't willing to let it go for a euro less."

My Tuscan home was a power symbol, a subtle way to impress and intimidate the men I worked for. There was nothing too expensive or outlandish. "The price is fair. We'll head to Milan and see the painting in person."

"Alright. Just let me know when."

"How about now?"

She was about to take a drag from her cigar, but she lowered it back into the ashtray. "This second?"

"Yes." I made my own schedule. I could do what I wanted, when I wanted. "We'll take my plane. We can leave in thirty minutes, arrive in Milan in an hour, and then have dinner before we return."

Siena wasn't as suave as she usually was. All of that information caught her by surprise. She knew I was rich, but she probably didn't realize how easily I could make things happen with the snap of my fingers. Her father had an impressive empire, but it was dwarfed by mine. "Alright. I'll call the museum and let them know we're coming."

———

THE EXHIBIT WAS CLOSED off to the public, so we could see it in private. Anytime I did anything, I usually shut down the building because I wasn't a big people person. I wasn't concerned about being assassinated or kidnapped. I simply liked my own space.

Siena stood by my side, and we examined the Monet masterpiece in silence. The watercolors were breathtaking, and even after all these decades, it was still marvelous. Time hadn't worn it down, not when it was so meticulously preserved. Most famous artists were penniless and starving, and I always wondered how they would feel about their work being revered—and sold for millions.

Siena was quiet beside me, her black dress stopping above her knees. She wore black stilettos that gave her several inches of extra height. Her posture was always so focused, always so perfect. She seemed like a model rather than an average person. She had more elegance than the Queen herself. "It's beautiful, isn't it?" She was stand-offish and cold most of the time, but right now, her sincerity was heavy. It was thick enough to have substance, to feel like a physical object. "I wish I could paint."

"Why don't you?"

"Because I'm terrible at it," she said with a chuckle. "Trust me, I've tried. My work looks like a child's finger painting. To paint something like this, you need to have a special quality. Whether it's in the hands, in the mind, or the soul…it has to be distinct. It seems like a lot of famous artists have deficits, but those inhibitions somehow give rise to something unique and beautiful."

I'd never been a conversationalist, but I loved listening to her speak. With other women, I asked as few questions as possible. Getting to know them was never on my to-do list. The less I knew, the better. "There are other forms of art. Pottery, poetry…"

"Being an art buyer is as close as I'm going to get. And it's the greatest job I ever could have asked for." Her hands came together at the front of her waist as she stayed several inches away from me. When we weren't alone in a bedroom together, she kept her distance, keeping it professional between us like we weren't sleeping together. "What do you think?"

I didn't think I could leave behind a painting that she admired so much. It made the image more meaningful to me, made me feel like I owned a piece of her. "I'll take it."

She turned her head my way, her green eyes beautiful under the art lights. If someone painted a portrait of her, I would buy it in a heartbeat—whatever the price might be. "You're sure? It's a big responsibility."

"Having a painting?" I asked incredulously.

"This isn't just a painting. It's a piece of history. Artwork isn't something you ever truly own. It's like a home. You keep it for a while, enjoy it for decades. But when you're finished, you sell it to someone else. It's never really yours to begin with. You're just paying to borrow it —for a period of time."

I hated listening to anyone talk, but I could listen to her talk forever. "Don't worry, I'll take care of it."

"It'll have to hang on the northern wall so it doesn't get direct sunlight. As long as no one bumps into it or anything, it should be okay. If any of your clients knows anything about art, they'll recognize it right away. And that could always be a good conversation starter."

There wasn't much talking that took place between my

clients and me—except about money. "Let's make the transfer. Then we'll have dinner."

"Of course." Siena left the hall to handle the deal with the manager of the museum.

I stayed behind and stared at the painting I'd just bought—something that would remind me of Siena every time I looked at it.

———

THE PAINTING WOULD BE CAREFULLY TRANSPORTED by car the following day, so Siena and I went to dinner at one of my favorite bistros. Giovanni called ahead and told them I was coming, so they set aside their private room just for me and my date.

Siena sat across from me with her shoulders back and her posture perfect. The menu was open in her hands, and her hair naturally settled across her shoulders with her slight movements.

I ignored the menu and focused on her instead. I could have taken her to my home in Milan and fucked her instead of taking her out to dinner, but spending the evening with her over a bottle of wine didn't sound so terrible.

It was the most interesting part of my day.

"I'm getting the lasagna." She shut the menu. "What about you?"

"The chicken." I filled my glass and took another drink.

She opened the menu again and took a peek. "That doesn't come with cheese."

"So?"

"Who goes to an Italian restaurant and orders something without cheese?" She examined the bottle on the table and read the label. "This is a good bottle of wine. You're a fan of the Barsetti vineyards?"

"They make the best wine. And no, I don't eat cheese."

"Lactose intolerant?"

"No." I couldn't eat anything with fat or carbs to keep up this appearance.

"If the doctors told me I couldn't eat cheese, I would just do it anyway. There's no consequence I wouldn't face." She swirled her wine as she looked around the empty room. The other side of the restaurant was full of people, but our side was nearly silent. Low-burning candles were at the empty tables, and the distant sound of classical music came from the other room. She looked out the window for a few seconds before her eyes turned back to me.

Brilliant like gems, her green eyes were as vibrant as the forest after a spring rain. They were so clear and bright, reflecting the light from the candles but also emitting their own sparkle. She wasn't just a beautiful woman, the likes of which could be found by the dozen. Her unique qualities made her unforgettable, like the sexy curve of her upper lip and the plumpness of her bottom one. Her beauty was easily dwarfed by her poise. While some women were vain about their appearance, she was simply confident. She didn't think too much about her looks, but not too little either.

I was so transfixed by her perfection I nearly failed to

notice the waiter approach our table. "The lady will have the lasagna. I'll take the chicken." I handed over the menus and listened to his footsteps as he walked away.

"So, are you excited about your painting?"

I'd stopped thinking about it the second we left the museum. "Not much to be excited about."

"You'll have a masterpiece in your conference room. That's a bold statement."

"I make bold statements every day."

The corner of her mouth rose in a smile. "Can I ask you something?"

"Anything." Conversations with her never seemed stale. She didn't ramble on like most people, choosing to get to the point and not drag her feet. There was nothing more obnoxious than listening to someone talk just to hear their own voice.

"Be careful, Cato."

"I'm not afraid of anything." I certainly wasn't afraid of the truth.

"That man you shot in your driveway… Do you really think he deserved it?"

I hadn't anticipated such an interesting question. I hadn't anticipated her bluntness. None of my men would be dumb enough to question the validity of my decision. She obviously felt comfortable playing with fire. "Yes."

"Why did you do it?"

"I have enemies in Russia. They infiltrated my security detail with one of their own. He was planted there to spy on me, to find any information that might be relevant. He was only there for ten days before my men caught on to his tricks. Once they shared their suspicions with me, I handled it."

She suddenly turned timid and quiet, the beautiful blush in her cheeks fading to the color of snow. Her posture was still graceful, but it took on a cowering appearance, rigid like all her muscles were tightening at the same time. Her eyes remained focused on me, not blinking for so long, it seemed like she forgot how to blink at all.

"I could have had my men handle it for me, but I like to do the dirty work."

She tilted her head down and grabbed a piece of bread from the basket. She placed it on the plate in front of her and tore off a piece. She dipped it in the dish of oil but didn't place it in her mouth. It was the first time she'd fidgeted in my presence. "Does that happen a lot?"

"When you're at the top of the food chain, everyone wants what you have. Some men are stupid enough to believe I can be overthrown. Those men aren't executed in a merciless way. Those men are tortured first. Their families are tortured. Everything they love is ripped apart before I finally put them out of their misery."

She pinched the bread between her fingertips and smeared it with more oil.

I watched the color in her cheeks move to her neck. I watched the way she lost her confidence, like she was actually afraid of me. "I'm a scary man, baby. The scariest man in this country. But as long as you don't betray me, you have nothing to fear. I'm a criminal, but I don't harm the innocent. They stick to their world, and I stick to mine." I had the power to make anything happen, to commit murder in broad daylight, and the police wouldn't touch me. Reporters would cover it up to protect their friends and family. The entire world turned the other cheek—since I let them be.

"You just told me you torture people. I think fear is a rational response."

"I torture liars, thieves, and assholes. Are you a liar, thief, or asshole?"

She popped the bread into her mouth and chewed slowly.

"I didn't think so." I drank the red wine before I set the glass down again.

Siena was quiet now, her interrogation barely surviving a single question.

"You have a lovely home. I apologize for not mentioning it before." I'd been too busy fucking her on the kitchen table and the bed to make small talk.

"Thank you. I love it there." She abandoned the rest of her bread on the plate, having her fill from a single bite. "I know it's a bit small, but I think it's the perfect size. As long as I don't have more than two kids, it should work."

She spoke of a family like it was the only thing in life she really wanted. She didn't discuss other ambitions, like starting her own company or pursuing hobbies. She just wanted a family to live in that cozy house.

"What?" she asked, addressing the quizzical expression that must have been on my face.

"Nothing."

"You had this look in your eyes, like you were confused by what I said."

"I guess I'm just intrigued by the certainty in your voice, like having a family is the only thing you want."

"It's not the only thing I want. But it's one of the things I want most."

I'd thought she was different from all the other women I met. Maybe she wasn't.

She cocked her head slightly, picking up on my tone. "Let me guess. You're one of those men who never wants to get married."

"And you're one of those women who has to get married."

She shrugged. "I don't have to get married. If it never happens, it never happens. But I want to meet the love of my life, fall madly in love, and sleep beside him for the rest of my life. If that makes me sound boring, I don't care. If that makes me sound unoriginal, so be it. Marriage to the wrong man sounds terrifying. It could be a trap with no escape, a commitment to misery. I never want to be married for the sake of being married. There would be no point when a man can't offer me something I can't offer myself. But a marriage to the right man…sounds like the greatest experience." She wrapped her fingers around the stem of her glass and brought her wine closer to her. "Think less of me for it. I don't care. Just as I don't think less of you for wanting to be a bachelor forever."

"You don't think less of me?" I asked, a note of surprise in my voice. "You aren't going to tell me all of that will change when I meet the right woman?"

She chuckled and shook her head. "Everyone is different. Not all of us are meant to spend our lives with one person. We're wired differently. And the second we start making people feel strange for being different, we're in the wrong. So if you want to be alone for the rest of your life, Cato, then be alone. If you don't want a family, don't have one." She sipped her wine then licked her lips.

My mother always told me how she wanted Bates and me to marry. She said even if she'd known my father would run out on her, she would do it all again in a heartbeat. Having all the money in the world didn't compare to sharing her heart with the two of us. She said I would never understand until I had children of my own. "Bates and I made a pact never to get married."

"Married to each other?" she teased. "Good. I don't have a problem with two men, but I have a problem with two brothers."

The corner of my mouth rose in a smile. Now that we'd stopped discussing murder, she relaxed. She turned into her flirtatious and playful self. "In our world, we can't trust anyone but each other. A bad marriage could affect the business. It could destroy our lives. Neither one of us wants kids, so marriage is unnecessary."

"So, let me get this straight." She grabbed the bottle and refilled her glass. "Marriage is off the table because of money?" She pushed the half-empty bottle back to the center of the table next to the candle. "Money has dictated your lives so greatly that you can't enjoy anything else? That you can't even share it with someone?" She spoke with emotion but not judgment. "I stand by what I said. Money is the root of all evil. Money destroys lives. It's the monster that swallows happiness whole. There're so many beautiful things in life that are financially intangible."

"Only poor people say that." It was an asshole comment to make, but it was the first thing that tumbled out of my mouth. I would never forget how cold it used to be on winter nights without the heater. I would never forget how raw my mother's hands were from working in the cannery twelve hours a day. Money had saved my family—not destroyed it.

She didn't show offense. "Wealth is supposed to give you advantages in life. But from what you're describing, it sounds like it's inhibiting you. You can't go anywhere without thirty armed men protecting you. You can't trust a woman to love you for you. Men all over the world are trying to infiltrate your ranks to trick you. You're a prisoner—the walls of your cell, your own cash. I admire everything you've accomplished, but above all else, I pity you." Her pretty green eyes bored into mine, and instead of harsh judgment, there really was pity.

No one had ever given me a look like that before. Women admired me. Men wanted to be me. My mother's eyes beamed with such pride that it usually turned to tears. Everyone thought I had the world by a string—because I did. But not a single person spotted the loneliness, the emptiness, and the boredom.

No one had ever noticed what I hadn't noticed myself.

Speechless, I held her gaze, thinking about those afternoons I smoked my cigar while hardly moving, reflecting on the moments I told my brother I was bored. He questioned my sanity. How could someone with so much power and wealth be bored? It was a question that didn't have an answer. I never regretted everything I had or the sacrifices I made to achieve it, but it did seem like something was missing.

She didn't display a victorious look in her eyes. She continued to stare at me like the conversation was continuing, just without words.

I forgot about my wine and everything else in the room around us. I was spending the evening with a beautiful woman, but my mind wasn't on sex. It was the deepest conversation I'd ever had with another human being. Her intellect was dangerous, and her courage was even more startling. She was the only person in the world who didn't care about the size of my wallet. Unintimidated, she treated me like I was anyone else. "We were very poor growing up. The kind of poor where going to the doctor was a luxury. My mother did hard labor to support us, shaving off years of her life so we could have food, clothes, and someplace safe to sleep. Ever since I could remember, I wanted to be rich. I never wanted to worry about my next meal, and I didn't want my mother to have to put up with bullshit from other people. My ambition caught fire and never extinguished. Maybe money is evil, but I wouldn't have it any other way."

Her knowing look slowly faded and was replaced by an emotional gleam. "That's inspiring."

"The worst part of being poor is being powerless. You're at the mercy of other people. People are far more evil than money, and they'll take advantage of you when you're down. By holding all the money, I have all the power. Maybe I sleep with one eye open, but I also control everything around me."

"It seems to me you're in the same situation as before,

just in reverse. You have to work hard to maintain your stature because everyone wants to take it from you. There's a middle ground you're overlooking. You can be wealthy and secure, but also disappear from the public eye. You can have everything you need—without looking over your shoulder all the time."

The only reason I was patient with her was because I knew her background. Money had obviously destroyed her family. Her father kept playing with fire until someone hit him where it hurt—by killing his wife. Siena had the wisdom to turn her back on that lifestyle and settle for peace. To her, there was no other option. "It's more complicated than that."

"Is it?" The glow from the candles illuminated her features in the most beautiful way. Her emerald eyes reflected the white light, making them shine like Christmas ornaments in front of a fireplace. "Let me ask you one question. And you don't have to give me an answer."

Regardless of what her question was, I wouldn't give her an answer.

She tilted her head slightly. "Are you happy, Cato?"

The definition of happiness was lost on me. My money made me feel secure. My power made me feel invincible. The women in my bed made me feel like a king. But happy...I wasn't sure if I'd ever felt that before. The only thing close was seeing my mother comfortable and safe. Sometimes when I stopped by the house, I saw her tending to her garden, wearing a floppy sun hat as she got her hands dirty in the soil. She was at ease, reading by the window in the morning and then making me lemonade when I stopped by for a visit. Giving her a life she deserved was the only thing that ever made me feel anything. Everything else was just momentary highs. Making money was exhilarating, but after a few hours, the effect wore off. Making two women come before I finished ballooned my ego, but once the fun was over and we lay in bed, I was back to my calm coldness.

The answer was right in front of me.

No. I wasn't happy.

―――――

WE GOT into the back seat of my car.

"To the residence." I hit the button and raised the shade between the driver and us. The summer sun had set, and Milan was illuminated with the brilliant lights from the historic buildings and churches. We could return to my plane and be home in an hour, but I wasn't in the mood to finish the journey.

Siena turned to me, her legs crossed and her safety belt across her chest. "Where are we going?"

"To my place." I wasn't going to ask if that was okay with her. Her preferences didn't matter.

"Aren't you going to ask me first?"

I stared out the window. "No."

She continued to stare at my side profile. "That's rude."

"You work for me, remember?"

"Yes, I work for you. But I'm not being paid to fuck you."

I turned my face to her, noting the way she looked

stunning regardless of the lighting. "After sitting across from you at dinner all night, the last thing I want to do is wait another hour and a half before I can get you on your back. I want to taste that red wine on your tongue. I want to remember how sweet your cunt tastes. I want to be balls deep inside you, fucking the woman who's teased me all night with her beauty. Maybe I'm impatient, but I have every right to be impatient. Do you have a problem with that?"

Her hostility faded away as desire entered her gaze. The cues she gave were always subtle because she didn't wear her feelings on her sleeve. She was too proud to be obvious, too respectable to be deciphered. But there were hints of her emotions in the subtle movements she made, the slight shift of her eyes when she tried to hide something.

When I didn't get an answer, I forced her to give me one. "Do you?"

She cleared her throat. "No. I don't have a problem with that."

———

I OWNED a five-story building in Milan. After I'd bought it, the inside had been remodeled into a three-story home. The bottom two floors housed my security and weapons. We walked inside and took the elevator to the third floor.

Siena looked around as we stepped into the large living room. With hardwood floors, couches as soft as pillows, and a beautiful floor-to-ceiling window that showed the city, it was cozy like my place in Florence. I had many homes in different cities, and that was because it was the only way to truly guarantee my safety. All my homes were bulletproof. All of them were full of a security detail. My private property was the only way to control the situation. Going to a hotel or a public place made me vulnerable to an attack.

Besides, my homes were more luxurious than any hotel.

Siena slipped off her heels right away and left them in the middle of the floor. Now she was several inches shorter, but her confidence still projected her at an impressive height.

I headed to the bar. "Would you like a drink?"

"No."

I turned back around and ignored the scotch calling my name. If she wanted to get right down to business, so did I. I walked over to her and saw the color rise in her cheeks. Her breathing had picked up, the intensity of our privacy rattling her. She faced me with the same confidence, but there was a hint of intensity that couldn't be denied. She'd already slept with me, but it seemed like this was the first time again.

I pulled the paper out of my wallet and handed it to her.

She unfolded it and read through the results. Apparently, my word wasn't good enough. She checked the name of the laboratory as well as the date before she handed it back. "I didn't know we were going to do this now. I didn't bring mine…"

"Your word is good enough." I didn't trust anyone. Any interaction I had with someone besides my brother was considered suspicious. Bates was the only person I could trust implicitly. But something about this woman made me step out of my comfort zone, made me take a chance I never would have taken with anyone else. All of this could be a stunt, but I didn't believe it was. This woman seemed to be real, seemed to be scarred by wealth and power. She wanted nothing to do with my money or connections. All she wanted was a job—and a good lay.

"You've never asked me about birth control."

I grabbed her wrist and turned her arm, revealing the slight scar on the inside of her upper arm. She had an implant inserted there some time ago. It had healed, but she would have those marks for the rest of her life. Other types of birth control were impossible to detect, unless I saw a woman take a pill every day. But this was obvious. I released her arm then moved to the back of her dress. My fingers found the zipper at the nape of her neck, and I slowly pulled it down, revealing the gorgeous skin along her spine. She was so thin I could see the small bones jut out underneath the skin. Her slender muscles shifted slightly as she breathed, and the most beautiful bumps emerged over her beautiful skin.

The zipper stopped at the top of her ass, and that's when the dress came free. It fell to the floor at her feet, leaving her in a black thong that contrasted against the fair skin of her gorgeous ass.

Something I'd noticed before but never paid attention to was the scar on her right shoulder. I'd pulled the trigger enough times to recognize exactly what it was—a bullet wound. She'd been shot—and the bullet passed clean through. It'd been stitched up and healed nicely, but the distinct scar was impossible to miss. The injury told a story, a story she hadn't confided in me. My curiosity wanted answers, and I imagined she'd received this wound years ago when she was on speaking terms with her father. Perhaps her mother had been murdered and Siena was the next victim on the list—but she escaped.

I hooked my hands under her arms and squeezed her perky tits as I pressed a kiss to the back of her neck. My crotch pressed right against her ass, and my cock pushed against the fly of my jeans. My lips cherished her neck and kissed the shell of her ear. My hands continued to grope her beautiful tits, feeling the nipples harden under my ministrations. Her breathing picked up, and so did mine. "I can't wait to fuck you." I'd never been with a woman without a condom. I'd never felt bare pussy before. Even when I lost my virginity, it was with a rubber. But now I was about to feel this beautiful woman so intimately. She already felt amazing with a condom. She would feel even better when it was just the two of us.

She reached her fingers down to her panties, and she pushed them over her ass and to her thighs. They fell the rest of the way and landed around her ankles.

I kissed her left shoulder and sank my teeth into the skin gently. My tongue caressed her, and my breathing filled the space around us. My cock was anxious to be free of the restraints of my jeans, and I was eager to deliver my come deep inside that pretty little cunt.

She turned around, heat in her eyes and desperation in her hands. She pulled my shirt over my head then unfastened my jeans. Her eyes took in my physical perfection, her fingertips feeling the grooves between the muscles and the hardness of my chest. Every time she looked at me when I was naked, she wore that same look, turning into a sex heathen who couldn't wait to enjoy me. All women looked at me like that, but it seemed like she really meant it.

She pushed my jeans down with my boxers, sinking to her knees in the process. Her lips found my length, and she kissed him with full desire, worshiping my dick like it was God's gift to women. She sucked my balls into her mouth then dragged her tongue up my length before she took him deep into her throat. She closed her eyes and moaned, as if sucking my dick was nothing but a pleasure.

No woman had ever sucked my dick so well.

She moved back to her feet, carefully sliding my dick through her sexy cleavage on the way up. She used my forearms for balance, relying on my strength as an anchor to move back to a standing position.

I could lift her into my arms and carry her into a bedroom, but my hand swept deep into her hair and I tilted her chin back so I could kiss her. It was a slow kiss, full of warm breaths and gentle tugs with our lips. My eyes studied her mouth as my fingers fisted her hair hard. I yanked her into me and kissed her again, my tongue greeting hers sensually. I could be fucking her right now, but this arousing kiss seemed to be enough. For once, I wasn't in a hurry to fuck. I wasn't in a rush to hit the finish line. All I wanted was this, this sense that time was standing still.

Her hands explored my chest as she kissed me back, feeling the rock-hard slabs of muscle and the firm biceps of my arms. Her fingers moved down until they wrapped around my length. She squeezed it hard then ran her thumb across the tip of the crown, collecting the drop that beaded at the surface. "I've never let a man come inside me before." She looked up at me with smeared lipstick across her mouth and desire deep in her eyes. My dick was still in her hands as she smothered him with her experienced touch.

My cock immediately twitched when her words registered in my brain. Now I wanted her even more, to give her so much come that she wouldn't be able to hold it all. It would make a mess across the sheets, and if she got up in the middle of the night, it would drip down the inside of her thighs. Once it was all gone, I would just give her more.

I scooped my hands under her ass and carried her down the hallway. She was light as a feather and soft as a rose petal. My eyes stayed locked with hers as I carried her into a bedroom. I knew exactly how I wanted to fuck her, how I wanted to take my time and enjoy that smooth cunt. I laid her on the bed with her head against the pillow then moved between her legs. My knees separated her thighs and kept her wide open so my enormous dick could pierce those pussy lips. I hooked my arms behind her knees, and I held my face close to hers, my dick twitching in expectation.

She breathed hard even though she hadn't felt me yet. Her nails dug into my biceps, and she moaned in my face, as if the anticipation was just as good as the real thing. "Don't make me wait…"

I pressed my crown between her pussy lips and pushed inside, feeling the squeeze of her cunt as I slowly sank into her warm flesh. She was wet and smooth, even wetter than the last time I had her. Bare pussy was the greatest sensation in the world. Nothing had ever made me feel more like a man. All the money and power in the world couldn't compare to this feeling. I released a moan that sounded like a growl and kept sinking, enjoying every inch even more than the last. "Fuck." I slid in deep until there was nowhere else to go. My balls rested against her asshole, and I felt my entire body shiver with ecstasy. It was so wet, so tight, so fucking good.

I couldn't use a condom ever again.

I locked eyes with her, seeing this beautiful woman spread wide apart so she could take my big dick. I wanted to fuck her like this all night, give her mounds of my come until she was too sore to take me.

Her fingers moved into my hair. "I'm already gonna come…" Her pussy throbbed around me confirming her confession was true. A woman had never wanted me so much, so deeply. They wanted to be fucked good and hard, but Siena had a different look in her eyes. Maybe it was because it was just the two of us and she didn't have to share me with anyone else.

I started to thrust inside her, shoving my dick deep until I pulled my crown to the entrance of her lips. Her wetness smeared my entire shaft and even collected at my balls. There was cream as well because her pussy was producing everything to accommodate my big dick.

I didn't even fuck her hard or fast. I just moved slowly, took my time, and enjoyed it. I enjoyed this woman's cunt like it was the most priceless thing on the planet. I would have paid a billion dollars to fuck it, to coat my dick in her sexy cream.

She made good on her word and came. "Yes…" Her pussy clenched me like an iron fist, and she looked into my eyes, showing a raging fire. Her soft fingers unleashed their nails, and she clawed at me like a tiger. "God…yes." Her cunt gripped me a little harder then released, her climax passing.

As a man with something to prove, I wanted to keep going. I wanted to send her into another climax that would bring tears to her eyes. But all I could think about was coming inside that pussy, pumping all my seed inside this woman.

She grabbed my ass and yanked me inside her, her legs wide open. "Come inside me, Cato." Her nails sliced into my skin. "I want to feel your come as you keep fucking me." She breathed in my face with her sexy moans, her legs spread and her pussy so slick.

"Fuck." I pounded into her and smacked the headboard against the wall. The rhythmic sound echoed like a steel drum. I pushed hard and felt the explosion start deep within me, a visceral pleasure that set every nerve on fire. It sank down into my balls, a fiery goodness that made all the muscles of my back tighten around my spine. Then the seed exploded out of my dick, giving me the kind of ecstasy that could make my knees buckle underneath me. "Jesus fucking Christ." I impaled her with my dick and released all the way inside her, my ass tightening as the convulsions rocked my body. It was my first time combining my come with a woman's, and now I couldn't imagine any other way.

The climax seemed to last forever. It wasn't a quick jolt of pleasure like it usually was. As if the sensation was on repeat, it just kept going and going. My dick twitched as it finished inside her, and instead of softening, I was still rock-hard. That fuck was so good, but I wasn't close to being done. I started to thrust again, my come mixing with her cream as it coated my dick.

She gripped my ass and rocked back with me. "Cato… that feels so good."

My cock slid through the hot wetness between us. So much slickness, so much come existed between the two of us. My cock was buried in the nicest pussy it'd ever met, and the last thing it wanted was another pussy to fuck. Why would I want two women when this single cunt was more than I could handle? "Let's see how much come this cunt can take."

14

Siena

CATO FUCKED ME.

And fucked me.

Never stopped fucking me.

A man had never screwed me like that in my entire life. Had never made me feel so wanted, so sexy. Had never made me feel like the sexiest woman in the world. His hands were always on me, and his dick never seemed to soften. When a normal man would have started to get bored, Cato just seemed invigorated.

I went to sleep with so much come between my legs that it stained the sheets everywhere.

My body slowly woke up, and I was aware of the sunlight hitting my eyelids. I was on my back with a heavy arm across my waist. Warm breaths fell on my neck as the giant snoozed beside me. I opened my eyes and looked at his meticulously sculpted arm as it rose and fell across my tummy. His powerful frame was next to me, all muscle, skin, and the smell of sex. He hugged me like a bear protective of his cub.

I stared at his profile, seeing the hair start to come in along his jaw. It was a faint shadow, a shadow that hadn't been there last night. His hair was in disarray from the way I'd fingered it so much. His cologne had burned off in the middle of the night, replaced by the smell of the sheets and my sweaty body.

I replayed last night in my head, thinking about the intimate dinner we shared and the sex that commenced afterward. My purpose was to lure him into confidence so I could betray him, but I found myself pitying my own target. I began to humanize him, regardless of his crimes. He was the best lover I'd ever had, and he knew exactly how to treat a woman. Even our conversations were pleasant because he was very particular about his choice of words. He might be arrogant, but he didn't spend all evening talking about his accomplishments. He had a fathomless depth to him, like the middle of the ocean that extended for miles underwater. There was a distinct sadness to his soul, an emptiness he didn't have to admit. I understood his hollowness all too well. I saw the greed and corruption destroy my family. Cato didn't have a single person he could trust because even his close allies would stab him in the back if they had the chance.

Of course, I pitied him.

That also made me doubt myself. I was doing this to save my father, but Cato didn't seem like the demon Landon described. He possessed streaks of evil, but he also had hints of humanity. He shot someone without hesitation, but he also took care of his mother and spoke highly of her. How could I vilify him when my father was guilty of the exact same crimes? My father had murdered people who got in his way. He prioritized money over my mother. He sacrificed everything for a fortune he didn't even need.

And I was the one risking my neck to save him.

If I thought about it too deeply, nothing made sense.

Cato took a deep breath when he woke up. It was a masculine sigh, a low moan that came from the back of his throat. His hand squeezed my hip, and before he even opened his eyes, he moved on top of me and positioned his hips between my thighs.

"Uh, good morning?"

He opened his lids and revealed his sleepy eyes, a look that was even sexier than when he was wide awake. He tilted his hips and pressed the head of his crown right between my pussy lips. "Morning." He shoved himself hard inside me, sliding through the come that still remained from last night.

My nails dug into his arms, and I moaned when I felt his violent intrusion. I'd never fucked a dick like his before. He wasn't just long, but thick, and those perfect dimensions hit my desire in the right spots. It was the kind of cock made for fucking, perfect in its shape and hardness. "God…" My toes curled, and I moaned against his lips.

He buried his face in my neck and fucked me in the laziest way possible, his warm, heavy body pressing me into the sheets. His hips bucked, and he ground his body right against my clit. He didn't even need to do anything to get me off because he was simply so well-endowed.

Getting fucked by a sexy man first thing in the

morning was one of life's gifts. It was a treat I'd never truly enjoyed until now. There had been some good lovers in my life, but none like Cato. And skipping the condom made the sensations even more heightened, made every thrust ten times more pleasurable. This was a man so beautiful it was painful, and I actually felt like the luckiest woman in the world to be underneath him at that moment.

I never had to wonder if he would make me come. I never had to wonder if I should touch myself to get to the finish line. Anytime he was inside me, I knew he was man enough to finish me off before he released.

That made me worship him.

My ankles dug into his ass as I came, my nails clawing at his back as I rode the high he created in between my legs. "Thank you…" The words slipped out of my mouth on their own, a plea to this god in the sack. I didn't realize how much I needed to be pleased until Cato came to my rescue. He fucked me the way I needed to be fucked, fucked the way every man should.

He grunted as he finished, dumping another mound of come deep inside me. He filled me so much last night there was no room left, but that didn't stop him from trying to give me more. He moaned again as he finished, his come seeping out of my pussy and dripping between my cheeks. "Fuck. This. Pussy." He pulled his big dick out of me then left me there. He walked into the bathroom and got in the shower.

I didn't care about the cold way he used me then carried on with his day.

I loved it, actually.

———

I FELL ASLEEP AGAIN THEN WOKE up when I heard his voice in the next room.

"I'm in Milan."

I sat up then ran my fingers through my hair. I squinted to make out the time on the nightstand. It was almost one in the afternoon.

Jesus, I hadn't slept in that late in… I couldn't remember the last time.

"Siena and I looked at a painting. I decided to buy it." A coffee mug tapped against the counter, like he was sipping it then setting it down again. "I'll be back later today." After a long pause, he turned cold. "I know, Bates. You've made your opinion perfectly clear."

I opened one of his drawers and found a pile of fresh t-shirts. I grabbed the gray one on top and pulled it over my body. It was baggy around the arms and extended past my knees. It fit like a blanket more than a piece of clothing. I walked into the other room and found Cato sitting at the dining table, looking out the window. A mug of coffee sat in front of him, the steam drifting toward the ceiling, his phone beside it. He was in a new t-shirt and jeans, his dark hair styled after his shower. He didn't turn around to look at me. "Coffee?"

"Please."

He walked into the kitchen and poured me a cup.

I took a seat in the chair across from his. The sunlight came through the large window and filled the chair with summer heat. It would be a warm and humid day, but summer in Italy was always beautiful. Some people couldn't stand it. But I loved it. It was the winter months I despised. The heating system in my house wasn't great, and the fireplace wasn't powerful enough to chase away the cold.

He placed the mug in front of me then sat across from me. His light beard was gone, and his tanned complexion practically glowed in the afternoon sun. He hunched forward and cupped the mug with both hands as he stared at me.

I took a drink as I kept my eyes focused on him. A more beautiful man I'd never seen. He wasn't just pretty to the eyes, but rugged and masculine like a cowboy. His criminal roots showed in his cold exterior, but no matter how many crimes he committed or lives he took, nothing could stomp out the light in his eyes. There was still a soul in there, a loneliness that was so deep it was impossible to miss. "Who were you talking to?"

He drank his coffee, his expression betraying annoyance at my question.

"Not asking to be nosy. Just trying to make conversation."

"Then ask how I'm doing."

I let the hostile rebuff slide. "I already know how you're doing. When are we returning to Florence?"

"Whenever you're ready."

"I just need an hour to shower and get ready."

"Then that's when we'll leave."

I cupped the mug with both hands to feel the warmth against my fingertips. A part of me wanted to go back to bed and spend the rest of the afternoon screwing. Cato had invigorated me with a new sexuality. I never knew sex could be that good, could be so simple and wonderful. I'd been more intimate with him than I had with anyone else, and while that should have made me feel guilty, it didn't because I enjoyed it so much.

He didn't take his blue eyes off me once. "I was talking to Bates."

"I thought it was none of my business."

"It's not. Now I'm telling you because I want to tell you."

"Or because you knew you were being a dick."

Instead of flashing me a hateful look, a hint of playfulness entered his gaze. "You got me."

"Every time I see you interact with your brother, it seems tense."

"We're focused men."

And Cato was the most intense man on the planet. "Are you two close?"

"He's the only person in the world I trust implicitly."

"What about your mother?"

"She doesn't count. Different kind of relationship." He took a drink of his coffee. "My mother will be gone in a few years. Bates and I will be side by side for decades to come. He's my blood and my business partner. I will never have a wife or children, so he's the only family I'll ever have."

That was the most depressing thing I'd ever heard. "Let me ask you something. Do you not want a family because you just don't want one? Or because you think it's not an option?"

He drank his coffee again and didn't answer the question.

I didn't press him on it. It was stupid to antagonize a bear that was already irritated. "If Bates is just like you, I don't see how you get anything done. That's a lot of stubborn testosterone for one room."

"We're both assholes. That's why we get along so well."

My brother and I weren't that close, probably because we were so different. But right now, he was all I had in life.

"He doesn't like you." Cato took another long drink of his coffee and finished the cup.

I stilled at the comment and the abrupt way he said it. "He doesn't know me."

"He doesn't trust you. Doesn't want me spending any more time with you than necessary."

I kept the same calm façade, but my heart was beating a million miles a minute. Thankfully, he couldn't feel my heartbeat. Otherwise, my pulse would be a dead giveaway. I defused the statement. "Neither of you trusts anyone, so that doesn't say much." I drank my coffee even though the last thing I needed was caffeine. It was idiotic of me to think I could manipulate someone like Cato. I made more progress than I expected because we were monogamous for the time being, but the second I stepped out of line, the Marino Brothers would be on me in a heartbeat.

"We don't trust anyone for a reason. It keeps us alive."

"I really seem dangerous to you?" I asked, forcing a chuckle I didn't feel.

"Just your pussy." He rose to his feet and grabbed both mugs to carry them into the kitchen.

Once he wasn't staring at me, I let out the breath that was packed deep in my lungs. My fingertips felt numb from the adrenaline. I was dancing on a fine line, risking my neck every single day I spent with Cato. If I didn't finish my task soon, he might dig a little deeper and realize exactly who I was. Or maybe the reason Bates didn't trust me was because he already knew exactly who I was.

———

LANDON WAS WAITING for me in the back of the bar.

Lights were low, and few people were drinking this late on a Tuesday. Landon was in all black, holding his glass of scotch like it was a crutch he needed to walk. He hardly lifted his gaze when I took the seat across from him.

He'd already ordered a glass of wine for me.

"What happened?" he asked, instantly inquiring about my relationship with Cato.

"Hi. Nice to see you too. What's new?"

He lifted his gaze and gave me a vicious glare. "I'm crashing with one of the women I used to sleep with. I pay for rent and food with sex and monogamy. All I have is the money I swiped from the vault and the accounts. That's what's new with me, Siena. Now, what's happening with Cato?"

That was more information than I needed to know, but since we weren't that close, it wasn't totally awkward. "We're exclusive."

Landon's furrowed brows softened into a look of surprise. "Did he ask for that?"

"Yes."

"Really?" he said. "You're monogamous?"

"Until I'm finished decorating his house. That's the plan, at least."

He rubbed his fingers across his jaw, feeling the thick beard he'd allowed to grow in since the last time I saw him. "Your plan is working. A guy like Cato doesn't quit a lifestyle like his without reason."

"I'm just as surprised as you are." I thought it would be a lot more difficult to lure Cato into a connection. This guy could have any woman he wanted—and as many women as he wanted. To put that aside just to enjoy me seemed illogical. "But I think he's grown tired of the repetitiveness of life. I think he's bored and unfulfilled. I'm the only woman in the world who's ever told him no. I've played hard to get. I've dated other men in the meantime. That's not something he's used to, and I think he's intrigued by it."

"Whatever you're doing, it's working."

"Yeah…"

"You think you can get him somewhere alone? Your house would be the perfect spot. It's quiet, and there are no neighbors. Damien and Micah could show up in the middle of the night while he's asleep and ambush him then."

"Even when he's at my place, his men establish a perimeter around the property."

"Tell him it makes you uncomfortable."

Even if I did, I would be too paranoid to see the plan through. "Landon, I don't know if I can do it. He threatened me. Not directly, but he did. Maybe he was stupid enough to fall for my ploy this far, but I don't think he's dumb enough to fall for this. Bates is on to me too. Said he doesn't like me or trust me."

Landon held my gaze as he listened, his hand returning to his glass.

"I'm on the edge of a knife. Cato clearly feels a connection toward me. He tells me things, and when I see through his bullshit, he appreciates it. There's clearly something between us, the beginning of something anyway. If I betray him and it doesn't work...I know he'll torture me and kill me. He said it straight to my face."

"That was exactly what I warned you about."

"So...I think I have a different idea."

"What?" Landon asked. "Kill him in his sleep and take his body to Damien? You'd never succeed. And I'm sure they want him alive."

"No." My new idea was just as dangerous as my original plan, but it might have a better chance of success. "What if I tell Cato about my dilemma? What if I tell him my father has been kidnapped and the only way I can save him is by handing Cato over?"

My brother gave me the same look he'd been giving me our whole lives—like I was the biggest idiot on the planet. "And you think Cato will happily hand himself over to make your life easier? Maybe you're good in bed, but no woman is *that* good."

"That's not what I meant."

"Then what did you mean? Tell me how this idea could possibly work."

"Cato Marino is the most powerful man in this country. You've told me that more than once, and I've seen it with my own eyes. He owns everything and everyone. What if I told him the truth and asked for his help? Who would be better to make that happen? Cato could snap his fingers and our father would be saved and Damien and Micah would be six feet under. They wouldn't stand a chance against him."

When Landon didn't argue right away, it meant he was considering my words. With narrowed eyes and focused thoughts, he mulled it over. "That sounds like a dream come true. But why would he want to help you after you admit this was all a ruse? You tricked him, and he fell for it. He's gonna be so pissed, he'll probably rip your head off."

"True…"

"Like, actually snap your neck. I've heard that's his favorite way to kill people."

At least it would be painless and wouldn't make a mess. I'd look pretty in my casket.

"Cato will never forgive you for tricking him. The guy could be madly in love with you, but the second he realizes everything was a lie, he'll rip you apart. This guy rules with fear and torture. You're not special. He treats all his enemies exactly the same way. He's not gonna allow you to make a fool out of him."

I knew Cato was the killing machine Landon described him as, but I also knew there was a small layer of softness underneath his hard exterior. He did have some good in him, some understanding. "I still think I have a better chance telling him the truth than going through with this plan. It's obvious I'm only doing it to save my father. I'm not after his money or his power. Any human being would understand that."

Landon shook his head. "I disagree."

I wouldn't make my move right this second anyway, so it didn't matter. I still had time to think about what I was going to do.

"You'll need to make a decision soon. You're running out of time. Damien and Micah won't be patient much longer."

"Well, it's way too soon. There's nothing I can do right now."

"If the guy is only sleeping with you, I'd say you have some leverage."

"But when my job ends, we're over. I can't stretch it out forever."

Landon took a drink. "Look at it this way. This is the first time in the guy's life where he's only wanted one woman. He went from threesomes to a twosome. Not only that, but he wants it just to be the two of you. That's called ownership. That's called possessiveness. That's called a man marking his territory. When a man gets to that point, he doesn't walk away. Maybe he doesn't realize it now, but he will eventually. So if you keep this up, you'll eventually break through his exterior. The question is, do you have enough time for that?"

———

I SAT in the living room with a glass of wine in hand. My laptop was on my thighs, and I was researching the artwork I wanted to put in the hallway on the second level. Cato's house was so enormous that finding enough artwork to fill every space was difficult. After I was finished with it, it would practically be a museum itself. Anyone who had the honor of visiting his home would be in awe of the masterpieces he owned. Just the Monet painting alone cost him ten million dollars.

The sound of the front door pulled my attention from the screen. It sounded like the knob was turning or the lock was being picked. Damien had no problem breaking in to my home, so I tossed my computer off my lap and grabbed the gun I kept hidden underneath the table. I clicked off the safety then faced the door, my gun aimed and held at the ready.

The lock was opened, and Cato walked inside.

Like he owned the place.

He was wearing black jeans and a gray t-shirt, and his height gave my vaulted ceiling a run for its money. His eyes moved to mine as he shut the door behind him. Unaffected by the loaded gun pointed right between his eyes, he sauntered into the room.

"What the hell are you doing?" My heart slowed down when I realized Damien wasn't there to shoot me again, but I kept my gun pointed at the asshole who was trespassing on my property.

He walked right up to me and let the barrel of the gun press against his chest. Fearless, he looked down at me, that distinct look of amusement on his face. He cupped my cheek then tilted my face so my lips were angled toward his. "A beautiful woman with a gun…that's pretty sexy." He pressed his mouth to mine as he pulled the gun out of my hand.

My fingers turned lifeless as I let him pull the metal away from my grip. His kiss immobilized me, like I was the one being held at gunpoint. His warm mouth was as comforting as I remembered, soft and full. He gave me purposeful kisses that nearly made me forget he'd barged into my house without knocking.

He pulled down the straps of my yellow sundress and pushed it over my chest so my tits were on display. His lips didn't break from mine as he gripped both of my breasts in his large hands and squeezed them. He moaned before he gave me his tongue. "I missed you, baby."

I loved how sexy his hands felt as they groped me. So large and warm. They were a man's hands, big and callused. They knew how to handle a woman's rack, how to squeeze and massage until I was running out of breath. His thumbs flicked over my nipples as he kept kissing me.

"Say you missed me."

I didn't have an urge for disobedience. I turned into mush in his hands, my hormones overriding my rage. This man had done something unforgivable, but I was letting him kiss me and feel me up. "I missed you."

He gripped my dress then pulled it over my head, revealing my choice of a white thong. He stared down at me in approval, his fingers moving to my slender tummy and my wide hips. He turned his hand over and trailed the backs of his fingers down my stomach and toward the apex of my thighs. When his fingers reached my clit, he rubbed it gently, using two fingers to supply the perfect amount of pleasure. He touched me better than I touched myself, as if he could feel my own pleasure. "Say it again."

I didn't hesitate. My desperation came out without shame. "I missed you…"

His mouth moved to mine as he kissed me again, his

fingers still working my clit with precision. He sucked my bottom lip into his mouth then grazed his tongue past mine. His fingers rubbed me harder until my hips moved into his body.

This man made me fall apart—and I hated it. "You can't just barge into my house like that." I pushed my hand into his hard chest, but he didn't move. Instead, I was the one who moved back, his fingers falling from my clit. "There's a doorbell."

"I don't like doorbells." His eyes stayed glued to my lips, like he was waiting for the next chance to kiss me.

"Then knock."

"I don't like that either."

"Well, that's not how this is gonna work." I crossed my arms over my chest, but that only pushed my tits higher up my body. "Knock, or I'll shoot you next time."

A charming grin stretched across his face. It should annoy me, but anytime he wore a grin, it was innately arousing. "Fuck, you're sexy." He pulled my gun from his back pocket and set it on my coffee table. His shirt came next before he tossed it on the floor. His chiseled physique became my obsession as he removed his belt and dropped his jeans.

It was impossible for me to stay focused with this guy.

When his boxers were gone and his ridiculously beautiful dick was on display, hard and ready, I really did lose my train of thought.

He moved to the couch and sat back, his proud dick lying against his stomach. He wrapped his fingers around his length and patted his left thigh with his other hand.

I should still be mad at him, but that was impossible. I moved between his knees and lowered myself to the floor.

Before I could get on my knees to suck him off, he grabbed my wrist and yanked me on top of him. "Baby, you're wet enough for both of us." He pulled me hard against his chest then directed his crown inside me.

I lowered myself slowly, sheathing every inch of his dick until I sat on his balls. He was so long that I had to raise myself high to pull him out of me. Then it was a long fall back to his balls.

He stared at my tits as he moaned, his masculine jaw tightening with his movements. He gripped both of my cheeks as he guided me up and down, making me move at a slow pace because he wanted to enjoy every bounce. "You really did miss me…" His hands moved to my tits, and he squeezed them as I kept moving up and down.

It'd been a few days since the last time I saw him, and now that his dick was so thick inside me, I wanted it every night. The sex was good and life was short, so I should fuck him every single day. Even when he did nothing but sit there, he was still the best lay I'd ever had. He was perfectly created, one of God's favorites. He would ruin me for all other men, because no man would ever be able to fill me like this.

He locked his eyes on to mine, and I continued to bounce on his dick. He clenched his jaw and released another moan as he enjoyed me. He gripped my ass cheeks in his hands and guided me up and down harder, thrusting his hips up at the same time.

My arms wrapped around his neck, and I rested my forehead against his. "Cato, I'm gonna come…"

He pressed into me harder, his large feet pushing against the rug under the couch. "I know, baby. Your pussy gets so tight...so wet." He pounded me into oblivion, sending me into another climax that made me forget how much of an asshole he was. It made me forget I was doing this for a reason. Now it seemed like I was fucking him because there was no other man I wanted to fuck.

"Yes..." I closed my eyes and enjoyed it, feeling like a real woman with a real man inside me.

He gave his final thrusts before he yanked me down onto his lap, balls deep, and then he came. He exploded his seed inside me, filling me with everything he had. He moved his face into my neck as he moaned, his cock thickening and twitching inside me. "Fuck." He lifted me as he rose to his feet. "Now I want to stare at your asshole as I fuck you again."

———

I DOZED off for a few hours, and when I opened my eyes, I realized it was nine in the evening.

And I was starving.

Dinner had been forgotten because Cato stopped by with no warning. We wound up in my bed upstairs, fucking like it'd been weeks since we'd last seen each other, not days. Now I had a gorgeous man beside me, the sheets bunched around his waist as his hand rested on his stomach.

I slid out of the bed and made my way back downstairs. His shirt was on the floor where he'd left it, so I pulled it on and stepped into the kitchen. I'd already defrosted the chicken, so I added the spices then threw it in the pan. After a few more ingredients, I had chicken piccata.

"You can shoot, and you can cook. Perfect woman."

I turned around to see Cato standing there in his black boxers. With lean muscle bulging everywhere, he looked even sexier naked than he did in a full suit. I turned off the pan then scooped the chicken, tomatoes, and pasta onto two plates. "You don't know if I can shoot."

"But you handle a gun like you can." He carried the plates to the kitchen table.

I opened a bottle of wine and poured two glasses.

"I thought you were a scotch kind of woman?" He sat down and took a drink of his wine.

"I am. But if I drank like that all the time, my aim would be off." I sat across from him then cut into my dinner.

"A lot of people break in to your house?" he asked incredulously.

"You never know."

He took a few bites while keeping his eyes on me. Just as he did when we were fucking, he watched me with that same hint of possessiveness. "You're a great cook."

"Thank you."

"You can fuck. You can cook. You can shoot. Triple threat."

"Not if you're the one who pissed me off. I might shoot you then cook you."

He grinned. "If you fucked me first, I probably wouldn't mind."

The more I got to know Cato Marino, the more I liked

him. He was cold and empty when I first met him, just a hollow shell with few desires. But now he was a real man, one with confidence and a sense of humor. He even smiled once in a while. It was a much better version than the one I'd originally met. "So, no more barging into my house, alright?"

"Why?"

"What do you mean, why? This is my home, my property, and my privacy."

"You watch a lot of porn or something?"

"Some. Not a lot." I pointed my fork at him. "And that's not the point."

He was about to take a bite, but he lowered his fork and stared at me with a searing gaze. "Whoa, let's back up."

"What? That I watch porn? Women like it too. A lot of women."

He set his utensils down like he needed all his bearings to continue the conversation. "Is that what you were doing before I walked in?"

"No. But it would be none of your business if I were."

"How often do you watch it?"

Maybe I shouldn't have mentioned it at all since that was all he could focus on because he was a pig. "Doesn't matter."

"I just don't see why a woman like you would need to watch it at all. You can get laid as much as you want, anytime you want."

I shrugged. "Sometimes you like to be by yourself."

He closed his eyes for a brief moment, as if he couldn't handle the comment I'd just made. "Jesus, you're killing me." He grabbed his glass and took a long drink. "I just eye-fucked your asshole while I fucked you, and now I'm so hard up it's like I didn't fuck you twice in the first place."

I continued to eat. "All of this wouldn't have happened if you'd just knocked."

"I learned my lesson—I'll never knock again." His eyes narrowed on me, full of unstoppable arousal.

"Well, if you pull a stunt like that again, I'll shoot you."

"That'll only make me want you more." It didn't seem like an idle threat. It seemed like he'd never meant anything more in his life.

I broke eye contact first because his intensity was too much. I'd never been with a man I couldn't match. But my strength, intellect, and wit weren't nearly as strong as his. This man had more power and confidence than I ever would. He fucked like he went to school for it, and he made me swoon like he was my soul mate. "It's crazy to think you let me walk out of your apartment that one night."

"Yes. Biggest mistake I ever made."

"And here we are…eating dinner together."

"An excellent dinner." He finished his entire plate then washed it down with his wine. "Baby."

My eyes moved up to meet his, instantly responding to the nickname he gave me at some point. I didn't like possessive nicknames like that, unless it was from a man I was madly in love with. I would have told him to stop, but he never would.

He nodded to my left shoulder. "Tell me how that happened."

I knew he was asking about the gunshot wound. It was still a fairly recent injury, and it would leave a noticeable scar forever. I was surprised he hadn't asked about it until now. He probably didn't bed too many women with gunshot wounds. "I had an accident a long time ago."

"An accident?" he asked incredulously. "You shot yourself?"

So he knew it was a gunshot wound. Making up something wouldn't work. "I don't want to talk about it, Cato." I turned back to my plate and finished the rest of it.

He kept his gaze on me, like that answer wasn't good enough. "Why not?"

"You want to tell me something deeply personal about yourself?" I countered.

"Sure. What do you want to know?"

I rolled my eyes, knowing this was a false challenge. "Just drop it."

"You really can't tell me?" He cocked his head slightly. "Because if someone did that to you...I could even the score."

My eyes lifted to meet his gaze.

He stood by his statement by continuing his deep and hard look.

I pondered asking Cato for help. I wondered if he would fix all my problems. But I also wondered if he would be so livid I'd used him that he might kill me instead. "My problems aren't your problems."

"As long as you're fucking me, they are. If someone is giving you a hard time, I can give them a harder time."

I'd never needed a man to protect me, but the idea of having a strong man like Cato in my life sounded like the nicest thing in the world. Cato couldn't be challenged. He was too powerful. Even Bones and Crow wouldn't mess with him. I could make Damien pay for threatening to rape me all the time. I could save my father and put a gun in his hand so he could kill his jailers. "It's getting late, Cato. You should go." I grabbed the dirty dishes and carried them to the sink.

"The only place I'm going is to bed." He dropped the subject after I dismissed it, and he left the dining table. His heavy footfalls sounded behind me, tapping against the hardwood floor as he headed to the stairs on the other side of the house.

I stared down into the sink—unsure what move to make next.

———

MISSIONARY SEEMED to be his favorite position because that's how he usually wanted to fuck me. He preferred having my legs pinned back so he could drive himself as deep as my body would allow him. He liked to stare at my tits as he shook them, liked to kiss me when he ground his body against my clit.

I'd never had a man fuck me with such enthusiasm before. It was as if this man weren't getting ass on a nightly basis, as if he couldn't pick up a random woman in a bar and nail her within the hour. He screwed me like I was the only woman he wanted in the entire world, the only place he wanted to stuff his cock all night.

"Cato." My hand started on his cheek and then slid into his hair. I felt the sweaty strands and fisted them as he kept pounding me good and hard.

He kissed me softly as he continued to give me his cock deep, his full lips lavishing me with purposeful embraces that never faltered. He sucked my bottom lip then gave me his tongue, his heavy breath coming out of his nose.

I knew he was a fucker, but I didn't know he was such a lover.

"Cato." Like our conversation over dinner had never happened, I worshiped this man by calling out his name as I rode another climax. I didn't want to fuck him in the beginning because he was such an asshole, but now I would pay good money to have him fuck me like this once a week. He was so good it was indescribable. It made me want to betray him even less because I didn't want this to end.

"This pussy…" He slowed his thrusts and made them deep and hard as he finished. His cock thickened noticeably inside me before he released. With a loud grunt and a small spasm down his back, he filled my slit with another round of come.

He slowly pulled out of me to make sure he didn't lose a single drop. Then he lay beside me in bed, the late hour casting the bedroom into complete darkness. With one hand behind his head, he stared at the ceiling as he caught his breath.

I closed my eyes, so tired and satisfied I could drift to sleep right away.

"Baby?"

I faced the other way, my ass to him. "Hmm?" I could feel the come seeping from between my legs.

"I've got to get up early tomorrow."

"You know where the front door is. You barged in hours ago." I kept my eyes closed. I was too tired to even turn over and look at him.

"Alright. Then I'll stay."

"Wait, what? I thought you were leaving."

"No. Just wanted to make sure you didn't care about me waking you up early."

"Well, I do care. So, don't."

His grin was audible in his voice. "I like sex first thing in the morning."

"And I like sleep first thing in the morning. Don't wake me up."

"I'll try not to. But the orgasm might."

I shoved my leg behind me and kicked him.

He chuckled like it didn't bother him at all. "Good night, baby."

"Good night, asshole."

———

HE MADE good on his word the following morning. I was on my stomach, so he moved on top of me and fucked me in the prone position. The second his large cock was deep inside me, I was wide awake.

But I didn't complain.

He fucked me hard and fast because he didn't have all the time in the world. It was a quickie on overtime. He ground me into the sheets and made me come before he released inside me. "Have a good day." He pulled out of me and hopped in the shower.

God, he was such an asshole. He fucked me when I was dead asleep and then used my shower when he was finished. Total prick.

By the time he got out of the shower, I was wide awake and unable to go back to sleep—even though it was six in the morning. I was never awake before half past seven. I put on a pot of coffee and sat in the living room in my robe.

He came downstairs minutes later, dressed in the same clothes he wore yesterday but still looking like a million bucks. "Came to see me off?"

All I gave him was a glare.

He grinned, as if my anger didn't bother him in the least. "I'll be back tonight. Don't expect me to knock." He headed to the door.

I jumped up and followed him. "That's not how this works. You don't just come by whenever you want."

"What? Do you have plans?"

"No, but—"

"Then I'll see you later." He leaned down and kissed me on the corner of my mouth.

"Cato, you don't own me the way you own everyone else."

He turned back around, his playfulness gone and his intensity bright. "That's where you're wrong, baby. I do own you. I've owned you since the moment you whispered my name and came around my dick. I've owned you since the moment I came inside you. You're my lady, and I come and go as I please." He held my gaze and dared me to defy him.

I was so pissed I couldn't think. So I slapped him hard across the face.

He jerked with the hit, and instead of displaying a fiery glare, he turned back to me like he'd never wanted me more. He calmly pulled his phone out of his pocket and made a call, his eyes glued to mine.

I had no idea what was going on.

"Push my meeting back to one." He hung up and shoved the phone back into his pocket.

I knew something was about to go down. I was actually a little afraid.

He took a step closer to me and pulled his shirt over his head.

I stepped back.

He yanked his belt out of his jeans and slid it through his hands.

What the hell was he going to do?

He suddenly grabbed me by the back of the neck and pushed me to the couch.

My natural instinct was to fight—but that didn't get me anywhere.

He forced me onto my stomach and tied my hands together at the small of my back with the belt.

"Cato, get off me." I threw my hips up to buck him off.

"No." He dropped his pants and boxers then yanked my robe up.

"I mean it."

"As do I." His heavy body moved on top of mine, and he shoved himself inside me violently, getting his girth within me in one swift move. He grabbed my hair and yanked me back, forcing me to curve my spine and look up at the ceiling.

Then he fucked me so hard.

My body shifted with the movement, but I couldn't rest my neck because of the way he'd positioned me. He fucked me like I was a whore he'd paid for. Treated me like I was just pussy for cash.

And it felt so good.

"I. Own. You." He pounded me so hard that my clit ached against the cushions. "Say it."

As much as I enjoyed being fucked like this, I refused. "No one owns me."

His dick was so thick inside me, about to burst because he hated and loved my defiance. With the endurance of an athlete, he kept going. He kept fucking me like he wouldn't stop until he got what he wanted.

I felt the climax begin. I didn't want to give in to the pleasure. That only made him the winner. But it was impossible to fight. I could feel it, could anticipate how good it would feel.

Then he stopped. "Say it."

That was when I realized what he was doing. This was his torture. I would be in this state forever until he allowed me to release—and only with my obedience.

I kept my mouth shut.

He started up again, grinding me hard into the cushions with his massive dick. "I've got all day, baby."

I bit my lip and tried to think of a solution, but my mind was so focused on that big dick inside me pragmatism was impossible. Then I felt it again, the burning desire between my legs. He'd just made me come an hour ago, but it seemed like it'd been an eternity.

He stopped before I could release, removing his dick altogether. Despite how hard he was working, he wasn't out of breath. "We both know how this ends." He pushed his dick inside me again and rested his lips near my ear. "Say it."

"No…" I yanked against the belt around my wrists.

His body smacked hard against my ass as he drilled into me. He gave me everything he had, stimulated my body everywhere.

I felt it again.

He stopped.

I screamed in protest. "You're such a fucking asshole. I hate you. I fucking hate you——"

He fucked me again, just as hard as all the previous times. "And you belong to this asshole. Say it."

I didn't want to give in. But I didn't see any other way out. He was a master at controlling his climaxes. Most men couldn't keep their reflexes in check, but he was a professional at it. "Please…"

He chuckled against my ear. "Begging will get you nowhere. Now, say it."

When he pushed me toward a climax again, I tried to pretend I didn't feel anything. I kept my body relaxed and my breathing the same.

But he somehow knew. He pulled his dick out.

Fuck, I really couldn't win.

He gripped my neck and breathed into my ear, his wet dick pressed between my ass cheeks. "Baby." He grabbed my hair and forced me to look at him, victory in his eyes even though I hadn't conceded yet.

I didn't want a man to ever own me. My mission was to manipulate him to get what I wanted. Giving him what he wanted accomplished that, but I somehow felt like I was signing my soul over to the devil.

Cato Marino was the devil.

He pushed his dick back inside me and slowly started to move, keeping his eyes on me. "Say it."

I turned my face away so I wouldn't have to look at him.

He yanked me back, his eyes full of gloating.

"You own me…"

He inhaled a deep breath, like those words were beautiful to his ears. He pressed his mouth to mine and gave me a soft kiss before he righted himself on top of me. Then he pounded into me hard, nailing me so good I would hit a climax in seconds. "Say it again."

I felt the climax hit—and it was so good that it was worth all the self-loathing. "You own me, Cato. You fucking own me."

15

Cato

I SAT IN THE CHAIR FACING THE DESK WITH MY LEGS crossed. The Beck Brothers were using my money to drill for oil in the east, and once rumors circulated that their venture was going south, I'd decided to take a visit.

Judging by the sweat on Connor's brow, he thought he'd been clever enough to hide it from me.

No one hid shit from me. "You know why I'm here. You know what's going to happen. So choose your words carefully—and don't waste my time. I already took the afternoon off to fly here." My men had hit the property hard, taking their positions like they were ready to go to war. Whenever I traveled anywhere, I had the kind of security a president envied.

Connor couldn't touch me. He drummed his fingers against the desk as he stalled, trying to think of the right choice of words.

If he made the wrong move, I would kill him—right then and there. His brother would be next.

"We anticipated a lot more oil."

Good. He wasn't gonna waste my time feeding me bullshit. "That's unfortunate. What are you going to do now?"

He kept drumming his fingers. "We have a few leads in the area. About fifty miles north."

"And how credible is this lead?" I'd worn my three-piece black suit, and I missed my jeans and t-shirt. I missed doing work from the house because I could wear whatever I wanted—or nothing at all.

"Credible. But we won't know until we look."

"And when will that be?"

"Next week."

I rose to my feet and slipped my hands into my pockets as I approached his desk. "We both know I don't really care if you find oil or not. I only care about the five hundred million I loaned to you—with interest."

Connor lowered his gaze, like a dog that had just chewed through my favorite pair of shoes.

"You know what will happen if that doesn't come to pass." I continued to stare at him, my eyes burning through his cheek. "You know what will happen not just to you and your brother, but your lovely wife Rose and your twin daughters."

His eyes moved back to mine, the horror in his gaze. "My family—"

"Everything is collateral when you borrow from Cato Marino. I suggest you figure it out. Otherwise, I will butcher every member of your family." I rapped the backs of my knuckles against his desk before I turned around.

"Figure out how you're going to get my money, Connor. Or start picking out coffins."

―――――

WHEN MY PLANE LANDED, I got into the back seat of my car and was taken away from the airport. After the long day I'd had, there was only one place I wanted to go.

Siena.

We'd established a monogamous fling that was supposed to mean nothing, but my grip on her seemed to tighten. She said I didn't own her like I owned everything else, and that was when I realized how much I hated that fact.

I did want to own her.

Ever since the beginning, her uniqueness caught my attention. Every time she pushed me away, I pulled tighter. My attraction turned to obsession. My obsession turned to possessiveness. Maybe this arrangement would burn out and my interest would die—but I'd never been this invested in a single woman in my life.

Maybe that meant something.

Bates called me. "What happened?"

"Connor was straight with me. Told me they'd found a promising spot for drilling. I'll get an update in a few weeks."

"You think he'll make it happen? They've burned through half our money."

I rested my elbow on the armrest while my hand kept the phone against my ear. I looked out the window and watched the sun disappear over the horizon. It was past eight in the evening, and nighttime had officially arrived. "I don't know. But I told him what would happen if he didn't."

"Mention Rose and the girls?"

"Of course." The second you took the money, you risked everyone you knew and loved. If the Marinos didn't get their money, all hell would break loose. No one was immune to those rules. That was how we kept our clients in line. It was rare when someone took a risk they couldn't gamble—and they always died in the same way. "I'll send a coffin brochure just to get the message across."

Bates turned quiet. Instead of hanging up, he let the silence linger. That meant he had more to say, but he didn't know how to broach the subject.

"What is it?"

"Siena. Giovanni told me you slept over the other night."

I kept tabs on people. I didn't appreciate when people kept tabs on me, especially my brother. "Where I stick my dick is none of your concern. Mind your own fucking business, or I'll burn my cigar on your cheek."

Bates didn't hesitate at the threat. "Did you tell her you know who she is?"

I didn't see the point. She clearly had no interest in her family's blood money. "Trust me, Bates. She wants nothing to do with that lifestyle. She despises money and power. She's happy living in a little shack. She doesn't want anything from me. She doesn't even like me most of the time…"

"Then why is she still fucking you?"

I grinned. "Because I know how to fuck." I thought

about the way I'd left her that morning, powerless underneath me while I forced her to surrender. Watching a stubborn woman give in was the sexiest thing I'd ever seen.

"Has she ever asked you about what we do?"

"Not once."

"Has she ever asked for anything too personal?"

"No, Bates. In fact, she's told me how much she pities me. She knows I have all the money in the world, but she sees how bored and empty I am." I'd never admitted it to her face, but the second she said those words, I knew they were true. I knew she understood me in a way no one else did. When we met, I wasn't looking for a connection. But I inevitably found one. Maybe that was why I wanted her so much—because she really knew me.

"You're just in a mood."

"Moods comes and go. I've been this way for a long time."

"Whatever. Don't let this bitch think she knows you. She doesn't."

The muscles in my forearms immediately tightened in retaliation. I didn't need to defend her honor, not when she was just a fling, but my reaction was so natural, it unnerved me. "Don't call her that. I mean it." I told her I would hurt anyone who hurt her. That applied to my brother as well.

He laughed into the phone, but it was a sad laugh. "Jesus fucking Christ, Cato. Please don't tell me you're falling for her game. You're smarter than that. At least, I thought you were…"

I was surrounded by liars and manipulators. My life revolved around staying one step ahead at every turn. The beautiful thing about Siena was there were no games. She only wanted one thing from me, and she got it. The rest of our time was simple. It was easy. We had real conversations that had nothing to do with money or power. "Good night, Bates."

"When the time comes, I won't be a gentleman. I'll be the asshole who said I told you so."

———

SHE THREW a fit when I didn't knock last time, but since she was sexy when she was pissed, I did it again. I picked the lock and let myself inside.

She stood in the entryway, the gun hanging at her side. She was livid like last time. "What did we just talk about?"

I loved the way her green eyes burned as if they were on fire. Her lips pressed tightly together like she was trying not to scream at me. Her petite frame was a direct contradiction to her enormous presence. Everything about her was sexy, including the way she held the gun like she knew how to use it. Even the scar on her shoulder was a turn-on. "Fuck, you're hot when you're pissed." I grabbed my tie and loosened it as I stepped inside.

"I warned you I would shoot you."

I grabbed her arm and placed the barrel right against my sternum. "Then do it."

She immediately lifted her finger off the trigger, scared she might accidentally pull it. She drew it back and set it on the table beside the door. "I'm serious, Cato. Stop just walking inside at night like that. You can have a key if you really want one."

"You want to give me a key?" I asked, shocked that she'd offered.

"It's better than having a heart attack every time you come to the door. At least I'll know it's you."

I knew she wasn't looking for a relationship, so there was only one other reason she would offer something like that. My eyes narrowed as I looked at her pretty face. "Baby, who bothers you?"

There was a quick reaction in her eyes, but it happened so fast, at the speed of a shooting star, I wasn't sure if I really saw it or not. She crossed her arms over her chest then moved to the door so she could close it. "No one. I live out here alone and…what the hell is that?"

I turned around and looked out the open door. The only thing I saw was the car lights from my security team. They spread out everywhere around the property, keeping a one-mile perimeter so no one could come and go without their knowledge. "My guys. They'll be there until I leave in the morning."

She poked her head out and took a look around, seeing the faint lights from their phones and cars. "How many are there?"

"Fifty."

"And they'll just stay there the entire time?"

"Yes." I didn't go anywhere without them following me. I didn't even pick up a cup of coffee without them trailing behind me. "You don't need to be uncomfortable with them."

"Ugh, there are fifty armed men around my property. That's pretty scary."

"They would never hurt you."

"Still don't like it." She walked back into the house.

I followed her then shut the door behind me.

"Would it be easier if we just went to your place?" She grabbed the gun on the table and returned it to its hiding spot underneath the coffee table. "Because it's pretty obvious you have an entire squad surrounding the property."

It would be simpler if we went to my place, but there was something about her quaint place I liked. I liked the paintings she had on the walls, the atmosphere she created with her presence. It was small, barely big enough for a man my size to get comfortable, but I still liked it. "Don't worry about it." I pulled my tie from around my neck and tossed it on the couch. I moved to my vest and jacket next before I could finally reach my collared shirt underneath.

She watched me undress. "Had a big day?"

"Something like that." I tossed my shirt on the couch and stood in my slacks.

She was in a tank top without a bra and little white shorts. Her makeup was gone, and her hair was in a ponytail. She didn't look as hot as she did in a backless dress and heels, but seeing her like this was somehow sexier. She didn't need any of that stuff to be totally fuckable.

What was sexier than that?

I undid my slacks then kicked off my shoes.

She watched me strip down to my boxers. "So, you're just gonna get naked in my living room?"

"Do you want me not to get naked?"

She pressed her lips together tightly and didn't answer. "I have some leftover dinner. Are you hungry?"

A woman had never offered anything to me before.

Maybe I never gave them a chance, but this was a first-time experience. The only home-cooking I'd ever had was my mother's. "I'm not hungry. But thank you."

"Wine or anything?"

"No. I just want to go to bed."

"Oh?" She crossed her arms over her chest. "You just come by whenever you want and—"

As much as it turned me on to watch her get pissed, I wasn't in the mood for talking. I'd spent the entire day on a plane, and all I wanted was pussy and a comfortable bed for fucking. My hands dug into her hair, and I silenced her mood with a kiss.

It worked. She kissed me back right away, falling for my soft lips and the purposeful way I embraced her. She liked to be in charge of her life, but the second we were together, she gave me the reins. She acted like she didn't care, but she liked having a man in charge, a man authoritative enough to put her in her place.

And I liked having a woman to put in place.

I scooped her into my arms and carried her upstairs to her bedroom. Just thinking about how incredible her pussy was made my cock twitch in my boxers. I'd been thinking about it all day, thinking about the moment I could sink deep inside it.

I laid her on the bed and pulled off her shorts and panties. The second those were gone, I looked at her perfect pussy, those succulent lips and that delicious nub. My boxers hit the floor, and then I pressed my face in her cunt, kissing the area I missed so much. I didn't go down on women because foreplay wasn't important to me. But Siena's pussy was just too intoxicating to ignore.

I didn't do it to make her feel good. I did it because I wanted to.

Her legs widened, and she moaned as she felt me suck her clit into my mouth. She writhed slightly, tilting her hips so her pussy could get farther inside me.

I loved the way she tasted, the way she smelled. I loved feeling the inside of her slit with my tongue. Two women used to bore me, but this single woman captured all my attention, and all the others were forgotten.

I moved up her body and pinned her knees back with my arms. Missionary was boring as hell, and I preferred having a woman on her stomach. Having a beautiful ass in my face was what I wanted most. But with Siena, I liked kissing her, staring at her tits, and watching every reaction she had to me. I liked shoving myself as deep as I could go and listening to her moan in response. "Miss me?" I sank deep inside her, my cock pushing through my saliva and her wetness as I descended. I couldn't keep the moan out of my voice as I sank deeper, finally getting the pussy I'd been thinking about all day. I'd always been a passionate man who needed sex constantly, but she elevated me to a new level.

When my cock was completely inside her, she dug her fingers into my hair. "Yes…I missed you." She breathed a deep sigh like it was her first breath of fresh air. Her fingers yanked on my strands, and her nails dug into my skull.

I'd conquered a woman who wasn't easily conquered. I put her stubborn attitude in check and made her surrender to me. Last time I was with her, I established the dynamics of the relationship—and put her in her place.

Now she was more responsive to me, becoming the subservient woman only a man like me could create. "I've been thinking about this cunt all day." I thrust into her hard, rocking her with my momentum as I took control of her headboard. Men had been where I was before, but now I wanted to erase them, to make her think of me when she took on a new lover.

I'd never been excited to be with one woman, to stare out the window from the back seat of the car and fantasize about her. A man like me could have any kind of sex he wanted. I could have women in whips and chains with the snap of a finger. But all I wanted was this woman, this small but fierce woman. "I've been thinking about your cock since the moment you left."

———

HER BEDROOM HAD A QUEEN-SIZE BED, a large window right behind it that extended into a nook, a master bathroom with one sink and a tub as part of the shower. It wasn't luxurious by any means, but it was well-decorated and reflected her personality. There was a vase of flowers sitting on her vanity, a picture frame with a photo of her and her mother beside it. There were different colored blankets at the foot of the bed and paintings of the Italian landscape on the walls. The entire room was the size of my closet.

I woke up the following morning with her sound asleep beside me. Her arm was hooked around my waist, and her leg was tucked between my knees. She snuggled with me like I was her favorite stuffed animal.

Women slept over all the time, but they didn't hang all over me like this. I needed my space, but with Siena, it never felt like she invaded too much of my domain. She seemed to fit beside me perfectly well, like a lock and key.

Her ponytail had come loose at some point, and now her hair spread across my chest. Dark like the wood of an oak tree, it was the most beautiful color. She had classic Italian features but with skin that was pale like a glass of milk. Some freckles dotted her cheeks and her shoulders, but the spots only added to her appeal. She was gorgeous but real. I watched her while I planned my day. I would head to the office in Florence and take care of business. Hopefully, I would be done before the late afternoon.

Siena was the only woman whose house I stayed at. I always had women come to my place because it was more convenient, but the second I visited Siena, I felt right at home. It was nice not to be waited on hand and foot by Giovanni, or to see armed men on my property on a regular basis. It was my home, but it was still a place of business. This house was a lot simpler. Made me forget about all the tedious aspects of my life.

When I couldn't lie around any longer, I lightly shifted her away from me then got out of bed.

Her quiet sigh announced her annoyance. "Sneaking out?"

"Didn't want to wake you."

"You never mind waking me up." She propped her head on her open palm and stared at me as the sheets were pulled over her chest.

"If I didn't have somewhere to be, you know I would." I went into her bathroom and brushed my teeth with her toothbrush before I put on the suit I'd arrived in. It was slightly wrinkled because I'd left it on the floor all night long, but I was too rich to care about my appearance.

I grabbed my watch from her vanity and slipped it over my wrist.

She stayed in bed, sleepy and sexy under the sheets. "I have to go to work too. But I could also stay here forever…" She pulled the sheets to her shoulder and closed her eyes. "It's nice and warm because of you."

I sat at the foot of the bed and pulled on my shoes. "That could save you money in the wintertime."

"My heater is so old that it doesn't really work. It's impossible to get heat up here. I usually use the fireplace, but then I have to buy the firewood and then carry it up here… I'm pretty lazy."

Sometimes I forgot what it was like not to have everything I needed at my fingertips. There was always someone there to fix my problems. "With me, you don't need a fire." Once my outfit was complete, I stood up.

She finally got out of bed and pulled on her purple robe. She ran her fingers through her hair and kept it out of her face as she came to my side. "I'll walk you out."

"That's awfully polite of you. Normally, you don't give a damn." I slid my hands into my pockets as I looked down at her, seeing those plump lips that I spent all night kissing. She was gorgeous, so gorgeous it was actually painful to look at.

"I don't." She smiled at me, the playfulness reaching her eyes. "But I need coffee." She turned away and walked out of the room, her bare feet hitting the hardwood floor lightly. Her hair shifted back and forth with her movements, the long strands reaching the middle of her back.

I stayed behind even when she was gone from sight, understanding just how transfixed I was by this incredible woman. It was lust combined with respect, and I'd never respected a woman before. I didn't just like fucking her. I liked talking to her, I liked dropping all the bullshit and being myself. I didn't have to be the coldhearted killer Cato Marino. With her, I could just be Cato.

I joined her downstairs and met her in the entryway. "Meet me for dinner tonight."

"Aren't you sick of me?" She crossed her arms over her chest while the corner of her mouth was raised in a smile.

I kept my hands in my pockets even though I wanted to grab her. I wanted to hold on to the back of her hair like a leash. Sometimes I wanted to be soft with her, but most of the time I wanted to be the dictator lover she'd turned me into. "Are you sick of me?"

Her smile slowly faded away, the seriousness entering her gaze. Something about my question struck her, chased away all the playfulness she had a moment ago. Her chest rose with the deep breath she took. "No…"

My fingers moved under her chin, and I lifted her mouth to mine. I planted a soft kiss there, an embrace that was gentler than any other. I kept my eyes open as I looked into hers, watching the emotion enter her gaze as the kiss continued. When I pulled away, it didn't seem like she wanted the kiss to end. "Me neither."

16

Siena

WHEN I FINISHED WORK AT THE GALLERY, I STEPPED outside and prepared to walk to the restaurant where we were meeting. Instead, a black car pulled up, all the windows tinted and bulletproof.

The man in the passenger seat got out of the car then opened the back door for me.

I knew who was waiting in the back seat.

I sat down and saw Cato beside me, his knees apart and his hands resting on his thighs. He wore a different suit than he had that morning. Now it was navy blue and crisp like it'd just been pressed. His blue eyes were more stunning when he wore the color on his hard physique. The more time I spent with him, the more terrified I felt. All of this was just a ploy to get what I wanted, and now that I actually liked the guy, I was so conflicted.

"Baby." He grabbed my hand and rested it on his thigh, holding me like a man held his wife. His thumb brushed over my knuckles, and he held me delicately, his enormous hand having the power to crush mine.

The words died in my throat.

The car took us to the restaurant, and we walked inside. Like last time, we sat in a private section away from the rest of the public. It was quiet, only the sound of the music overhead audible. I couldn't even hear the other guests from the restaurant.

Cato looked at his menu. "Something wrong?"

My pulse quickened in my neck. "Just hungry."

"Then what are you having? Something with cheese, I'm guessing?" He placed the menu to the side, a playful look in his eyes.

I forced a smile even though my stomach was full of acid. "You know me so well." I set my menu down and sipped my wine. Something about the way he'd left that morning made the guilt suffocate me. I thought about my father every single day, but now that I spent most of my time with this man, I felt torn. Betraying him didn't feel right anymore. Maybe he did criminal things, but he seemed like a decent human being to me.

He stared at me for a long time, his powerful gaze drilling into mine without a single blink. If this was how he stared down his clients, it was no surprise he always got what he wanted. A man was truly powerful if he could negotiate in silence. That was something I learned from my father, but Cato was a better example of it. "How was work?"

My job at the gallery was so simple it was boring sometimes. "Good. I've found a few pieces for your home. I'll show you the next time you're available."

"I'm always available for you."

My pulse quickened even more. "I'll bring them by tomorrow afternoon, then."

"Alright. Pack a bag."

The only time I'd slept over had been awkward. I was in a hurry to get out of there, but he wanted me to stay. I'd remained detached and indifferent, and that attitude worked well. It made Cato more interested. Perhaps if I hadn't been that way, I never would have been special to him. "Should I just barge in?"

When he smiled, he looked so ridiculously handsome. It was a rare sight because he hardly ever grinned, and when he did, it was breathtaking. Made him look more like a man than a villain. When we first met, he was such an asshole, but when he dropped his arrogant exterior, he was charming. It was the real him—and it was obvious he didn't show that version to anyone. "I think that's fair."

I took a sip of my wine then examined the bottle. "Barsetti Vineyards again."

"Can't go wrong."

"Do you know the Barsetti family?"

"I met Crow Barsetti once. It was a few years ago."

"Were you buying wine from him?"

"No. It was related to business." He didn't elaborate, no doubt because it involved money and threats. He didn't share that information with me, probably because he just didn't want to talk about it.

"How was your day?" I asked to be polite, not because I expected a real answer.

"It was another day," he said noncommittally. "I have

a lot of projects going on right now, and I'm keeping everyone in line."

"You're probably going to be pissed at me for saying this—"

"Then don't say it." His voice was as cold as ice. His blue eyes shared the same arctic temperature.

I stilled at the subtle way he threatened me, and I was reminded who I was dealing with. "Life is too short not to be happy. You're so rich that you don't have to do any of this anymore. Do you ever think about handing everything over to your brother and just walking away?" I shouldn't care about his safety, but there were dozens of men who wanted him dead at any moment in time. How could he sleep at night?

"Who said I wasn't happy?"

I didn't answer because it seemed rhetorical to me. I took another drink and gave him a knowing look.

"Bates and I are in this together. I would never turn my back on him."

"That's noble."

"We're family. You do anything for family."

"Yeah…" I stuck out my neck for my father, and the blade was so close to sawing through my skin. "So, what do you think about my bed?"

He cocked his head slightly like he didn't understand the question.

"I know it's small and old. Your bed is like…three times as big."

"I've never paid attention to your bed—just the naked woman in it."

I smiled. "Good answer. Where are we screwing after this? My place or yours?"

His eyes narrowed at the ballsy question. "How about yours?"

"That's fine with me." I was always worried that Damien would show up at the wrong time, but if he saw the perimeter of fifty men, he should be smart enough to stay away and not blow my cover.

"Good. Now I have the rest of dinner to consider exactly how I'm going to fuck you."

———

WHEN WE WALKED out of the restaurant, Cato's phone rang. He glanced at the name on the screen before he answered. "What?" He listened to whoever was on the other end as his car pulled up to the curb. "You're sure? Yeah, I'll be there in a second." He hung up and dropped his phone into his pocket. "I have business to take care of."

I'd thought I would be smothered by a gorgeous man all night and the following morning. I refused to be a brat and complain about it, but I was definitely disappointed. Now that I was getting the best sex of my life on a regular basis, I wanted it all the time. I wanted to enjoy it as long as I could. "Then I'll see you tomorrow. Good night, Cato."

He continued to stare at me on the sidewalk, his blue eyes smoldering like fire made of ice.

I had no idea what that look meant. "Really, it's fine. I understand."

He grabbed me by the elbow and pulled me into the

alleyway on the side of the restaurant. It was a narrow space between the two buildings, and there were no streetlights, so it was fairly dark.

"What are you doing?"

He led me around the corner to the most private spot then undid his belt and the top of his slacks. "I'm not going to be able to think straight until I've fucked you." He turned me around and pushed me against the wall before he yanked my dress above my ass. He shoved my panties to my thighs.

"I don't know what kind of woman you think I am, but I'm not the kind of woman who—"

He shoved himself inside me, his chest pressed against my back as he held on to my hips. Then he pounded me against the wall, slamming his dick into me like he didn't give a damn what I had to say.

I shut my mouth and gripped the wall as he fucked me. It felt so good that I wondered if I really was the kind of woman who liked to get fucked in an alleyway. I would never be stupid enough to go down a dark alley by myself, but with Cato there, I wasn't afraid at all. I enjoyed it like we were screwing in my bed at home. Even if the cops saw us, they would just look the other way—because Cato owned them.

Like he owned me.

"Fuck." He wrapped his arm around my neck and held me against him. "I have to fuck this pussy."

"Because it's your pussy." I grabbed his hip and guided him harder into me.

His lips rested against my ear, and he moaned in approval. "I own your pussy, don't I?"

"Yes."

"I fucking own it."

"Yes." I held on to the wall as I came, my fingers getting covered in dirt. My cunt squeezed him and bathed him in my wetness. I could feel every sensation between my legs, feel the heavenly explosion that made my fingertips go numb.

He didn't last much longer. He gave his final pumps before he released inside me, dumping all his seed deep within my cunt. "Fuck, baby." He let his cock soften inside me as he enjoyed the remainder of his high. Then he quickly pulled out of me and fixed his pants.

I felt the come drip down my legs, so I wiped it away with my fingers then licked it.

He went absolutely still, staring at me as if he couldn't believe what he just saw.

Like I still had the grace of a queen, I pulled my panties up and returned my dress over my hips. Then I fixed my hair and walked off like nothing happened.

———

I SAT between the two men at the bar. "Landon, this is—"

"I know who he is," Landon said coldly. "His reputation precedes him."

Bones stared at my brother coldly, looking like a madman with all those tattoos. "Too bad yours doesn't precede you."

The tension between the two of them was palpable. I had enough problems on my hands, so I didn't need my only two allies stabbing each other. "Look, I've been spending a lot of time with Cato, and I don't know what to do."

Bones turned to me, his eyebrows furrowed. "What the hell does that mean?"

"Yes," Landon said. "Explain."

"Cato isn't the monster you make him out to be," I said. "Maybe he does bad things, but he's not all bad. He's——"

"You're kidding me with this bullshit?" Landon asked. "That murderer has killed more people than you've met in your lifetime. He keeps the mob and the Skull Kings in line. He's the head honcho, alright?"

"Maybe he makes you come, but that doesn't change who he is," Bones said.

Spending all this time with Cato just made everything complicated. The idea of stabbing him in the back made me sick to my stomach. I didn't love him, but I certainly cared about him. He spent all his time looking over his shoulder, unable to trust anyone, but it seemed like he trusted me. I didn't want to throw that away, turn him into a more bitter man. "I think I'm going to ask for his help instead."

All Bones did was shake his head. "When he tortures you, you better not mention my name."

"He will torture you, Siena," Landon said. "And he will kill you. He's nice to you now because you're fucking him, but the second he realizes this was all a trick, he's gonna lose his shit. I'm serious."

"He's right," Bones said. "I understand what you're doing, but it won't work. Even if the guy were in love with you, he would still beat you to death then snap your neck. He won't go easy on you."

"If you want to save Father, you have to stick with the plan," Landon said. "There is no other way. But if you think you can't pull that off, there's still time to change your mind. Stop seeing him and just abandon this."

I didn't want to stop seeing him. And I didn't want to abandon my father.

"What are you going to do?" Landon pressed. "We're running out of time, Siena. I'm surprised Damien has given you a full month to figure this out."

"I can't trick Cato Marino in a day, alright?" I snapped. "Even when he comes to my house, he brings fifty armed men with him. He's never alone. He's too smart."

"Then you need to get him alone somehow," Landon said. "Tell him you want to bring him to Mother's grave—but you don't want armed soldiers with you."

I made a disgusted face. "That's terrible. I can't do that."

"Her anniversary is coming up. It would be the perfect cover, especially if he checks in to it." Landon held his glass but didn't take a drink.

Bones was silent, his eyes shifting back and forth between us.

I already felt like shit for betraying Cato, but I would feel even worse using my mother's death as a ploy. This was not the person I wanted to be. Even with my father's life on the line, I still felt like an evil person.

"Siena," Landon pressed. "What's it gonna be?"

I only had one parent left because the other had been

murdered. I didn't want to lose my father in the same way. Family came first, and I knew Cato would do the same to me if the situation were reversed. "I'll do it…"

———

WHEN I GOT HOME, I called Damien.

"Hey, sweetheart." His obnoxious voice boomed through the phone. "I missed you."

I ignored everything he said. "Don't stop by my house anymore. Cato comes and goes randomly, and he brings his whole army with him."

"Yes, I noticed that. You must be damn good in the sack."

Cato was the talented one.

"He hasn't been seen with another woman since. That's pretty impressive."

The guilt fried my stomach again, but this time, I thought I might throw up.

"But what's not impressive is how long it's taken you to get your shit together. We've given you over a month. We're tired of waiting."

This was such a nightmare. I thought turning my back on my family protected me from the corruption and violence, but I would forever be anchored to the underworld because of my blood. "I have an idea. I'm gonna ask him to visit my mother's grave with me next week— alone. That's when we'll do it."

Damien paused for a long time. "That's an excellent idea, Siena. Micah will be pleased. You bring him there alone, and we'll take care of the rest."

"And my father?" I stopped my voice from shaking, but the emotion was too powerful. I hated to think about the way he was being treated in that hellhole.

"We'll bring him. You just worry about bringing Cato." Click.

The second the line went dead, I dashed to the toilet —and barely made it to the bowl before I threw up.

———

"WHAT DO YOU THINK?" I set up the paintings on the table so he could get a good look at each of them.

Cato stood beside me, but his eyes were glued to me— not the artwork I'd selected for him. "Beautiful."

I hid my smile, but the grin still crept through. "I meant the paintings. I think they'll look nice in the upstairs parlor."

He shrugged. "I don't give a shit about the paintings." He moved in front of me, his back to the three gorgeous pieces, and he placed his fingers underneath my chin so he could lift my lips toward his. "I give a shit about you."

"Well, do you want them or not?"

"Yes." He leaned down and kissed me softly on the mouth. "I trust your taste, baby."

"This is your home. The only taste you should trust is your own."

His thumb swiped across my bottom lip before his fingers wrapped around my neck. "This is what my taste is. Naked portraits of you all over the house. In every room. So should we do it my way or your way?"

"Well, you wouldn't be able to afford all those naked portraits of me—because I'm not for sale."

He moved closer to me as his eyes narrowed. Now the emotions that were once mysterious were easy to read. His look was full of possession, a passion so hot that it burned the air around us. "Maybe that's why I want you so much —because I can't buy you." He moved into me and kissed me again, his hand snaking into my hair. We'd barely talked about work for fifteen minutes before it changed into this…our unstoppable attraction.

Bates announced his presence when he cleared his throat. "Hope I'm not interrupting."

Out of defiance, Cato finished the kiss before he slowly pulled away. "You would have to be important to be an interruption. And you aren't important."

Bates was in a black suit, dangerous and handsome like his brother. He had the same eyes and the same cold-ness—but he was definitely more arctic. His hands were in his pockets, and he glanced at me with obvious dislike. "I have Mr. Wong on a conference call. Thought you'd want to say a few words."

Cato pulled away from me. "You can hang these, Siena." He walked out the door.

Unfortunately, Bates didn't follow him. He came to my side and looked at the paintings I selected. "These are lovely."

"Thank you." I crossed my arms over my chest. "I think they'll be great additions to the upstairs parlor."

"Yes. A beautiful room that no one ever uses."

Bates had made me uncomfortable since the day I met him, but not because he seemed like a predator. He was just much more suspicious than his brother, much more paranoid. He didn't like me one bit, and it was obvious. I was terrified he would see right through me. I just hoped I would be able to save my father before that time came.

"Cato isn't just my brother. He's my best friend. He's my business partner. There's no one in the world I trust more than him—and that feeling is mutual." He turned his head my way slightly. "I don't understand his fascination with your cunt, and I also don't like it. My brother might not see through your lies, but I do. If you think you're going to play him for a fool, you're wrong— because I'll never let that happen. I'll carve your heart out of your ass and shove it up that pretty little cunt of yours."

Before I could respond, Cato reentered the room. He must have picked up on the hostility in the air because his eyes shifted back and forth between us, like an earthquake had struck and he could feel the aftershocks. "Everything alright?"

"I was just telling Siena the paintings are nice, but I don't think too many people will see them." As if he hadn't just grotesquely threatened me, he lied so easily, the words rolling off his tongue with no effort.

Cato's eyes shifted to me, like he didn't believe his own brother. "Baby?"

I suspected Cato would believe me if I told him the truth, but I didn't want to turn him against his own brother. Maybe Bates was an asshole, but he was trying to protect his brother. He was loyal—and right on the money. It didn't matter how much Bates insulted me, I still respected him. "Your brother doesn't appreciate art. I'll leave it at that." I gave Cato a smile in the hope he would believe me.

Cato did. "I could have told you that." His hand moved to the small of my back as he came close to me. "Let's get these paintings up. I'm sure Giovanni would be happy to help you."

———

"OH MY GOD. Your bed is so comfy." I rolled over three times and made it to the edge of the bed. Then I rolled back toward him.

"You've been in my bed before." He lay on his back with his head against the pillow, his hard physique lined with all the bulging muscles of his body. Despite his criminal ways, he wasn't covered in scars. He didn't have a bullet wound in his shoulder like I did.

"But I was too busy getting fucked to enjoy it."

I cuddled into his side and slipped my leg between his. "How do you get up in the morning?"

"Easy. I think about you." He moved his fingers through my hair and grinned.

I gave him a playful slap. "Perv."

"I'm a perv?" he asked. "I don't wipe away a man's come as it drips down my thighs then lick it."

"That doesn't make me a perv. I just didn't want it to go to waste."

"I'm glad you think my come is so valuable." His hand cupped the back of my head as he turned on his side. He faced me and pressed his forehead against mine, his hard chest pushing against my tits.

"It's Grade A come."

He hiked my leg over his waist and held me close, closer than we'd ever been before. His hand slowly grazed up my thigh to my hip before it moved back down again. We'd had dinner hours ago, and we'd been in bed ever since. Our lovemaking was only interrupted when we finished the third round.

Now we just lay together.

"If my brother was an asshole to you, I apologize." His fingers trailed through my hair then down the back of my neck. He gently stroked me, gently treasured every inch of my body like he'd never explored it before.

"He wasn't."

"You're covering for him. That makes me like you more."

"Why would I cover for him?" The guilt started to weigh on me again. I'd already confirmed with Damien what the plan would be, but I was lying in Cato's bed like that'd never happened.

"Because we're close. You don't want to cause a rift between us."

Perhaps Cato was more observant than I realized. I just hoped he wasn't too observant.

"You don't care about my money. You don't care about my power. If you did, you would turn me against my brother so I would distrust everything he said. Then it would be easier for you to get your way. Instead, you want to preserve the relationship—because you care about me. I know how you are, baby. If someone crosses you, you won't hesitate to cross them back. And I know my brother —he's a fucking asshole. But you put up with it."

I covered for Bates because he was only protecting his brother. I never thought my actions would make Cato trust me more—especially when I was a liar. All of this wasn't real. It was built on lies. Bates could see that, but Cato couldn't.

I hated myself.

Why couldn't there be a better way?

Even if I told Cato the truth and he took it well, Bates would kill me.

I knew that for certain.

I moved my face into his chest so I wouldn't have to meet his gaze any longer. In my heart, I knew this man only pretended to be an asshole to protect himself. He was cold to everyone around him because he knew they would use him the second he gave them a chance. He was the toughest man in the world in order to keep the other tough guys at bay. But he dropped all that hostility for me…because he trusted me.

God, I was going to be sick again.

17

Cato

I HAD A MEETING IN ONE OF MY OFFICES IN FLORENCE. It was in the building across the street from the coffee shop —the very one where I'd spoken to Siena for the first time. She had been reading a book and stalking me like an amateur. I always knew she was harmless because she was doing it alone.

I was only present at meetings when there was a lot of money on the table. These men from France were looking for someone to invest in their underground brothels, an underground world of sex. Unlike trafficking, this was straight-up prostitution. I'd paid for sex a lot in my life, so I didn't pass judgment.

Bates came into the room unexpectedly. He didn't even knock. "Cato, I need to talk to you." The vein in his forehead was throbbing dangerously, which told me he was about to explode in rage. Whatever pissed him off had really pissed him off.

"Can it wait fifteen minutes?" I was sitting across from the Frenchmen, with the contracts sitting on the table.

"No." He glanced at our clients then back at me. "I'm sorry, it can't."

I knew Bates wouldn't interrupt me unless it was important, so I cooperated. "I apologize, Mr. Beaumont and Mr. Champlain. Would you mind if I stepped out for twenty minutes?"

Mr. Beaumont nodded. "Of course."

I was letting them borrow a shit-ton of money, so they better be accommodating. I walked out with Bates and shut the door. "What the hell?"

Bates moved into a vacant conference room and shut the door behind us.

"Do you have any idea how—"

"Siena is a lying whore." He slammed his fist down onto the table, making the entire thing tremble under the force of his hand.

I stilled at the insult but didn't jump to her aid. My brother was too infuriated for that. He must be making those insults for a valid reason. "What are you talking about?"

"I knew she was full of shit." He pointed his hand at my chest. "Fucking whore."

I kept my anger in check even though I wanted to punch him in the face. "What did she do?"

"Her father has been missing for a month."

Stefano Russo ran a cigar empire. It was respectable but small. People went missing every day, so it wasn't surprising that didn't catch my attention. But it was concerning that he disappeared exactly when Siena and I started our relationship.

"I dug deeper and found out Micah and Damien hit his warehouse, killed everyone, and took Stefan as a prisoner. Siena's brother escaped, and no one has spotted him since."

My hands rested in my pockets and I kept a straight face, but my heart was starting to pound in my chest. My rage was growing slowly to match his, but I kept it hidden under my icy exterior.

"Siena stopped talking to her father when her mother died. I guess she blamed him for her death and wanted nothing to do with the family business. But Damien threatened to kill her father if she didn't turn you over."

Now it became harder for me to maintain my expression, to pretend this meant nothing to me. It felt like a knife was stabbing me through the gut, but I still couldn't react to it. This woman had been in my bed and I fucked her like she meant something to me, but she'd used me the entire time.

Fuck. I was an idiot.

"Her plan is to get you away from your men so Damien can grab you. They'll make the exchange then." My brother was livid, visibly enraged with that vein throbbing away in his forehead. He didn't have the strength to remain calm the way I did. If this happened to him, he probably would be more graceful about it. But since someone fucked with me, his brother, he couldn't see straight.

I was the most terrifying man in this country, but I let pussy cloud my judgment. She was different from the other women I met, and that intrigued me. But now I knew she was different because she was never seriously interested in me at all. I was just a farm animal she was fattening up before the slaughter.

Bates stared at me as he waited for me to say something.

I didn't have a damn thing to say. I turned away and walked toward the window, my hands sliding into my pockets.

"You better kill her."

I stared at the café across the street, remembering Siena sitting at one of the tables. Maybe she hadn't followed me for the job. Maybe she'd followed me because she was trying to get under my skin that entire time. "How credible is your source?"

"Very."

Everything made sense, regardless of how much I didn't want to believe it.

Bates came to my side and stared out the window with me. "I told you so, asshole. I fucking told you so."

"Yeah…you did." I was angry, but most of all, I was humiliated. I couldn't believe I'd allowed someone to get that close to me, allowed someone to mislead me like that. I fell for her lies like a dumbass.

He turned to me, his jaw strained with rage. "I'll kill that little bitch if you don't want to do it. I'd be happy to."

Breaking down her front door and shooting her between the eyes didn't sound like enough revenge. "No."

"Then you'll do it?"

"Yes, eventually. But I have a better idea."

"Rescue her father so we can execute him in front of her?" he asked, his eyes brightening with crude violence.

"No. I'll let her think she fooled me. And just when she thinks she's gotten away with it, I'll be the one to fool her."

"I like that idea. Teach that bitch a lesson."

I felt no urge to defend her honor anymore. "And then I'll kill her."

18

Siena

THE NAUSEA GOT WORSE BECAUSE THE GUILT STARTED to crush me.

I couldn't believe I was going to do this.

Cato didn't deserve this.

I threw up every morning for three days because the dread was killing me. I had to choose between my father and Cato, and the choice seemed obvious. But that didn't make me feel better about my decision.

It only made me feel worse.

I'd just finished making dinner in the kitchen when the front door opened. Now I knew it wasn't Damien, so the only person who could barge into my house was Cato. His heavy footfalls were unmistakable.

"I'm in the kitchen." I turned off the stove and put the meal on two plates.

He rounded the corner and came toward me, wearing jeans and a t-shirt. His suits looked flawless on him, but the thin cotton of his shirt was much better. Showed off his chiseled forearms. When he spotted me, he stilled, his head slightly cocked and his eyes narrowed. It was the same intense look he always gave me. It just seemed a little deeper than usual.

The stare almost made me uncomfortable because he resembled a predator so much. I felt like a cornered gazelle, and he was the leopard about to rip me to pieces. He didn't greet me with a kiss or a look full of arousal. He just stared me down like a statue, like he wasn't truly real.

I tried to defuse the tension. "Are you hungry?" I held up the two plates.

He kept his eyes locked to mine. No answer.

"Alright…" I walked past him and set the plates on the dining table. "Well, if you want something, it's there." I moved behind him and grabbed a bottle of wine and two glasses. His cold behavior was unusual, but I didn't want to ask him about it. Once I opened that can of worms, I didn't know what would come out.

I poured wine into his glass and added water to mine.

He joined me a moment later, his eyes focused on mine as he placed the food in his mouth.

"Long day?"

"You could say that."

I kept eating like everything was normal, but deep inside my chest, there was a storm of emotions. The guilt ate me alive and chased away my appetite. Then it made me throw up the food I managed to get down in the first place.

He drank his wine then kept eating. "No gun today?"

"I assumed it was you."

"You didn't assume that before. What changed?"

I shrugged. "I guess I just got used to it."

He chewed slowly, his blue eyes locked on to mine like targets.

Was he always this intense? Or was it just a warm evening? I grabbed my water and took a drink.

"No wine?"

"Trying to cut back. My stomach has been upset lately."

"Stressed?" He drank his wine again.

"No. I'm not sure."

"It's natural for the body to shut down under stressful situations."

I was in the most stressful situation of my life. "Decorating a three-story mansion isn't as easy as it sounds."

"Among other things…"

I didn't even finish half my meal because my stomach couldn't handle it. The cramping got worse the second he walked into the house.

"Everything alright, Siena?" He ate every single bite on his plate without looking at his utensils.

"Yes. Why do you ask?" Was I that flustered?

"You said your stomach hurt. You're quiet. You aren't pointing a gun at me. Not exactly yourself this evening."

Neither was he. "My mother's anniversary is in a few days…" I couldn't believe I was doing this. Now the plan was set into motion. It was time to commit to it. "The anniversary of her death. It's been five years."

He rested both elbows on the table as he stared at me, his hands coming together in front of him. "I'm sorry to hear that. Anniversaries are hard."

"Birthdays too. But those make me remember her

when she was alive. The anniversaries just make me think of the day she was gone."

He massaged his knuckles slightly as he stared at me. Throughout the entire meal, he'd only blinked a handful of times. "It's rough."

"She's at the cemetery outside of Florence. I was going to go visit her." I waited for him to offer to accompany me. That would make it less obvious than me asking him outright. "Bring her some flowers or something."

"That sounds nice."

Maybe he wouldn't offer to go with me. "If you aren't busy, I would really like it if you came with me. Going alone is always hard…"

His eyes narrowed instantly, like the question meant something more to him than it should. He pulled his arms off the table and sat back against the chair, his wide shoulders as expansive as a billboard. "You want me to go with you?"

"You don't have to if you don't want to…" If I didn't get him alone, then the plan would never work. I wouldn't have to feel guilty for not saving my father, not when I tried. So if Cato didn't cooperate, it wouldn't be the end of the world. He would make the decision for me.

"No." He leaned forward over the table, his brilliant blue eyes settling on mine. "I would love to."

My heart immediately broke in two. I hated myself more than I ever had. I hated Damien for putting me in this position. I hated that Cato was so strict I couldn't just ask for his help instead. No matter what decision I made, it was a bad one. "Thank…" I cleared my throat to keep the emotion out of my voice, but it was no use. I felt like dirt—felt lower than dirt.

He reached for my hand on the table and held it. "Baby."

Oh god. His hand was so warm as it enveloped mine. I closed my eyes for a brief moment, treasuring the way his affection felt, but also battling the guilt at the same time. I didn't know what he would say next, but I suspected my heart was about to melt into a huge puddle.

"Everything you said about me was right. I'm unfulfilled. I'm empty. I have everything, but I had nothing at all...until you. I live in a world where women only want me for sex or money. Then I met you and all of that changed. With you, I don't have to look over my shoulder. With you, I don't have to wonder what your motives are." He held my gaze as his thumb brushed over my knuckles. "Because I trust you."

———

CATO DIDN'T SEEM interested in missionary anymore. All he wanted was to fuck me from behind, pressing my face into the sheets as he slammed into me. They were always hard screws, contradictions to the gentle words he said to me.

He fucked me like he hated me.

I liked it, but I also missed the old way.

He slept over then left the following morning, still quiet and brooding. Despite the sweet things he said at dinner, his mood still seemed strange. He wasn't quite himself, staring at me with a slight look of concentrated anger.

Or maybe I was just imagining it.

The night before we were supposed to visit the cemetery, Damien called me. "So, everything still ready to go?"

"Yes."

"What time will you arrive?"

"Two." It was the middle of the day when everyone was at work. It was quiet out in the countryside, and hopefully, no one would be there visiting loved ones. I wanted this to be clean and easy. Even though my stomach hadn't been either of those things.

"We'll be waiting past the gates. I'll have all my men with me—so don't pull anything."

"What could I possibly pull?" I was bringing the most wanted man right to them. "My father better be there, Damien."

"Sweetheart, I'm a man of my word. Just make sure he comes alone. If he doesn't, I'll shoot your father in the stomach and watch him slowly bleed out and die."

That was an image I didn't want to picture. "Fuck off, Damien." I hung up and tossed my phone aside before I sat on the couch. Just like earlier that morning, the nausea got to me. It was so common that I wondered if there was something serious going on with me. Guilt could do strange things to people, but to make me so physically ill? That didn't seem likely.

I hardly slept that night because all I could think about was the following day. I stared out the window and watched the sun slowly pierce the curtains and blanket the room with light. The entire night had passed—and I'd hardly closed my eyes.

I got ready for the day and did my best to cover the bags under my eyes. I looked paler than usual, like all the blood had drained from my face and neck and gave me a vampire-like appearance. I wore a black dress with white pearls around my neck, a necklace my mother had given me.

The pain I would normally feel over losing my mother was absent because I felt so much other pain. Cato was good to me, and I was about to throw him under the bus. He told me I was one of the few people in this world he could trust…and I was about to stab him in the back.

But also save my father.

I was downstairs when Cato walked in the door.

This time, I kept it unlocked so he didn't have to pick the mechanism in the door.

"That was quicker than usual." He was in black jeans and a black shirt. It was way too hot for a black suit or a blazer, so his casual attire was appropriate. If the heat didn't get you, the humidity would.

"Would you prefer I lock it?"

"I like to time myself. A challenge." He leaned down and gave me a soft kiss on the corner of my mouth. "You look lovely."

"Thanks…" I avoided the sincerity in his eyes because it felt wrong to enjoy it. I grabbed the bouquet of flowers I'd gathered from my garden and carried them outside.

Cato followed behind me, his arm circling my waist. "My driver can take us."

"Ugh, I would rather drive, if that's okay. I don't want to visit my mother with strangers in the front seat."

Cato didn't put up an argument as he led me to the old car in the dirt driveway. It was almost eight years old and small. Even in the front seat, Cato's legs would have a hard time fitting. He got into the passenger seat without complaint.

I started the car. "Your fifty men aren't going to follow us, right?"

He looked out the window. "They always accompany me."

"I know, but I'm not sure if that's appropriate. We're going to a cemetery…" Hearing myself talk just made me hate myself more. Was it as obvious to him as it was to me?

Cato didn't seem suspicious at all. "Alright." He dug his phone out of his pocket and made the call. "Wait for me here. I'll be back in thirty minutes." He returned the phone to his pocket and stared at my house. "Done."

I didn't expect that to be so easy. I expected a further argument, at least a few questions.

But Cato trusted me implicitly.

———

AFTER A SHORT DRIVE, we were about two miles from the cemetery. The radio was off, and we sat in comfortable silence while my flowers lay in the back seat. Both of my hands gripped the steering wheel until my knuckles turned white, and the air didn't seem cool enough to combat the sweat that formed on the back of my neck.

Cato was quiet, looking out the window without making conversation. His knees were apart, and his hands rested on his thighs. My car was far too small for a man his size, but he never insulted my piece-of-shit ride.

My pulse was so powerful in my neck, I could actually hear it.

I wondered if he could hear it too.

The closer I got to the gates, the worse I felt. My gut told me this was wrong—and my heart was in agreement. I wanted to save my father, but I didn't want someone else to take his place.

Especially Cato.

Cato had been good to me, even when he behaved like an asshole. He respected me, treated me well, and he had a good heart. Sometimes his true selflessness was lost in his work, but I knew he wore his heart on his sleeve. He took care of his mother when other men would be too greedy to share their wealth. He would take a bullet for his brother. And sometimes I wondered if he would take a bullet for me.

I knew he didn't love me. But he cared about me.

And I cared about him.

I'm sorry, Father. I slowed the car down until it came to a stop in the middle of the street. There were fields around us and homes in the distance. The sky was too beautiful for a tragedy to happen today. Both of my hands were still on the wheel as the self-loathing hit me. I hated myself for turning my back on my father, but it was his fault he was there. I'd told him to walk away from the business—but he didn't listen.

"What is it?" His voice was particularly cold, a direct contrast to the summer heat.

I turned the wheel and turned the car around. "Cato, there's something I need to tell you."

From the left came a squadron of black cars, along with a tank in the front. An actual tank. They turned the corner in the road, hidden from my view just a moment ago when I drove in the opposite direction. "Oh my god." I slammed on the brakes, and my eyes went to the rearview mirror. A brigade exited the cemetery and came this way, a string of equally armored cars.

We were in the middle of a war.

Cato turned to me, giving me a look so cold there were shards of ice in his gaze. His jaw was clenched with the same tightness as his fists, and he looked so livid, like he didn't know what to do with himself. He couldn't decide how he wanted to kill me—if he wanted to strangle me or shoot me. "You aren't as clever as you think you are." He stepped out of the car.

The pulse in my neck exploded into a raging panic. My chest couldn't keep up with my need for air, and the adrenaline was so strong, I thought I might pass out then and there. Cato knew about this the entire time. I thought I'd played him—but he played me.

He opened my door and unclicked my safety belt. "Out."

"Cato—"

He grabbed me by the hair and dragged me out of the car.

I screamed as the hair was yanked from my scalp and I was pulled from the car like an animal. My body hit the hot asphalt, and my knees scraped against the rough surface.

He grabbed me by the neck and pulled me to my feet before he guided me past the militia and to his private car. The back door was already open, and he pushed me inside, making me fall across the leather seats as he slammed the door behind me.

"Shit."

When he opened the door on the other side, that's when the gunshots went off.

The war had begun.

The second he got in, the car took off in the opposite direction, taking us away from the battle that raged where we'd sat just moments ago.

As if nothing had happened at all, Cato looked out the window. He didn't scream or yell. He didn't pound his fist into my face. He was unnaturally still and quiet, and that made him far more terrifying.

"Cato, it's not how it looks—"

With lightning speed, he struck me across the face and made my head smack into the window. "Be silent, bitch." His arctic gaze burned into mine, and now he was the asshole I'd met a month ago—only worse. Now he was a monster, a demon. He was the Cato Marino everyone warned me about.

"Please listen to me."

He moved to hit me again.

I blocked his hit and pushed back. "I changed my mind. I turned around. I couldn't go through with it."

He got his fingers around my neck and squeezed me so hard I couldn't breathe. "I don't give a shit if you changed your mind. When we arrive at my estate, I will put you on your knees and execute you like the traitors before you. Your blood will seep into the soil and bring new life to my garden. Your body will be dumped in the landfill where I put my enemies—and you will rot like the trash that you are."

I tried to push his hand away, but the lack of oxygen made me weak. I couldn't put up a fight to match him— even if I were fully prepared for it.

Just when I was about to pass out, he released me.

"I did it to save my father. And if I refused, they were going to rape and kill me."

He faced forward, indifferent to my statements. "Your father is already dead. Perhaps if you were smarter, you would have figured that out."

"What…?"

He didn't look at the emotion on my face. He didn't care about me at all anymore. "They killed him the second they had him. You did all of this for nothing. You could have asked for my help at any time. Instead, you conspired against me and actually believed you had a chance to accomplish the impossible."

"I wanted to ask for help, but I was afraid you would kill me."

He looked out the window, his hands resting on his thighs.

"You would have killed me, Cato. I had no other option. I had to save my father…but in the end, I changed my mind. I couldn't do that to you. You didn't deserve it… and I couldn't go through with it."

"Maybe you turned around because you knew I was on to you."

"I didn't."

"We'll never know," he said coldly. "And I don't care either way. You made your choice, and I've made mine. Enjoy your last few minutes of life—just don't shit in my car."

———

THE CAR PULLED up to the roundabout where the fountain stood, the exact place where he had executed a Russian traitor just weeks ago. His men stood there with their guns on their hips, and Bates was in the center, looking even more pissed than Cato. With his arms across his chest, he stared at my window like he could see me through the tint.

I knew Cato didn't unleash empty threats. He would drag me out of that car and force me to my knees like a prisoner of war. I'd done this to save my father, but now I realized, no matter what decision I'd made, I was destined to wind up dead anyway.

When Cato stepped out of the car, the men opened my door and yanked me out.

Bates was on me fast. "What did I say?" He grabbed me by the neck and punched me hard in the face.

I dropped to the ground instantly. I'd never been hit like that in my life. My lip bled and vertigo started. The pain didn't knock me off my feet right away. It was the momentum packed into the punch.

Cato did nothing.

"I told you not to fuck with my brother." He yanked my hand off my face then punched me again. "You fucking whore."

My head snapped back at the impact of his fist. Now the pain kicked in—and it was excruciating.

Cato grabbed a pistol from one of his men. "Stop."

Bates punched me again, making my nose bleed.

"Enough." This time, Cato grabbed him by the arm and pulled him off.

"You should be the one doing this." Bates yanked his arm free. "Make that bitch suffer."

"Not interested. Not worth my time." He cocked the gun and walked toward me, the weapon hanging at his side. There was no pity in his eyes for the way his brother had beat me. The second Cato's eyes settled on me, that same rage took over. He raised the gun and pointed it at me, aiming for my skull.

On the ground like an animal, I was defenseless. All I could do was look at the barrel that would give me the release of death. I'd lived my life fearlessly, but in that moment, all I felt was fear. There were no words to describe how it felt to have a gun pointed at me like that, to see the man's hand not shake at all. "I did it to save my father...what else was I supposed to do?" I refused to cry or shake. My last moments on earth would be full of dignity...at least as much as I could possess with blood dripping down my face.

"Don't care."

"You would have done the same."

"And I would have paid the price for it—and not begged for my life." Cato was the stone-cold killer he was rumored to be. He'd fucked me and shared private moments with me over dinner, but none of that mattered now.

Now that I had nothing left to say, I said the only thing that might matter. I wasn't completely sure it was the truth, but based on all my symptoms, I couldn't find a more logical explanation. "I'm pregnant."

The gun shook as he narrowed his eyes.

"Liar," Bates barked. "And even if you aren't, you think we give a damn? Two birds with one stone."

The gun continued to shake in Cato's hand. "I expected more out of you."

"I'm not lying, Cato. You know I've been sick for over a week."

"From the guilt—of being a lying bitch."

I placed my hand over my stomach, like that would make a difference.

He still didn't pull the trigger.

Bates stared at his brother, his arms over his chest. "Cato, kill her."

Cato continued to hold the gun, but his resolve faded.

"She's lying," Bates said. "And even if she isn't, who gives a shit? Kill her or I will."

The rage remained in Cato's eyes as he lowered the gun to the ground.

"You've gotta be fucking kidding me." Bates stepped in and snatched the gun out of his hand. He pointed at me and fired.

Cato managed to push the gun away from my direction at the right second. "What the fuck are you doing?" He snatched the gun.

"You're too much of a pussy to kill her. So I'll do it."

Cato emptied the bullets out of the barrel. "We can't."

Bates stared at his brother furiously, his jaw tight and his head shaking slightly. "Who gives a shit, Cato? Even if she is pregnant, and even if it's yours, it doesn't fucking matter. Kill them both and be done with it."

Cato lowered his voice so the men wouldn't overhear his words. "Father left us. He turned his back on us because he was a coward. I'm not a coward. I'm not like him."

Bates turned silent, and his eyes shifted back and forth as he looked at his brother. "It's not the same—"

"It is the same. If she's telling the truth, that's my blood in there. That's my family. You don't turn your back on family."

Bates sighed loudly, furious at the turn of events.

Cato nodded to one of his men. "Get her a pregnancy test."

Now I really did hope I was pregnant. If I wasn't…I would be dead.

Bates turned to me, a disgusted sneer on his face.

Cato approached me and squatted down so our faces were closer together. "Take the test. But if it's negative, I will torture you before I kill you. So, if you're lying, you might want to reconsider."

I could either get a quick death now—or a painful one later. "I'll take the test."

He stepped back and didn't help me to my feet. One of the men escorted me inside, put the box in my hand, and then stood outside the door while I did my business.

Armed with rifles, the men would blow my brains out the second I stepped out of line.

"God…please be positive." I peed on the stick and then waited for two minutes to pass. I always knew I wanted a family, but I didn't expect that time to come so soon. I'd imagined I would be married to a man I loved for years before it happened. I'd never anticipated a moment like this, that being pregnant could save my life.

When the two minutes were up, I looked at the results.

Pregnant.

Thank fucking god.

I held the stick in my hand and felt the tears well up in my eyes. I'd been on birth control for years, but somehow this happened—a little miracle. My baby was about to save my life. I walked out with the stick held in my hand and was escorted to the front by the armed guards.

Cato snatched the stick from my grasp and read the results. He gave no reaction.

Bates came to his side and read it too. "Fuck." He turned to me. "She did it on purpose."

"I didn't." I spoke with a weak voice because my words didn't seem to matter. It wasn't on purpose, but of course, I looked guilty. I couldn't blame either one of them for assuming that. "I know you don't believe me, but I didn't."

Cato stared at the pregnancy test again, like he needed to check it once more.

Bates looked like he wanted to strangle me. "Check to make sure it's yours."

"I will. But I already know it is." Cato slipped the stick into his pocket.

Bates shook his head and walked off.

Cato stared me down, his expression impossible to read. He used to let me read his soul, decipher the emotions he worked so hard to hide from the world. But now he treated me like an enemy. "You'll live here with me until the baby comes. It's not safe for you to live alone. Once people find out, you'll be a target. I'll provide for you and protect you."

There was the man I knew. The compassionate and caring man. "Okay." I didn't want to live there with him full time, but I was so grateful I wouldn't be dying that I didn't dare argue.

"But once the baby is here, I'll finish this." He raised the empty gun so I could see it. "Enjoy the last nine months of your life. They'll go by quick."

"What...?" He was going to take my child and then kill me? "You can't be serious—"

"I'm dead serious." He stepped closer to me, his face nearly touching mine. "My son or daughter is living inside you. They're the only thing I care about. You're just a surrogate, and once your job is fulfilled, you will serve your punishment."

"Cato, they can't not have a mother—"

"Shut up."

It was the only time in my life when I obeyed.

"I grew up with a single parent, and I turned out fine. We don't need you."

Tears flew out of my eyes and streaked down my cheeks. The migraine behind my eyes didn't affect my tears. The pain from being thrown around in the car and onto the concrete had nothing to do with it either. But the idea of never knowing my baby, spending nine months carrying it, only to have it taken away…was unbearable. "Please…Cato. No. Don't do that to me. You can't… please. Mercy."

He kept up his cold expression, immune to my emotional plea. "I'll let you hold the baby once. That's the most mercy you'll get from me."

The story continues in The Dictator...

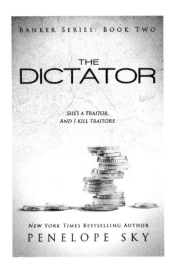

The only reason I'm still alive is because of the baby growing inside me.

My baby saved my life.

Now I'm a prisoner inside Cato's fortress. He's pissed at me, livid every time he looks at me. He refuses to sleep with me because now I'm the enemy.

But I miss him...and he misses me.

I only slept with Cato to save my father, but now he means something to me. I care about him, and I know he cares about me.

Can I earn his forgiveness? Can I earn his trust?

But even if I do, will he shoot me anyway?

Order Now

Printed in Great Britain
by Amazon

86641194R00171